The Bridge of Olin

PENELOPE S. HAWTREY

ONE

Five years later . . .

J umping from rock to rock, water licks at my ankles. Arms outstretched, I use them to maintain my balance, so only my toes get wet. Mom follows me, mimicking my movements.

Watching Mom, she shifts, stumbles, and lurches forward. I shout, "Mom!"

Right now, I'm eleven again when I found out Mom had cancer. It also reminds me of the time Abelard, Laurence, and I fought Isetan in the Gudrul Sea in Canonsland when I had my hands around the grip of my sword, and I froze because fear had left me numb.

Pressure sinks into my chest. Even though it's been more than five years now and Mom's still cancer-free, I worry about her.

Laughing, Mom looks at me and says, "I'm fine, Jayden. Good god, girl, you need to relax." When Mom's beside me, she puts her arms around me and pulls me close.

"Mom!" I whine, freeing myself from her embrace. Looking around, I search for witnesses. If Dave or Rob were here, or Ava or Hannah, that would be fine. But other kids from my school, well, that wouldn't be so good. Sure, I talk to my friends about Mom and Dad because my friends know them, and they think Mom and Dad are cool. But I don't share anything with the other kids about my parents because I've overheard comments in town: *His truck is a piece of junk. Can't he afford new jeans? Did you see Jayden's mother's hair? I think she cuts it herself.* So, I don't want to give anyone else more ammunition to say stuff about them. But I may have made a mistake when I told some kids I liked my parents.

At my high school, on breaks between classes, there are always guys lined up in the hallway who'll chant as I walk by: *Jayden, Jayden, won't leave Mommy and Daddy. Living in Calgary, she'll be the new cat lady!*

"So, David?" Mom says with her hands on her hips. I roll my eyes at her. "He's the boy who pushed you off the swing when you were younger, right?"

Sighing, I say, "Mom, stop it." Mom and Dad have bugged me about Dave so many times. "We're just friends," I add. We're biking, hiking, and boxing buddies. I walk along the path beside the Bow River with Mom beside me.

Mom's lower lip puckers, her eyes sparkle, and she says, "I thought . . . "

"Thought what, Mom?" I ask. Sometimes, I wish I could tell her I have a boyfriend. I think my parents just want me to be a normal kid: Go to school dances, find a man, get a job in Calgary, get married, have babies.

But how can I possibly do that?

That might have been my life if it weren't for the mirror, Wyndham, Enisseny . . . Not that I blame them. Wyndham's been a second father to me, and Constance and Petronilla are the sisters I never had.

"I had a conversation with Mr. Sharp. He said you need to think about whether you're going to college or university."

Lowering my head, I bite my lip. I thought we were going for a hike because Mom had a day off. Not because she wanted to talk to me about my future.

"Mom," I say, waving my hand at her. "Do we have to talk about this today? It's your first day off in weeks."

"Honey, you really need to start thinking about it. Your education is important. You don't want to end up like me and your father, do you?"

"What? Hard-working? Good parents? No, of course, I wouldn't want that!" Stepping back from Mom, I tighten my jaw.

Shaking her head, Mom folds her arms. "Flattery, my dear, will get you nowhere. Trust me." Taking a breath in, she says, "You know what I mean. You've always known."

And there it is—Mom and Dad's guilt at not being able to afford to buy me Nike shoes or an iPad. They can't afford to send me to ballet school. *Not that I want that.* Although, I guess if we had more money, I might hit them up for fencing lessons. Then again, I don't need those, either. I have several tutors in sword fighting. *Thanks.*

"Jayden, do you want to struggle like your father and I have? We're always worried about paying the gas or the hydro bill. Will we have the heat turned off again like we did when you were little?"

"Mom," I say, "you and Dad are doing fine now. You're working. I can even go to the dentist, and it doesn't cost that much because we have insurance."

"Yeah, but Jayden, if I lost my job tomorrow, we'd lose that. Your father and I, we have some money in savings but not that much. It's taken us so long to get out of debt," she says, her eyes narrowing at me. Taking a step closer, she touches my arm and says, "And if I got sick again—"

"No! You're not going to—you're not going to get sick," I say, shaking my head and swallowing the sudden lump in my throat.

Mom looks away from me, and when she turns to me again, her eyes are cloudy.

"Do you even know what you want to do?" she whispers.

I hate making Mom upset. But if I tell her, she might laugh at me. And then how do we come back from that? Then again, if she supports me, it might kill her when she finds out I'll have to move away because my studies will take me across multiple provinces in Canada.

I can't tell her. Not yet.

"I don't know. Do I really need to choose right now?"

"Well . . . ," she sighs, "I mean, you don't have to know for certain. You can change your mind later on if you want. Lots of people do that," she says, nodding and folding her arms across her chest. "But, if you don't have a path, I mean, somewhere you want to get to, there's a chance you won't get anywhere." Sucking in air, she says, "I don't mean to pressure you. I just want you to have the best life you can."

Maybe if I gave her a tiny morsel of information, that would help. Make her see that, *yes, Mom, I do have a plan.* "Mom, I'm looking at a couple of options. I just need to do some more research first."

A wisp of a smile forms along Mom's lips, and her eyes shine like the water beside us.

Oh no, I know what's coming next.

"Like what?" she asks, taking a step closer to me.

"Mom, I don't want to talk about it right now," I say, raising a hand to her. What's with my parents? Or all parents, for that matter. My friends and I compare notes, so I know our parents ask the same nagging questions. Although my situation is different because my answers wouldn't be the same as, say, Dave.

What are you doing now? (Sleeping, I'm exhausted. Kemena kicked my butt in training.) *Why don't you clean up your room?* (See earlier answer.) *Why aren't you eating your Brussels sprouts?* (I ate two dinners with lots of vegetables at both. Give a girl a break, Mom.)

"Why not?" Mom says.

"Mom, this one time, can you drop it?"

"Jayden . . ."

"Mom, please . . . ," I say. "I'll tell you when I'm ready, okay?"

Looking away, she stares out at a Douglas fir. I hate this.

Nodding her head, I notice her eyes glisten like dew on the grass on an early summer's morning. Facing me, she says, "Okay."

I always try to be honest with my parents. So, if there's something I don't want to share with them, I don't. Mom's killing me, though, with her shifting, her distant smile, the way her arms are hooked together, protectively.

Eustace has been great at helping me pick up on body language. So now, I have a clue what Mom might be thinking.

This one time, I'll lie. But I'll piggyback the lie on a truth.

Shoving my hands in the front pockets of my blue jeans, I say, "I was thinking about becoming an accountant." Mom's eyes sparkle, and the lines in her face soften. "Or maybe join the Canadian Armed Forces to become a pilot—and if I can, a fighter pilot." As soon as the word *fighter pilot* drops from my lips, I swivel and make my way down the path before Mom can say anything.

"Jayden?" Mom calls after me.

I continue down the path, arms swinging at my sides. After I've put some distance between us, I wave and say, "Come on, Mom!"

"I'm not surprised," Mom says. When I look back, Mom's hands are on her hips. She hasn't moved. Squinting, she holds a hand up and looks at me through the sun, and says, "I want you to be happy, Jayden."

The air in my nose burns, and I don't know why. Nausea washes over me. Isetan, the sea monster, has returned.

Mom's face scrunches at me. There's a whisper of a smile at the corners of her lips. "Is the accountant thing even true?"

"Not really," I admit. Both feet in, there's no way out now. Rubbing my forehead, I shake my head and add, "I didn't think you would like it."

"What? That my daughter wants to be a pilot?" Mom says. When I was younger, and a plane would fly over our house, Mom would lift me into the air, spin me around, and say: *Where do you want to go? BC to see Grandma and Grandpa? To Italy for pasta?*

Fairyland! I would squeal.

"It's cool, Jayden," Mom says, stepping towards me. When she's in front of me, she wraps her arms around me and squeezes me tight.

"I don't know if it's possible," I say.

"We'll look into it . . . ," Mom's smile shrinks away like marigolds along our walkway on a warm July day when she's forgotten to water them. Mom's eyes look over my shoulder, and her mouth forms a small o. It's some expression that could be amazement or shock.

So, I turn around—

A tidal wave of white-water blasts from above us, but it's not from the sky because I saw the Winter Dragon—Enisseny is here! And he's dumped waves of river water on us when he shot out of the Bow River. Blinking, I wipe the water away and see Edric the Knight hanging onto the dragon with one hand while a woman clothed in an emerald dress with dark flowing hair grips his other arm.

I use one hand to hold Mom while I try to steady my feet as a vortex of wind and water spins around the dragon, Edric, and the woman, dragging Mom and me closer to the river. Mom's head leans forward, and she cries, "Oh my god!"

"Hold on, Mom!" I scream.

I grip Mom's arm tighter and yell, "Edric!" as the dark-haired woman lifts a dagger to him.

Where did that come from?

I step forward to help Edric but stop when Mom squeezes my hand. Standing there, water and wind rush over us, and between waves, I see the woman plunge the blade into Edric's chest. Edric struggles to push the woman away with his free hand, but then she yanks the knife out as Edric cries, "Witch!" and a stream of crimson flows from his wound. Enisseny and Edric disappear back into the Bow River. As the water recedes, the woman stands in front of Mom and me on the path, clutching a blood-soaked blade.

The brown-eyed woman has a red mark close to the bottom right-hand corner of her mouth. Strolling toward us, she pushes her limp hair back as a trail of water follows her and says, "Hello, my dears." Clutching the knife, she spins it around at us. I place my hand on my right side, touching my waist. And there's nothing there.

My sword is in Canonsland.

"Oh, are you a traveler?" the woman coos.

"Get behind me!" I say to Mom, shoving her backward.

Mom's breath is in my ear. I stand in front of her. Her hands are on my arms. I bend my knees and separate my feet. The dark-haired woman lunges forward with the knife and jabs it at us. Mom barks in my ear, "Get back, Jayden!" and throws me to the ground.

Hitting the ground, I cry, "Mom!"

Mom skips back, dodging the woman's knife. I'm still on the ground, so when she's closer, I kick my leg high and with as much force as I can, and my foot catches her in the stomach. The dark-haired, knife-wielding woman groans and leans forward. So, I kick her again—knocking her behind the knees, and she's sent sprawling to the earth.

Somehow, the woman still holds the knife when another wave of water washes over us. Screaming, I say, "Mom!" as I choke on water. I see a flash of gold that glimmers before her plaid shirt rises and then splashes into the river. "Mom!" I cry as the dark-haired woman is grabbed by her shoulder, and behind her is Edric's blanched face, and then Enisseny's wing clips the back of my head, and I stumble backward. The dragon's war-cry pierces the air and slowly fades. Getting to my feet, I look around and see Enisseny, Edric, and the woman are gone—and so is Mom.

My hair drips. Shaking, I yell, "Mom!" as I stand on the shoreline and look into the river.

"Mom!" I cry. Searching the water, I see her. She's face down in the river before she rolls and disappears beneath it.

"Oh my god, are you okay?" a man says, running down the path clutching his cell phone.

"Call 911!" I say as I toss my coat on the ground and jump into the river.

***

The water's cold. I gulp it in and then choke on it. Gurgled words come from me. "Mom!" I scream again.

Searching the rolling waves of the rapids, I see the spot she was before I dove into the water. I watch the spiraling waves, the way it drifts, rises, and sinks, and the way it cuts and pushes things along like logs, branches, the odd fast-food wrapper, and pop can.

I see something . . . red, plaid fabric—

"Mom," I whisper. There's no response. I push my hands into the water and kick my legs and keep my eyes on Mom. Digging into the waves of the water with my hands, I drink in the air between breaststrokes.

A few feet from her, I lose her. Frustrated, I splash the water, and then her head bobs up again. Her eyes are closed. I'm close enough that I can see blood streaming from her forehead.

Treading water, I wait for some sign of life—a word, even *honey, help me.* I would take anything right now.

Bravery is about doing what is difficult and sometimes what we most fear, and when at times there is no hope of success. In those moments, swallow the terror and step forward—no matter what monsters lie before you.

"Mom!" digging into the water with my hands, I kick my legs and grab her wrist. I place her head against my shoulder, keep one arm around her waist to keep her head above the water, and use my legs and my free hand to move us toward the embankment. When we're close to the riverbank, two men help me drag Mom up. The blue-green water changes to a slight pink as Mom's blood seeps into the waves.

Two men in sports clothes carry Mom up and place her farther up the riverbank.

One man touches her neck and then places a hand onto her chest. He pushes down on her chest then up. Down, then, up, down, then, up . . .

I don't remember which man it was or what they looked like. I don't know how much time passed before I was in the police car.

Someone says, ". . . tornado. But there were no alerts in the area. Was it a tornado?" Police Officer Wilson asks me.

"I don't know," I say, shaking my head. I'm wrapped in a blue blanket and sit in the police cruiser beside her.

What was I supposed to say? There was a dragon that sprayed water over Mom and me when he rocketed out of the river. Oh, and by the way, there was also a knight who got stabbed by a woman dressed in green. She had a red birthmark beside her lower lip. You should be looking for them, too.

Dad's truck rumbles and then jolts to a stop. I grab the car door handle and push it open as Dad steps out of his vehicle and looks around.

"Jayden," Officer Wilson says.

"Dad!" I yell. Waving, I take a few steps forward. Before I know it, I pick up the pace, and then I'm running and crying. When Dad turns around, I see his pale face, and when he sees me, he runs, and we meet halfway.

I want to tell him I'm sorry. I never thought something like this could happen. You see, Wyndham never told me there were other ways Enisseny could travel between worlds. I'm sorry, I didn't know. I'll fix this.

"Jayden! Jayden!" Dad says. He wraps his arms around me in one of his bear hugs. I hear the gurgling of liquid in his chest, the raspy huffing of his breath—his attempt to even it all out. Be the man he's always been, a man who's in control and able to solve almost every problem.

Embarrassingly, I'm sniffling. The wimpy version of me has returned. Blinking furiously, I tighten my lips. And with that, I'm able to shut down the wide-eyed, fearful kid in me.

She doesn't belong here. Not now.

"Are you okay?" Dad says as he pushes me back. He leaves one hand on my shoulder, though.

I clasp my hands into fists and say, "Yeah."

"Your daughter's a hero," Officer Wilson says. "She jumped into the river and saved your wife."

Nodding, Dad stands beside me and squeezes my shoulder

before letting go. Dad's eyes are red-rimmed.

Is that anger? Does he know this is my fault? No, he can't. It must be something else. Some other emotion I'm not reading right.

"My wife?" he says.

"They took her by helicopter to the Foothills Hospital. Two joggers revived her before the paramedics arrived."

Dad's face breaks apart like glass. "Thank god," he says, covering his mouth with his hand. I look away and breathe in the smell of the spruce and poplar trees that's mixed with Dad's sweat, and stare at wild roses and bluebells along the path.

"We should go see her, Dad," I say.

"Yeah, of course," Dad says.

"Do you want me to drive?" Removing the blanket from my shoulders, I roll it up and hand it back to the police officer. "Thank you," I say.

"You've been through a lot. I can drive you home," Dad says, nodding.

"I want to see Mom," I say. I extend my hand and add, "I can drive if you want me to?"

"No, Jayden. I can do it. But listen, if you want to come . . . ," Dad pauses, and this one time, I don't rush him, "we should go home and get you some dry clothes."

"I'm fine, Dad. Look, I'm already dry!" I say, patting my pants and shirt.

"Alright," he says. His eyes are searching for something. Some answer, some reason, some explanation. I can't look at him. His stare haunts me. "I'm so proud of you, Jayden. You saved your—your," running his hands across his mouth, he says, "—your mother. I can't imagine what it was like . . ."

"It's okay, Dad. I'm alright," I whisper. Dad runs his hands over his mouth again. Then a choking sigh comes from him as the officer asks him several more times if he's okay. Dad insists he is, and the officer gives us directions to the hospital. Officer Wilson said cell service has been spotty out here the last couple of days, so we might not be able to use our cell phones for directions. I take a breath in, grateful the cell phones for the two runners worked when they did.

Dad's arms are folded in front of him with his finger hooked around his keychain ring as he listens to the directions. It's his habit to make sure he doesn't lose his keys. It backfires, though, when they fall to the ground. He doesn't notice. Dad listens, asks questions to clarify the best route with his brow scrunching as he takes in the information from the officer.

I wait one minute, maybe two. Then I scoop down and grab the worn metal keyring with the "R" on it with twenty different keys, some Dad knows which doors they open, and others he doesn't. "Okay," Dad says. "Thank you," he says to the officer, and she turns and leaves. "Jayden, you ready to go?" he asks.

"Yeah, I'm ready."

"Okay." Dad's face twists as he pats his pockets in his shirt and pants. "Where are my keys?" he says, shoving his hands in his pockets.

Dangling the keys in front of him like a hypnotist, I say, "They're right here, Dad."

"Oh, how did you get those?"

"You dropped them, and you didn't notice." Shaking my head, rolling my eyes, I walk toward the truck with Dad trailing me. "And that settles it—I'm driving," I say, opening the door for the driver's side.

Dad snort-grunts, and runs a hand down his face, and tugs the loose skin of his neck. I reach for the driver-side door, already open, and jump inside. Dad opens the passenger-side door, gets inside, and once he's belted in, I turn the key, and the engine rumbles to life.

"I'll come back with Uncle John tomorrow and get your Mom's car," Dad says, nodding, "as you don't have your full license."

I nod. But I don't admit to Dad that I forgot about Mom's car that she parked at the beginning of the trail. I guess it's a good thing there are two of us.

TWO

"Enisseny?" It's the second time I've whispered his name. Leaning closer to the mirror, I repeat it, and there's still nothing.

"Jayden?" Dad says through my bedroom door. "Are you awake?"

"Yeah, Dad . . ." I run a hand over the mirror. It's a sad attempt to summon Wyndham, Enisseny, or for that matter, anyone. They've all disappeared, and now, I'm left alone in this world for the first time since—I don't remember the last time. And this is when I need to get back to Canonsland.

I have questions that I need answers to.

"Any chance you can help, Bob?" I mutter. Bob's white-haired speckled eyebrows arch at me, and he gives a low moan.

"Jayden?" Dad says again.

"Sorry, Dad," I say as I walk over and open the door.

"Hey, I thought I might make some hot chocolate. Did you want some?" Dad leans on the door frame, his cheeks changing to pink like the rosé he and Mom drink after I've gone to bed.

"Sure," I say as I glance back and search the mirror for some hint of Constance or maybe Petronilla. There's nothing.

So, I pull the door shut behind me.

Bob steps lightly down the stairs. Bob had one slight mishap about a month ago where he slid down the last four steps, so he's learned to take the stairs at a slower pace. Wyndham never really explained how the mirror works except that Enisseny always decided when I could be contacted. Until today, I worried that Bob had some part to play in it—that if something happened to him, I would lose my connection with Wyndham and his family and would never be able to visit again.

Now that I know the Winter Dragon can charge out of the Bow River, I guess it's not up to Bob.

"Good boy, Bob." Leaning over him, I pat him on the head at the bottom of the stairs, his mouth widens, and he pants and shows me his slightly stained teeth when he grins. "Did you want me to make the hot chocolate, Dad?" I ask as we enter the kitchen.

"No, I've got it," he says as he pulls out a pot from the freshly painted white cupboards. That was Mom's doing, not mine. She's much more patient with a brush than I am. The smell of the drying paint, the memory of Mom in her overalls, carefully brushing paint onto the cupboard doors makes me nauseous. "I think I can warm us some milk and dump in a package of hot chocolate," Dad says, smiling.

I slide the chair out from under the table and take a seat. Bob lies down and places a paw on top of my feet and rests his head on them, too. My toes warm from the weight of my old Pup's body. "Are you alright?" I ask.

"Yeah," Dad says, "just a long day, that's all." Standing over the stove, he stirs the milk with a wooden spoon. The sweet smell of warming milk spreads throughout the kitchen. It reminds me of warmth, goodness, my parents—all the things I love about home.

The thought of Edric, Enisseny, and Canonsland stabs through the safety of my home. This other world that I've become a part of nearly took my mother. *You must put aside emotion. Think logically.*

Alright, I know it's not the dragon, nor Wyndham or Edric.

It was the dagger-wielding woman in green with the red birthmark on her face. I drum my fingers across the table.

"Jayden . . ."

"Sorry, I know you hate it."

His eyes are distant, as if he sees a ghost behind me. Shaking his head, he says, "No, that's not what I was going to say." Dad stirs the milk with a wooden spoon in a medium-sized silver pot as steam rises above the stovetop. Then Dad opens a package of instant hot chocolate and pours it in with the milk, and the decadent scent of chocolate is everywhere. "Are you okay?"

"Ah, yeah, just tired, too."

"I noticed you hadn't changed yet. That's the reason I was asking."

Looking down at my shirt, I stare. *I could've sworn I changed my clothes?* On my blue t-shirt, I notice something dark. Using a fingernail, I pick at it. When I have it between my fingers, I rub them together. Red bits of dry, crumbly stuff fall from my fingers onto my jeans.

Is it soil? Or was it blood? I shake my head and pull my eyes up to Dad's gaze instead.

Dad places a cup down with a *thump* in front of me and disappears into the living room. Alone again, I touch the crumbly bits again.

A plush blanket is draped across my shoulders. Looking up, Dad's there, and he squeezes my shoulders, kisses me on my forehead, and sighs. When he lets go of me, Dad says, "Jayden, what would your Mom and I do without you?" he says, sitting across from me.

"Have more money, move to Hawaii, be living the dream . . ."

Dad chokes, sputters, and sprays hot chocolate onto the table and into my face.

I shove my chair back and accidentally kick Bob in the head. "Oh, gross, Dad!" I say as I use my palm to wipe sticky milk and chocolate off. I push the tablecloth back to check on Bob. He's got a, *what did you do that for?* look on his face. "Sorry, Buddy," I say to my old Pup.

Dad coughs into his hand, chokes, and wheezes.

"Are you alright?"

"Yeah, but if I'm not, I'm sure you know how to do the Heimlich maneuver." Dad gives me one of his winks—it's the same one he gives me when I'm helping him with a roof, installing windows, or replacing siding that means I've done a good job.

"Maybe . . . course," I raise my nose and smile, "you shouldn't need the Heimlich maneuver to unclog hot chocolate from your throat."

Dad grabs my arm and gently squeezes with some conflicted smile of happiness, sadness, and worry that's tugging at his lips and eyes.

"Jayden," he says, "I—you must have been so scared. I'm sorry," he whispers. "I should have been there. You could have been killed," he says, squeezing my arm again.

Rage and fear burn in Dad's eyes, and it reminds me of the swirling coral water at Red Ocean Pass in Canonsland that brightens to a darker shade of red whenever they get the white rainstorms. The storms aren't like we get here. Instead, it's some mixture of hail-rain that's soft and warm. It's safe to be out in it, and even though the water is spinning, it doesn't come with the same amount of ferocity that levels houses in the prairies like a tornado will. The hail-rain doesn't destroy anything but drenches crops with warm water and makes fruit and vegetables grow larger.

"Jayden?"

"Sorry, Dad," I say. I've never had my two worlds collide before. Now, I struggle to keep them separate.

"Did you hear what I said?"

"Sorry."

"I don't want you to ever take a chance like that for me. You're all we have, Jayden. Do you hear me?"

Leaning forward, I rub the back of my neck and pull the

tablecloth back. A low grumble of a snore comes from Bob, who whimpers, and his tail wags. "What do you mean?"

"If you ever find me in your mother's position, don't risk your life for me. Got it?" He's leaning back, and a *slurrrppp* comes from his lips as he inhales the hot chocolate.

I love my father. But man, does he have some annoying habits. "Of course, I would do the same for you."

"Jayden?"

"No, Dad, you can't make me promise that. I'll always help. *Always.* I don't care about the risks."

"Jayden, something could have happened to you, too. Do you understand that? Then, what would I have done?" Dad covers his face, and then a gurgled moan comes from him. Sucking in the air, he covers his nose and lips with his hand and looks up at me.

"Dad, I'm really good at calculating risk." Okay, it's sort of a lie. Dad scrunches his eyebrows and goes quiet.

"Really?" he says, tilting his head and raising his bushy brows.

I'm too tired to play these games. I lift the green ceramic cup I made last year at the City of Calgary's ceramic course I took with Mom. She was annoyed we weren't spending enough time together. *I spent too much time with Dad hanging shingles.* The handle on the cup has a blotched mark of my thumb on it. And the whole thing is slanted. "This is ugly," I say, running a finger over the warped mug.

"It is," Dad says, grinning, "but she loves it."

I breathe through my nose, holding back tears, and say, "Dad, I don't really calculate risk."

"I know," he says, staring down at the table.

"But I can't walk away. I have to help if I can." The words catch in my throat. "Please, don't make me make promises that I don't intend to keep."

Dad grabs my hand and squeezes it once. "Fine. But you and your mother are not allowed to go hiking again without me. Got it?"

Tears slide down the sides of my cheeks. I brush them

away before he spots them. "Okay."

"Okay. Now drink your hot chocolate before it gets cold." Lifting his cup, he gulps the last bit back.

I chug from the crooked cup, and then hot chocolate dribbles down the side of my face. Stupid, angled cup! "I hate this cup!" I whine.

Standing at the sink, Dad leans against the counter as I wipe my face and clothes. Dad crosses his arms in front of him and looks away. "That's the other reason your mother keeps it around and gives it to you so often."

"What?"

"She loves watching you spill stuff all over yourself." Laughing, Dad wipes away tears and shrugs.

I snap my mouth closed. *Oh my god. My mother has a sense of humor? When did that happen?*

***

I take a quick shower because I can't stand the seaweed and sewer stench on my clothes anymore. Now, I sit cross-legged on my bed in blue jeans and a sweatshirt and stare into the mirror.

Where is Enisseny?

It's been hours, and there's still no sign of anyone.

Where's Wyndham? Why was Enisseny with Edric? Is there more than one portal between our worlds? Wyndham told me that Enisseny was the key to the other realms. He never mentioned there was more than one way in or out.

I flop backward against my mattress and stare at the ceiling and squeeze my hands into fists. Should I go to the Bow River? Is that where Enisseny will be? Did he know I was there?

I stare at my bedroom door. If my Dad finds me missing in the morning—I shove the thought aside. I hate always doing the right thing. If my Dad wasn't here, what would I do?

That's an easy answer. I would go to the Bow River.

But David told me that he learned in cadets that if you get lost in the woods, one of the worst things you can do is keep walking because it will be more difficult for a Search and Rescue Team to find you. Then again, doesn't Enisseny know where I am all the time? Wyndham said that *Enisseny knows a person's heart and decides who needs him or the people of Canonsland need.*

"Jayden?" a gruff voice crackles, and then there's wheezing. I bolt up from my bed and stare at Wyndham. He lifts his armor over his head, and it crashes to the stone floor. Enisseny's white wing is extended in the background, and his head is flat against the stone.

"Wyndham!" I hiss into the mirror. "What happened?"

Wyndham's arm is through the mirror, and I reach in and grab it. I stare down at my bed, and Bob raises his head and then flattens it again.

"Okay, Bob," I say, "you stay here and take care of Dad." With that, I slide through the mirror alone. I step onto the stone floor and see candle wicks in corners of the room burnt down so low they give little light. I take a deep breath in as the image of Bob sleeping on my bed shrinks, and then the sight of Bob goes dark.

Wyndham and I are the only two reflected in the mirror. I frown at the sight of our image. This is the first time I've ever been to Canonsland without Pup. And there's some feeling I can't quite explain. Then I know.

It's some heaviness in my chest that twists at my heart and spreads to my stomach. Stepping forward toward the mirror, I touch the glass and place a hand on the spot where I last saw Bob.

"Jayden, how is your mother?" Wyndham asks.

"She's okay," I say, taking a deep breath in as I let go of his hand. "What happened?" I ask. I circle Wyndham as random images spin in my mind—Mom in the water, me dragging her up the riverbank, the two men trying to revive her . . . "How could Enisseny do that? How could he put my mother at risk like that? He should have known. He almost killed her . . ."

"Jayden?" Osgoode's voice stops me mid-rant. I stare

down at the hallway stones. For the first time, I notice a black puddle of liquid on the floor that I've stepped in, and there are black imprints from larger and smaller treads from boots too that are everywhere.

Wyndham's hand is placed on his abdomen, and he holds it there as blood soaks through his shirt.

"Oh my god, Wyndham!" I cry. I run up to him and brace him with my shoulder to steady him and place my hand over his abdomen.

"I told him to lie down!" Dr. Eastwood shouts from the other side of Enisseny.

"Wyndham!" Laurence cries as he runs down the hallway, throwing his sword and shield aside. As he passes by Enisseny, Laurence steps into the black puddle and whispers, "Enisseny?"

"Is that blood?" I ask Osgoode, my eyes wide with fear.

"Yeah, it's blood," the doctor says. Beside Dr. Eastwood, I notice Constance, Idonea, Petronilla, and Osgoode for the first time, and they're covered in black sludge from Enisseny. Dr. Eastwood raises a long red metallic cover, placing it over Enisseny's neck, and holds it there.

"Laurence!" I shout as my knees buckle under Wyndham's weight. My mind spinning, the hair on my arms prickle, when I think about what's happened: *Both worlds? People I love in both worlds got hurt!* "Laurence!" I say again. Wyndham's face changes to ghostly white, and his eyes roll back. Laurence snaps out of his trance, runs over to us, and places his shoulder under Wyndham's other arm. Together, we hold him up, and with Wyndham's body leaning forward, we drag him through the doorway and into the dining room.

"Put pressure on that wound until I can tend to it!" Dr. Eastwood shouts.

"Seriously, how are we going to do that right now?" I snap. "Hugo! Emma!" I say. "Get out of the way!" When I see their wide-mouthed, angelic, four-year-old stricken faces, I shake my head and turn and say to the white-haired cook who was busy clearing off the table so we could place

Wyndham down on it, "Walter?"

"This way, my dears," the long-bearded man says as he grabs each one of the children's hands in his and leads them out of the dining room.

Laurence and I slide Wyndham onto his back as blood pours from his wound. I place a hand over it, apply pressure as Wyndham's eyes open, and he grunts, "Aaaaaa!"

"Sorry, sorry, sorry . . . ," I say. When I raise my hand to my face to push my hair back, I see it caked in sticky red blood, and the scent of iron hangs heavy in the room mixed with the smell of rotting flesh—the pungent odor of death and birth that's tied together.

From behind us, there's a screech.

"Get back! Get back!" Constance says from the other room. Then there's the sound of boots running across the stone. Looking up, I stare out the other doors—the ones that lead to the main entrance—and peer over Laurence's head and out the window as I try to figure out what Constance is talking about.

"Get back!" she barks. Constance shoves Laurence back against the wall, and runs around the table, grabs me around the waist, and yanks me against the other wall with her.

"What the—"

There's a wave of white air that blasts across the table, and I turn my head to the side to avoid getting hit. When I look up, Enisseny's head is in the doorway. His eyes are brown, and he blinks at Wyndham, who lies asleep on the table. Wyndham's wound is covered in a sheet of ice.

"Well, I'm glad you're feeling better," Dr. Eastwood says as he squeezes past Enisseny's head. Enisseny blows air through his nostrils at him. "Good, god, dragon, what did you eat today?" he asks as he waves his bag at him. The doctor's hands are drenched in black blood, and he snaps his surgical gloves off, tossing them on the ground.

Opening his bag, he pulls on a new pair of gloves and says, "Okay, Wyndham, hang on."

"Kent!" Doctor Miriam Wretchell cries as she runs in

carrying buckets of water and bandages.

"Miriam!" he says, "Please this way." When she arrives, he squeezes her arm once and says, "Thank goodness."

"Enisseny," Osgoode says, "they will take care of him. Go rest." Osgoode strokes the Winter Dragon's nose with one hand, and Enisseny maneuvers back into his room.

"What shall we do?" Constance asks, clinging to my hand tightly while Osgoode closes the door to Enisseny. My heart aches. Staring down at Wyndham, I know he's Laurence and Constance's only parent. When I was younger, she held my hand to reassure me. I squeeze it, so she remembers I'm beside her.

I stare up at Laurence, who leans against the wall, his mouth open, his eyes wide, and he trembles.

"Get cleaned up," Dr. Eastwood shrugs and says.

Osgoode places a hand on Idonea and Petronilla and pulls them out of the dining room. He looks back at us and says, "Constance?" Placing a hand on Constance's shoulder, I use my other hand to urge her out of the room.

"Laurence," walking Constance to the door, I say, "let's leave the doctor to do his work."

Laurence doesn't move from his spot. "Laurence?" I say again as I hand off Constance to Osgoode.

Placing a hand in Laurence's, I tug at it, "Laurence?" I say. "Please?"

His chin punches out. It's a proud look. Or maybe it's a stubborn stare? I don't know. "I'll find out who did this to him."

"We'll find out together," I say. "Whoever did this might also be responsible for nearly killing my Mom, too."

"What?" he whispers. Laurence's eyebrows droop, and lines form along his brow. Confusion maps his face.

"Come on," touching his elbow, I say. The sound of his footfall behind me assures me that this one time, he's following me, and I know I don't need to answer his question right now.

THREE

"What happened?" Osgoode asks. He stands with his arms crossed against his chest.

"I do not know," Laurence says, pacing around the room. He looks at the curtains and the wooden sofa, which Osgoode was working on the last time I was here. "I had gone East with Eustace to Ikansterup to ensure all was well with the Ikans. Wyndham had gone west with Edric and Enisseny as ongoing tension on the Xyidak-Trygolish border was escalating. Edric said he overheard a conversation in his travels that the Xyidaks were planning an attack on the Trygolish to take more land. The King did not want to send troops, fearing the Xyidak and Trygolish would think he was mounting an offensive. So, he sent only Edric, Wyndham, and Enisseny in the hopes that they could reason with the Xyidaks."

Throwing wood in the fire, I watch it burn. Placing a hand against the mantel, I stand and say, "Do you know if they ever made it there?"

He shakes his head and says, "I do not know."

"You mentioned your mother—something had happened to her in your realm?" he asks.

Osgoode's leaning against the doorway, and he straightens,

standing at his full height. Biting my lower lip, I say, "My Mom got pushed into the Bow River," hesitating, I add, "by Enisseny."

Osgoode's head tilts, and he says, "Have there been any reports of others who were scavengers as Droart and Fulke who plan to travel to other realms to take resources?"

"We have heard nothing of it from either our friends or informants, if there are," Laurence says. Laurence picks up the picture of Wyndham and him on his Knighthood Day and says, "And King Nicholas has given us clear direction to check continuously." Laurence places the photo down on the table. Facing me now, he says, "How is your mother?"

Leaning on Wyndham's chair, I stare down at my red-spotted blue shirt. *What a bloody day.* The pun makes me grimace. I run a hand across the top of the chair. "She's alright," I say, "but she has a concussion. So, she'll be in the hospital overnight. The doctor said she should be able to come home tomorrow." The time difference always throws me off. I clarify, "Well, my tomorrow, at least."

Tapping the top of the chair, my mind drifts back to the things I said to Wyndham. I didn't know he was wounded. *What kind of knight am I going to be if I can't control my temper?*

"Jayden?" I hear someone say. But the word doesn't mean anything to me. It's the touch of light fingers on my shoulder that tears me away from that past me—the hateful child who threw accusations at the knight who's always been kind to me. "I have prepared your clothes," Constance says, threading her hand into mine.

"Thanks," I say. Following Constance, I stop. I take in all the photos in the room of Alwyn, Eustace, Constance, Laurence, and Wyndham from all the years they've spent together as a family. Alwyn, Eustace, and Constance were all older when they lost their parents. In Laurence's world, though, Wyndham might be the only father he remembers.

I try to remember the details of what I saw at the Bow River. Frowning, I say, "Edric got stabbed by a woman who wore a green dress. She had black hair and dark brown eyes," there was something else, "and she had a red mark at the corner of her mouth." That's what Wyndham's taught me to do—relay the facts. *Do not make assumptions.* "It may have been a birthmark." After the facts, I'm allowed to speculate.

"What has happened?" Alwyn's voice cracks through the conversation. He peers over Osgoode's shoulder, stares at Constance, and then faces Laurence.

Laurence's chin drops. Constance pulls me forward and out of the room. As we leave, I look back. Alwyn's hand is placed on top of Laurence's shoulder. Osgoode's face is the last I see before he closes the door to the study.

***

I return to the study with Constance and Ella following me. My head's filled with rage, heart splintered. *Emotions occur, and you cannot always separate yourself from them. Recognize them but keep them in their place,* Wyndham's said. It's easier said than done.

Taking a breath in, I turn the steel latch, and the wooden door creaks open.

"Jayden," Osgoode says, standing, "you mentioned that there was a woman on the—river?"

"Yeah," I say, "she had a dagger and stabbed Edric. Does anyone know what happened to him?" Taking a seat beside Alwyn, I add, "Is he okay?"

"No one knows. It was only Enisseny and Wyndham that returned to Rumbling Town."

Gripping the cushion of the sofa, I squeeze it when the door to the study opens again. We all stand when Dr. Eastwood enters.

"Okay," Dr. Eastwood says. "I've had to remove Wyndham's spleen. It was damaged beyond repair." He pulls on a long black coat that Miriam hands to him. "Thank you, my dear," Kent says as he plants a kiss on her cheek. "I could not have done it without you." Miriam's bronze skin shines with the glow of the candles, and her cheeks flush pink.

"Beautiful and brilliant," Dr. Kent Eastwood says to his new bride.

"We are so thankful you were both here," Alwyn says, shaking his hand.

"Me, too," he says to Alwyn. "As luck would have it, I was visiting my bride. Unfortunately, Miriam had left several hours before Wyndham and Enisseny arrived to purchase food at Wringing Sound Station for our return trip to the King's Acres. Thank goodness, she returned when she did." Lifting Miriam's hand, he kisses it. "Miriam's replacement should be here before we leave tomorrow," Dr. Eastwood says.

"How is Wyndham?" Petronilla's dark brown eyes shine, thick with tears.

"He's doing well," Dr. Eastwood says, helping his wife, Dr. Wretchell, with her coat. "Enisseny has helped greatly. His wound has begun the healing process."

"I can stay with him," I offer.

Laurence lifts an eyebrow at me, and I smile at him as my cheeks warm. We do that a lot. Say the same thing almost in unison. Except Laurence says things differently: I can tend to him, were his exact words.

"I will take care of Wyndham," Constance says, touching my arm. "You have said there was a woman who injured Edric. She may have also been the person responsible for Enisseny and Wyndham's wounds. You must share the details of what you remember." Walking to the door, she places a hand on the handle, faces Laurence, and says, "And you must tell us when we can expect the other knights." She gives one of her crooked smiles and says, "Besides, neither one of you are good at nurturing another."

"I burn the stew once—" leaning back, shaking my head, I cross my arms in front of me.

There's no laughter. But I do get smiles all around.

"Aunt Constance, may I help?" Petronilla says.

"Of course," Constance winks at me as she opens the door. "We will see you out, Doctors," Constance says to Dr. Eastwood and Dr. Wretchell. Then they disappear through the door.

"So," Alwyn says, "Laurence, you have said that Wyndham traveled west with Edric and Enisseny to help settle some dispute?"

"Yes," Laurence says. "Eustace and I had gone east to the City of Ikansterup to ensure the Hunters—" shaking his head, he says, "sorry, the Ikans—old names are difficult to forget—that the building of the Southern Gateway Road was going accordingly. We were there to ensure that they had sufficient supplies, to pay the builders their wages, and to provide an update to the King."

"Where is Eustace?" Osgoode asks.

"I sent him back to King Nicholas to tell him what happened."

"Alone?" Alwyn asks, arching his eyebrows.

I snort and half-laugh. Then my face flushes. I know this isn't the right time to joke about how terrible Eustace is with a sword. "Sorry," I say.

Laurence's hands are crossed behind his back. His lips are tight, curled into one of his hidden smiles. "Gamel is with Eustace. He had traveled with us as he wished to provide an update to the King directly on the progress of the road—and he thought it wise to provide additional protection to Eustace as well," Laurence says.

"Good," Alwyn says. "Otherwise, I would send out a Search Party to find him. Reports from travelers who have passed through Wringing Sound Station say thieves are in the area—who take more than a person's coins."

The room falls silent. Gamel, the Captain of the Ikansterup soldiers, is a good fighter and friend to Eustace, who's saved Alwyn's brother's life before.

"The reports are true," Laurence says. His jaw pulses as lines in his forehead form.

"So, if you and Eustace were returning from Ikansterup, how did you know that Wyndham was injured?" Osgoode says.

"We were at the crossroads, Center Corner, I believe, and from above us, we saw Enisseny lurch. In all my years with the dragon, I have never seen him struggle to fly before." Raising an eyebrow at Alwyn, he adds, "Not even when you have flown on him, and he tried to make you see your breakfast for a second time."

Laurence turns away and stands at the window, looking out. Behind his silhouette, I see the blinking of lanterns from the villager's homes. Smoke drifts above their chimneys. The arms of windmills twirl close by, providing electricity to the people of Rumbling Town that powers the streetlights.

"The calmness of an early morning whispers secrets to those who would listen," Laurence says.

"Wyndham's words," Alwyn says with a catch in his voice.

Folding his arms, Laurence stares out the window. I want to help. I want to say something to all of them. But what can I say or do? So, I don't say anything.

"Yes," Laurence says, facing us. "There was some black and red liquid that dripped from above us as Enisseny passed over." Laurence's eyes stare down at the ground. I know his mind is somewhere else. Nodding in my direction, Laurence looks at me and says, "Wyndham told us of the color of Enisseny's blood when he had been injured long ago—and I remembered it from our conversation."

"Yes, and 'tis good that Constance remembered the blanket," Osgoode adds.

"It heals Enisseny?" I ask.

"It helps," Alwyn says. "Now, about the woman—"

"You mentioned she wore a green dress, had dark hair and dark brown eyes and had a red birthmark on the right side of her lower lip?" Laurence says.

Breathing in, I stand, nod, and say, "That's right."

"I have never heard of such a woman," he says.

I squeeze my hands into fists by my sides, fighting the urge not to overreact. Sure, Laurence knows I have a history of getting things confused when my mind turns to mush in a crisis. But not this time—this time, I memorized every detail even though the dark-haired woman was holding a knife and had already stabbed Edric.

The sound of horses' hooves running through Rumbling Town stops me.

"The other knights have arrived. And so quickly," Laurence says. "Gamel and Eustace must have ridden hard to the King's Acres." Laurence walks out of the room, and we follow him through the hallway. When he gets to the front door, he unlatches it and walks out onto the road at the front of Isons-Lydric Castle.

And just like that, I've lost my opportunity to say anything more.

***

Slouching in a chair next to Wyndham, I'm frustrated at being shut out from the meeting with the other knights. *You are not a knight yet,* Laurence said before closing the door on my face. I'm old enough to take responsibility but not old enough to be taken seriously. Shaking my head, I recline in my chair.

"Jayden?" Wyndham says.

Straightening, I lean forward, place my hand on his, and say, "Wyndham, you're awake!"

"Yes," he says, squeezing my hand. "Remind me again, how is your mother?"

Shrugging my shoulders, I wave a hand and say, "She got a little bump on the head, that's all."

"You said that your mother was hurt?" He shifts and uses his palms to push on the mattress and moves into a seated position, and then he reclines back and places his head against the headboard.

I move from my chair to the edge of his bed. "Mom went for a little swim and bumped her head and got a small concussion. She'll be fine," I say with a tight-lipped smile.

"That is good," he says as his eyes crinkle and crow's feet form in the corners. Wyndham looks at me and shifts his gaze to the orange glow of the light. "You are changed," he says when he faces me again.

My head gives a half shake. Then I stare at him, not quite sure what he means. *Changed? Changed in what way? Better?*

Worse?

Then I know. Blinking back tears, I say, "Wyndham, I'm sorry."

"Why do you apologize?"

Lifting my chin, I brace myself and stare at him. *If you apologize, always mean it, and make sure you say the words like you mean them.* Those aren't Wyndham's words—they're my dad's. "For the way I spoke to you in Enisseny's room. I was angry that Enisseny put my mother in danger."

"Yes," he says as he gives me a sideways glance. "Well, I did not bleed from the words you spoke."

I wipe my nose to suppress a laugh. I've got such a bad habit of laughing at the worst times. "I didn't know there were other ways, other—" sometimes, I have a hard time finding the right word for things. Remembering the word, I say, "—gateways to my home. I thought the mirror was the only way."

"Yes, there are many," Wyndham says. "I rarely speak about these things—not even to my children. The few who have visited Canonsland and chose to make this place their home or travel back and forth know they cannot tell anyone. The knowledge is dangerous." Wyndham groans, shifts, straightens his blanket, fluffs his pillow, and places it behind his back. Once he's settled, he leans his head against the headboard again. "As you know, it risks those in other realms." There's a picture of a man with long thick hair, clean-shaven, dressed in his red ceremonial regalia with a flapping red and black cape with a white dragon that's stitched on it. It's the King's crest because it's the same one Laurence wore when he was named a knight. Next to him is a woman who has her hand around the man's elbow, and the woman's dressed in a long red and white flowing dress with flowers that crown her loose curly red hair.

Staring at the photo, I say, "I thought the connection was between Enisseny and Bob and that if Bob—"

Wyndham's eyes gleam from the dark room and light from the candles. Or maybe he's in pain? If he is, he'd never admit it. "No," he says, "should something happen—" Slouching forward, he places a hand on the bandage around his wound and gives a small grunt.

"It's okay," I say. "I know Bob," the words catch in my throat. I need to finish the sentence, though. Bob's just a dog. Taking a breath in, I whisper, "I know he won't—"

Wyndham lifts a hand to me. "No one will," he says as he reaches a wrinkled red-spotted hand for the framed photo. "She was my wife. On the day we were married." Placing a finger on the image of the woman, he outlines her face. "Why discuss the inevitable? It comes for all of us. There are things to do—some things, better than others." Placing the photo back on the table beside his bed, Wyndham says, "There are brides who walk down aisles, children to share stories with, songs to be sung, dancing to do—and battles that must be fought. That is life."

"I've never seen that photo before," I say.

"No, I had stored my possessions at the King's Acres. The last time I traveled there, I asked Eustace to prepare them so that I might bring them back here. Eustace did one step better and had them sent to me."

"Oh, that reminds me . . . some other knights have arrived. They're meeting with Laurence in your study. I didn't see Edric, though."

Wyndham says, "You would not." Wyndham's jawline pulses with Edric's name, and his eyes are once again distant. "I must dress," he says, "then we should speak with Laurence and the others. Wait outside my room. When I am ready, we shall go there together."

"Sure," I say. "I'll walk you there in case you have any problems."

The lines in Wyndham's face deepen. His eyebrows may have disappeared with the grey hair, but the wrinkles have sharpened his expression with age. "You will attend," he says. "After all, you are a knight-in-training."

"Laurence said that because I wasn't officially a knight yet, I wasn't allowed into the meeting."

"He did?" Wyndham says, squinting. "We shall see about that."

FOUR

I rap my knuckles on the oak door. Wyndham leans against the wall as we wait.

Golden light seeps through the windows and creates shadows in some corners. A couple of mirrors reflect the sun's rays, and it's odd to me how everything always seems darker in darkness, but in light, even the most terrifying moments aren't that bad.

Vik, a new knight, peers around the open door. He says, "Laurence has said . . . ," his words trail off as Wyndham looks at him over my shoulder. Stepping away from the door, "Wyndham, you are awake," he croaks.

"Yes," Wyndham says, pushing the door open with his hand and stepping into the doorway. "Come, Jayden," he says in front of four other knights in the room.

Laurence is seated on the sofa with Kemena. Kemena Knoxwell's dark bob haircut swivels in my direction. She's one of only three female knights that make up the Knighthood. My bad luck follows me here too because she's one of the knights I've studied swordsmanship with who barks orders at me like, *Move faster! Stay alert at all times! You are clumsy on your feet! You move with the same stealth as naderbers!*

Naderbers are an odd bear and groundhog combination

and move with the same noise level as a herd of rhinos on a rampage. They're also as trusting as koala bears. But if something or someone tries to hurt a fellow naderber, they'll kill them with their twelve-inch retractable claws. It's happened before.

With my hand, I push my hair back that's come undone from my ponytail and swipe along the scar that Kemena gave me in training.

"Wyndham!" Laurence cries as he gets to his feet, grinning. "It is good to see you up and about!"

"Yes, I would say so," Wyndham says. Laurence recoils his hand from Wyndham's shoulder that he'd placed there as if he's been stung by a hornet.

"Jayden?" Laurence says. I don't say anything. Instead, I stand there and try to keep my hands loose by my sides and fight the urge to fold them.

"Jayden is a knight-in-training," Wyndham says, "and she brings to us important knowledge of the woman." Wyndham raises his chin as he stares up at his son. Up until Laurence was eighteen, it was the other way around. As soon as Laurence hit that age, though, he gained several inches on Wyndham.

"I am relieved you are feeling better, Father," he says.

"We sent Laurence to pass the message on," Kemena says, standing from the couch. She walks toward Abelard and stands beside him. Abelard, an older knight with thinning hair with the rest cut short, runs his hand over the top of his head. "You know how emotional she can be," Kemena says, crossing her arms. "And we assumed—"

I don't dare interrupt. Instead, I just stand there.

If I react, Kemena wins. If I don't, she still wins.

Also, she's not wrong.

Wyndham lifts his hand. "Do not—" he says, cutting her off. "I should have known," Wyndham says through clenched teeth. Shaking his head, "We waste time with egos," Wyndham adds, looking at Laurence.

Kemena's cheeks flush pink. I stare down at the floor and

notice the trail of mud from the knight's boots.

"He is right," Abelard says with a heavy sigh. "As I was the most senior knight here, I am responsible. I should not have barred Jayden from attending the meeting. Forgive my lapse in judgment."

"'Tis forgiven," Wyndham says.

"Wyndham, did you see the woman that Jayden spoke of?" Laurence asks.

"Only from afar," he says. "We left Enisseny on the outskirts of the Xyidak and Trygolish border for his protection. Edric said he had a source and would take me to speak with the Xyidak, who claimed they were mounting an offensive. Instead, we faced waves of Xyidak soldiers that Edric and I fought. But we were separated by the onslaught of soldiers, and I summoned for Enisseny. Enisseny did not hear me. It was only from a distance that Enisseny saw Edric and I were under attack, and he came to help. Enisseny planned to do as he has done before to limit the loss of life— to throw ice on the Xyidaks and freeze them, but a woman threw a spear at him near where Edric was fighting. Edric charged the woman, and Enisseny grabbed them both. Disoriented from his injury, Enisseny used the link he had with a knight-in-training in hopes they might help." Wyndham faces me and says, "Enisseny believed you to be alone and did not sense your mother's presence—I do not know why." Sighing, Wyndham says, "The dragon's heart is filled to the brim with remorse for placing your mother in danger."

I nod. Sure, I blamed Enisseny a little. But I know who's really responsible. *We need to find that woman.*

"What of Enisseny? Did he see? Can he share with you the woman's features? Clearly?"

Wyndham chuckles, his eyebrows twitch, and he says, "Have you ever heard Enisseny speak?"

"No, I have not. I thought—" Laurence's eyes sweep across to everyone in the room, searching for someone to help him.

"You're connected to Enisseny, and we know you share some thoughts," I say, hesitating. I'm doubtful Enisseny can clearly describe the woman telepathically, but I'm open to the possibility. Laurence and I, in our private conversations, have discussed it. No one here really understands how Enisseny shares things with Wyndham. "So, maybe Enisseny knows what she looks like and can somehow communicate with you through your connection?" I say. Turning to Laurence, I add, "Is that right, Laurence?"

"Yes," he says. "But I am not questioning your ability to recall the woman." Laurence shifts uncomfortably.

"No, it's okay," I say, lifting a hand, "a lot was going on. Mom and I got sprayed with river water when Enisseny came up, and then the woman held a knife at Mom and me—" I stare at the bookcase and add, "And Mom nearly drowned . . ." My cheeks warm, and I blink back tears with the memory.

Admitting this in front of Kemena is hard. She'll have grounds to call me too emotional to be a knight. I can't even think of a defense right now.

Wyndham tilts his head, and the lines in his face deepen. "You said your mother had some small bump on her head?"

Twisting my lower lip, I forgot that I hadn't told him everything. I shift in my spot. Rubbing my eyelid, I say, "She hit a rock when she fell into the river. She was knocked unconscious." I lift my chin and straighten my back.

"How did she survive?" Laurence whispers.

I roll my shoulders back and focus on the grandabier grandfather clock in front of me that's a mix of wood and metal that occurs naturally in Canonsland. The wood part makes it malleable to carve, and the metal gives it its shine. I say, "I had to save her."

"Vik," Wyndham says. There's shuffling close to me. I refuse to look at anyone. It's a new tactic of mine—if I can steady my mind and not be swept away by another person's emotions, I have a better chance of controlling my own. The hardest thing for me when I'm coming undone is when someone else is sympathetic. Like when Dad arrived and said, *you must have been so scared.*

No. I won't think about that right now. I lift my chin higher.

"Vik," Wyndham says again, "speak with Petronilla as she has a friend in the village named Matthew, who is good with portraits. He is skilled at creating images from only words and memories. See if he might come to the Isons-Lydric Castle. Ask him to bring his sketching paper and pencils." Facing me, Wyndham says, "Between Jayden and my recollections of the woman, Matthew may be able to use his talents to sketch an image of the woman that would allow us to search for her." Sitting on the couch now, Wyndham adds, "Once we find her, perhaps we can find Edric—or perhaps find out what happened to him." Placing a hand on his bandaged abdomen Wyndham, shifts and says, "Assuming he still lives."

***

Matthew arrives, and Wyndham and I give him whatever description we can. Memories are faulty little traps, infected with distractions, and sometimes misconceptions. Everyone does this. And I know that I'm no better. Scraping butter on my bread, I watch Osgoode as he lifts a spoon in the air and sails it down, pretending he's Enisseny flying into town as Emma, his daughter, opens her mouth and gobbles up the porridge.

"Jayden, you say nothing at breakfast," Constance says, snapping me out of my memory of my first encounter with Osgoode. That first meeting, when I thought Osgoode might have been responsible for Wyndham's disappearance and for imprisoning him in the Tower in Ikansterup.

Pushing the porridge around, I let out a loud sigh, louder than I'd intended. The woman, Edric, who was injured, Enisseny's wounds . . .

Glancing down the table, I see Wyndham staring at me. Of course, there's also Wyndham's missing spleen now, oh, damn—then I shift uncomfortably . . .

I'm not allowed to swear here, so I try not to, even when

I'm working things out in my head because I've accidentally said the words out loud before. And then there's Mom's concussion—so, there's a lot to think over. Finally, there's the whole perpetual ticking clock that hangs over me when I'm here, and will anyone notice I'm missing (right now, that's Dad), before I can make it back home?

"How's Enisseny doing?" I ask Constance.

"He is doing well," Constance says. "He has recovered quickly. If I were to guess, I would say he will fully recover in the next day."

At the other end of the table, Kemena, Vik, Abelard, Laurence, and Wyndham discuss what they will do next. Between the conversation with Constance and being distracted with her children, as well as my guilty memories of things I did years ago, I've only caught snippets of the conversation between the knights.

They've devised a plan for Abelard, Kemena, and Vik to check with neighboring cities to see if anyone has seen either Edric or the woman. After, they'll return to the King's Acres. Wyndham and Laurence will go directly to Stock Castle.

"And Jayden, you will come with us," Wyndham says as he places his napkin on the table and reclines back in his chair.

I flip my wrist over to check my watch. When I look up again, Wyndham's watching me. "Sorry," I say. Guilt sweeps across me like an icy polar vortex wind. I shift in my chair. Will Wyndham think I'd prefer to be somewhere else instead of helping him find Edric and the woman?

Leaning forward, Wyndham says, "Do not worry, Jayden," he says with a wave of his hand. Placing his elbows on the table, he leans forward and hooks his fingers together, and says something to Abelard.

Conversations are happening all around us: Constance and Osgoode with their children; Petronilla and Matthew chatting at the other end of the table about their last day of school and friends; Abelard, Kemena, Laurence, Vik, and Wyndham making plans of what the next steps will be.

I've always been the outsider, whether it's here or at home.

Not rooted enough in Calgary like Hannah and Ava. And I don't know that I'm made for the realm of knights and dragons either. When I first came, I believed because Enisseny brought me here, I definitely belonged. Now, I'm not so sure.

"Did you speak with your mother before you arrived?" Wyndham asks.

I say, "Yeah, she'd just woken up. Dad and I only talked to her for a little bit before visiting hours ended, and we had to go."

"Before we leave," Wyndham says, "we will check to make sure that all is well at home. That you are not missed there."

"Jayden!" Hugo shouts, and the sound of his pretend gruff voice startles me.

"Hugo!" Wyndham snaps back at the four-year-old. The boy's curly hair bobs at Wyndham, and he places a finger to his lips. He doesn't cry, though. Hugo and Emma rarely do. Hugo, with big eyes, watches Wyndham, and I notice Emma has gone silent along with the rest of the table.

Wyndham winks. Hugo throws his hands up in the air, squeals, and says, "Aaaaaaa!" grinning at Wyndham. Hugo's triumphant relief spills across each person at the breakfast table—even Kemena and Abelard smile and laugh.

***

"We will leave early tomorrow morning." Wyndham's words are an order, not a suggestion. I let go of Petronilla's hand.

"Safe travels," Petronilla says as her fingers slip from my hand. Before she leaves, she plants a kiss on my cheek as she's done ever since my first outing with Wyndham as a knight-in-training when—let's just say things didn't go so well.

Ever since we were young, she's always been warm like that to everyone. Other people have noticed it: Ella's sincerity, her ability to diffuse difficult situations, and at the same time to lead people. She's finished her final year of schooling in Rumbling Town, and in the next few days, she's going to leave and will attend Diplomacy School on the King's Acres. With her leaving, I long for more moments when we can ride horses together, chase each other around the Castle, or pick berries.

"It will be difficult for Idonea and Alwyn . . . ," Wyndham's eyebrows arch, "as she is their only daughter." I stare at the closed door my friend disappeared through, wishing that she'd come back. Wishing I could talk her out of Diplomacy School and leaving Rumbling Town.

Would that be fair to her, though? We all go in separate directions, eventually. Even my friends in Calgary can't wait to leave the city so eager to see what comes after high school. My friends are always talking about what schools they'll be going to, jobs they want to do, and where they hope to live.

My chest burns as Wyndham and I walk down the hallway. When Wyndham unlatches the door, Enisseny lifts his head, bolts up, and races toward Wyndham and gives him a thump with his nose.

The gentle "thump" from the dragon's nose causes Wyndham to fly to the other side of the room. Bending forward, I can't help myself as tears roll down my cheeks. Laughing, still, Wyndham's legs and arms are spread out across the stone floor. Enisseny blinks a few times. And I don't know. Is that a smile across his face?

"Wyndham?" I say, wiping the smile from my face. "Wyndham?" I say louder. "Damn it, Wyndham!" I shout.

"I am here." One of Wyndham's black gloves is in the air as he slowly rolls over. "And do not use those kinds of words here," he adds.

"You could have killed him, Enisseny!" There's nothing from the dragon—not a hint of remorse, not a curled lip, not a slinking away into a corner like other animals do when they know they've been bad. Instead, Enisseny flaps his wings once and staggers towards Wyndham.

"What are you doing?" I ask Wyndham. He has his arms hooked behind his head as if he's staring up at the stars. He doesn't say anything.

I look up to the ceiling. Above us, there's a view from my world of clouds and Snowbirds with CAF Pilots in the cockpit and a roaring sound that thunders as jets speed over us. When they're gone, the wooden ceiling fades back to the image of several Winter Dragons flying above a small village where below them there's a baker that holds a long loaf of bread while small children play in the meadows and men and women work in fields side-by-side.

"I have never seen anything like that before," Wyndham says.

"And neither have I," Laurence says from behind us.

"It looked like our Snowbirds—they're jets, from my country," I say, glancing at Enisseny. "But they have jets in other countries as well. So, they could have been from somewhere else, too." *But I doubt it—because I'm sure I saw a maple leaf on those jets.*

Wyndham stands and dusts himself off. "Let us check the time," he says.

Enisseny opens the portal, and I take Wyndham's hand and step back through the mirror. Bob's sleeping on my bed, I stop and pat his head, and he doesn't move. I check the time on my clock, and it shows a little past twelve. It's dark, so I guess it's only been a couple of hours. To be sure, I grab my cell phone and check the date. It shows the next day, and the time is 12:23.

"Jayden? How is everything?" Wyndham says from the other side of the mirror.

I have twenty-six missed text messages. The problem with living in a small town is that word gets around fast. My fingers flick through the messages, and I skim them:

Dave: Jay, I heard about your Mom. You okay?

Hannah: OMG! I heard about your Mom. Is she okay? Are you okay?

Rob: Heard what happened today. Glad that your Mom's okay.

Ava: Jayden, call me!

Rob: Wow. You're uh, some kind of badass. Can I get swimming lessons from you?

Smiling, I can't help myself. Rob's always ready with a joke. So, all of my friends have heard about Mom . . . Then again, I only have four close friends. I know I should respond to them...

Right now, though, I can't.

I plug the phone back into the charger. Facing the mirror again, I say, "Everything's fine." Enisseny breathes ice crystals, Wyndham extends his hand, and when Wyndham's hand appears through the mirror, I take the black-gloved hand and slide back into the mirror.

As the window to my world closes, I notice Bob never moved from my bed. And that thought, the one friend I've had this whole time and who has followed me everywhere, now doesn't, makes me feel more alone than I've ever felt before.

FIVE

I throw the saddle on Lyra, straighten it, and tighten the buckles just like I learned when I came to Canonsland and visited with Grandma and Grandpa in British Columbia. It's odd when I see Grandma Imogene in British Columbia because she doesn't live on the farm anymore. What started as me staying with them for one summer when Mom was diagnosed with cancer became a yearly trip for a few weeks each summer.

Last winter, though, Grampa Sydney died. A stroke took him and took him quickly. Nana knew she couldn't take care of the farm, so she sold it and bought a two-bedroom condo in Kelowna. Now, there's no more horseback riding. Instead, we go to Bingo.

I only have one grandparent left now. I toss the reins over Lyra's head and clip her in the nose with the bite. "Sorry, Lyra," I say, rubbing the spot on her nose.

"Abelard, Kemena, and Vik have left," Laurence says, leading his horse by the reins. Laurence's Knights Travelling Bag is secured to the back of his saddle that carries small amounts of food and a canteen to scoop water from rivers, lakes, streams, and such. For a knight, it's all about traveling light. Laurence wraps the reins around a nearby post and says,

"Do you need help?"

"Noooo," I say, buckling the last parts. Hiding behind Lyra, I stop moving. I take a breath in. Lack of sleep makes me impatient. And snappy. Laurence always irritates me. I don't know why.

Peering under Lyra's neck, I say, "Sorry."

Laurence doesn't say anything, but he gives me a half-nod. When we're out of the stables, Constance is there, holding a bundle in her hands. "I have packed you some fresh scones and jam," she says as her daughter Emma squints up at me.

"Thank you," I say. "But you didn't need to do that." I take the bundle and add it to the back of my saddle, where I've tied some clothes and a blanket to sleep on if Laurence and I don't make it to the first town.

"I wished to," she says.

"Yes, and I do not object," Laurence says, grinning.

"No, you would not," Constance says. With her hands behind her back, she squints at Laurence and smiles. "You will find the woman," she says, turning to face me. Emma places her hands on her hips, sighs, and waits.

Constance and Osgoode are definitely not typical parents. Sure, they take care of Hugo and Emma well. Otherwise, their children are free to run, play, and figure out who they are. I suspect that's the reason why Emma and Hugo seldom cling to Constance or Osgoode's pants. At four, they have more confidence in themselves than I've ever had.

"Yeah, I'm sure we will." Placing my hand on the horn of the saddle, I take a step forward to sling my foot into the stirrup. Constance places her hand on mine, and I stop. Standing beside me, she squeezes my hand once. I stare at her, but I can't find the right words to say. The warmness of Constance's hand gives me some comfort. Then she turns and walks away. I swing myself up into my saddle.

When Constance stands next to Emma, she snaps her fingers at her daughter and offers her hand. Emma looks up, slides her fingers into her mother's hand, and they climb the hill back to Isons-Lydric Castle. Emma chatters away and says she's going to ride out to the blue weeping willow. Constance says, "If I bring yellow berry scones, could I come, too?" and that's the last thing I hear.

As we leave the outskirts of the Castle, I stare at everything more closely—the blue weeping willows, the brown fields, and the lights that are strung across the village. Steam rises over my lips from the cool air. Smoke billows from chimneys as the morning sun wakes the sleeping town.

"What are you thinking?" Laurence says, his saddle swishing back and forth, the hooves of his horse clopping alongside Lyra's. When I look over at him, his eyes are moist, and he shifts in his seat. He glances back at the weeping willow that's maybe a couple of hundred feet from the stone wall that surrounds Rumbling Town before he peers at me, still waiting for an answer.

There's a look I can't describe—some uncertainty in his face. It's the smoothness of his skin, the way he's leaning in his saddle, and the way his chin is dropped. "Nothing," I say.

"Same," he says with a sigh while he stares at the still waking town.

I want to say something. *Do you feel it? That something's shifting? Something is coming for us? We're not prepared. And now, I don't know . . . It feels like we're out of time.*

A rare green five-foot lenis eagle soars down from the sky and perches himself on the wall. Flexing his wings, he expands them as he bobs his head up and down, looking from right to left but never at us. Shy by nature, they're rarely seen. Then the eagle turns and stares at us. I tighten my grasp on my reins and glance over at Laurence. He runs a hand across his horse's shoulder and stares at the bird too.

And as quickly as the lenis eagle arrives, it's gone. There was no flapping, no sailing up to the clouds, nothing. It was there one minute, and then it wasn't. A song from the clouds catches my attention, and that's when I see the large green wings disappear through scarlet, round clouds in the sky.

Sighing, I say, "Let's go."

***

Kneeling down to the river, I fill my canteen. Cupping my hand, I drink from the Golden River, named so, because the water looks like gold. Below the surface is a metal with a yellow glow to it, and on the right day, when the sun is burning bright unhindered, the water appears with the same golden shine.

The metal under the water is worthless—it's not malleable, and it can't be bent like steel to build weapons or cutlery. Neither does it have the same value as crystal, gold, or diamonds. (All are used in Canonsland, too.) The sole purpose of the blondel is to deceive people and make them believe it's valuable when it's not.

"Jayden?" Laurence's voice comes from above me. I squint and hold a hand over my forehead to block out the sun's rays. Laurence's hands are on his hips. "'Tis important one remains vigilant as one may never know when danger is imminent."

Sighing, I say, "Uh-huh."

"Why are you dismissive of me?" Laurence says, folding his arms.

"Defensive, much?" I mutter.

"You do not listen to the advice I have to offer," he says. "When you are not in training with Kemena or Wyndham, when they are not available to guide you—I wish only to help," he finishes. Laurence stares off at Mount Saint Agatha, a mountaintop rising high in the northeast. You can't always see it every day, but it's visible on a crisp day like today.

The mountain is the original one, the birthplace of all life of Canonsland. Or at least that's how the story goes. I remember this was the fable: Once upon a time, two sister mountaintops, Agatha and Eithne, created all of Canonsland—from the flowers, trees, rivers, lakes, animals, and people. But for everything Agatha made—the Golden River, the Winter Dragons, the lenis eagle, all those things that were good—Eithne created the opposite—the River of Fire, the black dragon, the warlock eagle. At first, it wasn't so bad, and Agatha tried to encourage her sister's creations. This carried on for many years.

Over time though, Agatha noticed her creations were slowly destroyed: The River of Fire gobbled up Agatha's meadows; the black dragons shredded the waving tree. Agatha tried to negotiate with her sister and suggested dividing the world into half where Agatha could work on her creations and Eithne could do the same. Eithne, however, refused.

So, the situation carried on. Until one day, Agatha, boiling from the inside and who never had gotten angry before, struck Eithne and sent her flying to the north.

There, Eithne survived. However, buried beneath ice and snow, Agatha's sister could never create anything again, and whatever Eithne made died away.

"You don't have to tutor me," I say. "Wyndham and Kemena have taught me enough." Standing up, I grab my water container and walk past him.

Stepping in front of me, Laurence whispers, "Jayden? I was your age. I know what a difficult time it can be—wedged between the world of adult and child."

"Do you?" I ask. *Do you really, Laurence? Do you know how hard it is for someone like me, a girl, to want to join the CAF and become a pilot? Do you know that there's a good chance I'll get laughed at and no one will take me seriously?*

It's bad enough that my school guidance counselor doesn't think it's an appropriate career for a girl. *Jayden, how about a Business Degree at the Community College?* he'd said. Welcome to the 1960s.

"I wish only to help," Laurence says. He walks beside me to where our horses are grazing by the river. He ties his water canister to the horse, pauses, and glances in my direction. "Are you angry that we did not travel with Wyndham? As he said, we would?"

"No," I say with a huff. "I understand Enisseny might not be able to carry all of us because he was injured." Grabbing the reins of my horse, I add, "Of course, I also know that we should check with the smaller villages and the unmapped ones because Abelard, Kemena, and Vik were only stopping at the larger towns." There's more I want to say but can't because of who might be listening. Sticking my foot in the stirrup, I say, "I'm angry that you assumed I wasn't paying attention." I swing myself up into my saddle. Leaning forward, I breathe into Laurence's ear, "I saw the mander that was nearby. I don't know why you assumed I didn't. I was prepared if he decided to attack."

Laurence stares forward and says nothing. Then he swings his leg over his horse and sits on Sigmund. Seated now, he says, "I am sorry. I should not have doubted you."

"Well," I say, "maybe you can tell Kemena that I'm observant?"

"I would be happy to," Laurence says as he searches the haunting trees and the redena wildflowers that are wrapped around them. "We should be able to stay at the Inn at Ludswup this evening."

"Yeah, we've got about four more hours of daylight." I crane my neck as I watch the sun's light dip below the horizon. Time is a sneaky creature that gives you the impression that it's on your side. Until the day it isn't.

I catch Laurence mid-nod. I guess it's the best he can do. He doesn't disagree with me about my estimation in time, but he doesn't agree either.

***

I carry my bag up to my room and toss it into the corner. Lifting my sleeve, I glance at the time. Dr. Eastwood nor I have been able to determine the ratio of the time difference between Canonsland and our world. It's not one day equals two days. Or one day equals three days. Time is constantly shifting. Sometimes, one night is one night. And sometimes, two weeks in Canonsland is one night.

Dr. Eastwood has settled in Canonsland permanently since he married Dr. Miriam Wretchell. He's managed to close off his ties to the other world. Both Dr. Eastwood's parents and siblings are gone, and his nieces and nephews won't be looking for him. He's sold his property and donated the money to charity. Now, he resides on the King's Acres and lives in a newly built stone house on the outskirts of the village that surrounds Stock Castle.

Me? I'm still straddling two worlds.

The door opens, and Laurence carries his bag in his hand. There's a pause. "I see you have decided on that bed," he says, tossing his satchel into the other corner of the room where there's a second bed as he scans the room. "Mander?" Laurence whispers.

"Yes," I say, pulling the curtains back. I look behind them before I close the plaid drapes. Laurence bends forward and lifts the blankets back and onto the bed, and peeks under the mattress. When he's done, his lower lip puckers, and he chews it. I've checked underneath my bed already when I unlaced my boots.

Laurence scans the room, searching. Placing one hand on the doorknob to a closet, I put my other hand over the dagger strapped to my thigh. My boots, belt, and sword are next to my bed on the other side of the room. Okay, I know I shouldn't have done that. If there is someone here, I only have my dagger. It's a junior mistake.

Laurence lifts a hand to me. Frustrated, I swing the door open.

There's nothing there besides one old moldy and worn red suitcase.

Shaking his head, Laurence says nothing.

"What?" I demand.

"I have a new appreciation of how Wyndham felt when I was your age. That is all."

"I'm not you," I say. "Stop comparing me to you—we don't have the same life."

"Of course, we do not." Laurence continues to dissect the closet, laying his palms on boards on the walls and tapping the floor with his foot calmly.

And it's infuriating. "There's no one here, Laurence. Do you really think there's a hidden entrance behind one of those boards? This place used to be a barn. Well, before they converted it to an Inn."

"I have the same history of Ludswup as you," he mutters. I cross my arms in front of me, no longer caring what he thinks.

"That was clever of you," he says.

"What was?" I ask.

"The man who was following us, you called him a mander snake, so he would not know you saw him—clever."

"Clever and . . . ?"

Laurence places a hand on a board in the closet. Kneeling down, he shifts the suitcase over and pushes on one of the floorboards. "And nothing," he says, looking up to the shelf at the top of the closet. I huff. There's the smell of day-old sweat on him, and his skin glistens with perspiration. Covering my nose, I watch Laurence as he places a hand on a wooden bar and says, "It was good of you to use a code word. So, as not to alert the man—"

There's a rush of air that blasts from below my feet. Laurence disappears through a hole that opens there. I want to scream, *Laurence! Laurence!*

Instead, I grunt and chew my lower lip. I swivel my head in the direction of my bed where I'd kicked off my boots and where my sword sits. *Yeah, I don't think I have time to go back for either.* The wind hissing through the open floor subsides as the wooden floor begins to snap shut.

I place a socked foot in the spot where Laurence had stood and force the wooden bar up. The hole in the floor reopens, and I fall through it.

SIX

"O w," I grunt. I'm barely able to grasp where I am. Bouncing along a dark stone tunnel, I slip along greasy mud that digs into my clothes and scrapes against my skin. With a *swoosh*, I'm ejected and land on my back. Staring up, I take in the view around me.

There's sloppy, black sludge all over me—and a lot of it. If I'd landed ten feet to my right, I would have missed this heap of slimy goo. I use the back of my hand to wipe bits from my face. Looking around, there's a partial wall a short distance away that leads to another room, and I see several heads in there. *Clanking* and *banging* sounds are everywhere. I slow my breathing and crane my neck when I hear footsteps and muffled words. Placing a hand on my right side, I search for my sword. I tighten my jaw. *Right, I left it in the room.*

Rolling onto my stomach, I inch forward. I keep part of my body submerged in the mud, and sludge drenches the front of my shirt and my pants. I creep up to the wall. I notice the sloppy earth has disappeared, replaced with moss-encrusted bricks under my feet. With my missing boots and the lower temperatures, even though we're in the south of Canonsland and I still have socks on, my feet sting from the cold bricks.

"Is there someone else with you?" a long brown bearded man says, wearing a lop-sided straw hat.

"No," Laurence replies. I shouldn't be surprised it's so easy for him to deny my existence. Laurence berates me for always getting into trouble, losing my direction, and never being a good partner because I sometimes follow too far behind whatever knight I'm teamed up with.

"Liar!" the man barks as he swings his fist across Laurence's chin, sending him sprawling into a nearby steel drain. "We know there was a woman with you!"

Laughing, Laurence gets to his feet and says, "Ah, yes, the woman. She is no one. For certain, she is not someone a man like you should fear."

Shrinking against the wall further, I grind my teeth. I understand that Laurence is keeping them from searching for me. But, at the same time, I know he believes there's some truth to what he's saying.

"Why have you come to Ludswup?" the man says. "You know Ludswup does not welcome knights."

"Yes, I know." Laurence wipes blood from his lip. Standing, he says, "We search for a woman. And a knight named Edric."

"You come to Ludswup, anyway?" the man says, grinning.

"We were tired," Laurence says, lifting one eyebrow. His eyes glisten with his pathetic joke.

"Still, trying to get yourself killed?" I whisper. Peering over the wall, there are three men to Laurence. Two men are behind Laurence. One man's grey-haired, and he slouches and sighs loud enough that even from where I am, I can hear him. Water swishes around an open drain. The drain runs around the outskirts of the room, and if I had to guess, I suspect it's the water that supplies either the Inn or the town of Ludswup. Another man stands directly behind Laurence. He's close enough that Laurence most likely knows what he had for dinner.

"Have you seen them?" Laurence asks.

"Who?" Brown Beard says.

My back is against the wall as I look around.

Bent forward, I inch along the wall as my toes cramp. Leaving my boots in the room makes things uncomfortable. At the same time, it might be a stroke of good luck. Without the soles of my shoes clopping against the stone, no one can hear me coming.

When I get to the slopping water in the open drain, I sink into the water. It's freezing! I suppress a shiver. Keeping my eyes open, I slow my breathing, relax my body, and let the water push me along the drain right into the path of the man that sits close to the gutter.

My eyes are wide. As I slowly drift in the direction of the man, I keep my breathing slow and remind myself not to blink.

Laurence is still doing his thing. *Whatever that might be.* Then, I see—his mouth isn't moving. My ears are underwater, so I can't hear a thing. I keep my mind calm while I continue to stare at nothing. Laurence is in front of me. His outstretched hand reaches for me. From behind him, there's movement. Laurence disappears from my eyesight. Brown beard's back is turned away from me. I take a chance, blink, and search for Laurence. Laurence is face down on the ground. Again.

The man who was sitting on the edge by the drain is standing. *Did he see my eyes move?* No matter.

I leap from the water charging at the grey-haired man. I knock the wrinkled man to the ground and release my dagger from my leg. Dragging the man to his feet, I place the knife against the elderly man's neck and hiss, "If you want him to live, I wouldn't touch the knight again!"

"Miss, we don't want any trouble here!" Brown Beard says, backing into a corner.

"Laurence," I stutter. My hand shakes from the cold water as I hold the dagger to the man's throat. "Ask your questions." Laurence's face is ashen. *What's the matter with him?* I drag the man into a corner, keeping my arm wrapped around his neck. My eyes rest on the other man who stands in the corner. Laurence gapes at me.

"Laurence!" I bark.

Laurence shakes his head and clears his throat. "Have you seen a knight in Ludswup?"

"We have not seen the people you search for!" Brown Beard says. "Now, let my Pop go!"

I glance at the man that I have in a chokehold. His body is bent backward, given how short I am. When I see his eyes, they're watery. Dark lines run deep into his skin, showing his age.

"Laurence, show the man the picture of the woman!" I snap.

Searching the front pocket of his shirt, he pulls out the sketch of the woman that Matthew had drawn.

Brown Beard glances at the picture of the woman and shakes his head. Then, Laurence shows him the sketch of Edric, and the man says, "I have not seen them!"

I unhook my arm from Brown Beard's father's neck. "We're taking him with us!" Tugging the old man's collar, I pull the worn fabric toward me. *Pop*, the man had said. Remorse rolls over me like one of those paving machines. I want to let him go. But the senior man is our only insurance that Brown Beard and his thug won't kill us the first chance they get.

Grabbing the man by his arm, I walk backward with Laurence following me. We run along a corridor, and then we enter another room. I place my fingers to my lips and keep the dagger close to the stubble of the man's neck. "I can show you another way out," the man whispers. His palms are raised in surrender. Laurence and I look at each other. "I do not wish for anyone to get harmed."

"How can we trust you?" I say.

"You have no choice. My son, he knows these tunnels well. He will find you. My son is a good boy, but King Nicholas' Knights have charged him several times with laws that do not apply in Ludswup. And he is protective of me. He has never killed before, but I am the last of his kin—the death of his wife last winter and then his son's murder by Xyidak thieves near Mt. Lieuschanean—he may now. His temper is like a spark, ready to ignite."

"Jayden, lower your weapon," Laurence orders, pushing my dagger down. I return my blade to the sheath strapped to my leg. He turns to the old man. "We have had reports of thieves on that road."

Squeezing his palms together, the man says nothing. His eyes redden, though. Walking over to a wall in the room, he faces us. "My son knows his way well, here. However, he does not know all of Ludswup's secrets. The man touches a spider web, and in front of him, a ladder drops. "Go up," he says, "and once you are there, you will see a young man with red hair and eyes to match. His name is Olin. He will ask you a question so you may enter his world to escape." The wrinkles around his eyes link together as he focuses on Laurence and me. Glancing at the ladder, he says, "Now climb!"

"Jayden," Laurence says, scanning the room, "please, go first." And bossy Laurence has returned. Hooking my foot into the rope ladder, I start to climb up. Laurence is right behind me, and the ladder begins to swing.

"Laurence, stop bouncing," I hiss.

"One more thing," the elderly man says. Laurence and I freeze on the ladder. "Do not lie to Olin," the man says, peering up to us. With a flick of his wrist, he swings another cobweb, and the ladder rushes up.

✳✳✳

Grasping the rope ladder, I hold on tight as we speed upward. I know I should be terrified. I'm not, though. Wind rushes between my fingers that cling to the rope. Bits of mud blow off my face.

"Jayden!" Laurence cries.

Staring down, I see Laurence grips a wrung of the ladder with only one hand. His legs are flailing underneath him. "Laurence!" I shout. Slowly, I go back down the ladder. I wrap my knees through the wrung and hang upside down when I'm close to him. Extending my hand, Laurence reaches for it, grasps my fingers, and I pull him in. Laurence grips the ladder with the other hand and wraps both arms around the rope. "What were you doing? Trying to show off?"

Laurence sucks in air. Looking away, he says nothing. Then he gives me a slight smile, and says, "Of course. I am a knight!"

I start to laugh. It ends when I skid across the dirt.

My face stings as if it's been burnt. Wiping a finger across it, I notice, as usual, I'm bleeding.

"Sorry about the difficult landing," a red-haired man with red eyes says. He looks roughly the same age as Laurence.

"Olin," Laurence says, getting to his feet. I'm in a seated position, knees bent, and I watch incredulously as Laurence strides past me. Extending his hand, he says, "'Tis good to meet you." The man's hands are folded in front of him. He says nothing to Laurence. "The elderly man, he told us of you," Laurence adds.

"Yes, he is one of the few who knows about me and this place." Laurence retracts his hand and stares out at the stars that surround us. Otherwise, darkness is everywhere.

Stepping past Laurence, the red-haired man says, "Do you need help?" he asks, extending his hand.

Taking it, I say, "Thank you," as I get to my feet. My lips tighten at Laurence. *See? See, Laurence?* That's what you should have done.

"Oh," Laurence mutters. His cheeks glow pink.

Some days, he really does fail the knight chivalry challenge.

"I must ask you a question before I can permit you to enter my world." Olin's hand unclasps my hand.

"Yes, we were told. What world is this?" Laurence asks.

"It is a world within Canonsland."

"And you are the Gate Keeper?"

"No. The man you met is the Gate Keeper. He decides who I should see or who might need help. An escape, if you will—so that someone might get themselves together." His eyes rest on me. For the first time, I have some sense of how I might look. I stare down at my fingers and notice a thick layer of mud under my fingernails. Gooey bits are everywhere on me; down my black pants and up my brown shirt— pushing my hair back that's come undone, there are crunchy chunks in my hair—and the weight of the sludge squishes from my socks. You would think soaking in the water would have helped. It didn't. Running a hand along my face—yup, it's there, too.

I peek over at Laurence. His knees and elbows are splattered. But I guess he landed in a better spot when he shot out of the tunnel . . .

Olin smiles and says, "Now, before I let you in, you must answer a question. And a warning—you must be honest in your answer."

"And, if we do not?" Laurence asks.

Olin chuckles and folds his arms. Sighing, Olin's eyes sweep across Laurence's clothes, and he says, "Do you make it a habit to lie?"

"No. Of course, I do not." Laurence throws his hands up and says, "But my position does require me to be discreet. So, there are things I am not at liberty to say."

Slapping him on the shoulder, Olin puts his arm around Laurence and places a hand on the back of his neck, squeezing once. "Do not worry. I am not after King Nicholas' secrets."

"I'll go first," I say.

Olin walks towards me and says, "You are not afraid?"

"I've got nothing to hide."

"Everyone has something to hide," Olin says.

I want to be a fighter pilot. My face flushes with heat. Blinking at him, I can't say anything.

"What happens if we lie?" Laurence asks.

"Your internal body temperature will warm up. It is what happens when most people lie."

"Where is the threat in that?"

"If you continue to lie, your internal body temperature will continue to increase . . . and if you lie again . . . ," Olin's red eyes rest on me. "Let us leave it at it will increase until you either tell the truth or do not."

"You are a wizard?" Laurence says.

"Sir Laurence asks many questions," Olin says with a playful smile. "It is surprising he manages to get anything done."

Covering my mouth, I try to stop myself from laughing. But I can't. Laurence shifts awkwardly.

"What do you do?" Olin asks.

"I'm in school," I say. "But Wyndham, Laurence, and a few of the other knights think I might be okay as a knight someday. So, I'm in training," I say, shrugging.

"You are from another realm?"

"Yeah. How did you know that?"

"You say words differently," Olin says. "As for your question," he stares down at Laurence, "I am not a wizard. Consider me the Officer of Trepid Divide. I ask the question, and the gates decide whether you speak the truth." Olin crosses his arms, arches an eyebrow, and says, "It is an easy question, Jayden. Are you ready?"

"Yes. One question, though."

"You will be a good knight," Olin grins.

"Right, the knights that ask too many questions," I say, nodding. "How did you know my name?"

"Neither one of you were, how shall we say, *discreet* on your way up on the ladder. Hopefully, you are not like that in battle. I heard two names: Laurence and Jayden. I guessed which one applied." I watch Laurence deflate like a tire that's got a nail in it. I can't help but feel the same way.

"So, Jayden, this is the question—" Olin says, eyeing Laurence. "And it is always the same question. What is your greatest fear?"

"Why tell us the question is always the same?" Laurence says. "If you tell us, then we will know how to answer next time."

Spinning around, Olin glances at Laurence. His childish,

playful smile is gone. His eyes cool. Then the curve of his eyebrow and the arrogance in his jawline dissipate. "Your answer will change. With time . . . ," he says.

"So, Jayden, your answer?"

***

"I can only say one thing that I'm afraid of?"

Olin's pupils move back and forth. He's hunting. Searching for an understanding of why I would ask that question. Then it occurs to me. I just gave away the fact that I'm afraid of multiple things.

"The question is: *What is your greatest fear?* It is one thing that you are the most terrified of above all else."

"One thing," I whisper. Several things come to mind, like losing Bob, Mom, or Dad; or the door to Canonsland being permanently closed to me. All of this, all the things I learned in Canonsland, all the people I met, will be gone. Not being allowed to be a fighter pilot. There are too many things to choose from.

"'Tis difficult to choose only one, sometimes," Olin says.

"No, it's easy . . . losing my Mom." Looking at him, I raise my chin. *I know what's important.*

The wind blows across my face. The breeze is cool on my skin. It's refreshing after the mud, the swim, the ladder—all of it.

"Good," Olin says. Swiveling around, he says to Laurence, "and, you? What is the thing you fear the most?"

"Not being a good knight," Laurence says.

"Excellent! You have both done very well! See, the question and the answers—were easy!"

Running a finger across my lips, they're warm. And they're swelling. It's the same thing that happens when I have the flu. "Are you alright?" Olin's eyes flicker at me as he leans forward.

I touch my forehead with my fingertips, dabbing the sweat away. "Perhaps, not so easy . . . ," Olin's words trail off into the darkness that surrounds us. He peers over at Laurence. Laurence's face glows red.

"Jayden," Olin says, "not everyone lies deliberately. Sometimes, a person's greatest fear is not known to them either. They have concealed it from themselves."

Gulping, a headache makes me blink. Laurence collapses to the ground.

"Ah! Perhaps we should work on him first! Men do not always have as much time!" Olin shouts as he kneels beside Laurence. Touching his chest, he leans into Laurence. "Laurence, what is the thing you fear the most?" Laurence's mouth opens, then closes, and he gasps.

Bending forward, the darkness makes me dizzy. *Where's that breeze when I need it most?* I collapse to the ground beside Laurence. "Laurence," I say. "I won't tell anyone, just tell Olin what you're most afraid of." Staring up, Laurence chuckles, but a cough makes him stop laughing. "Laurence," I whisper.

"Laurence and Jayden," Olin says, holding my hand and Laurence's. "Most of the time, it is the thing that first comes to mind. Now, Laurence—what is the thing that you fear the most? Do not think or weigh each thought. Many times, from what those who survived have told me, it was the first thing you will think of before you have time to consider."

I don't hear Laurence's answer. "Jayden?" I see his red eyes and his red hair. My body is light on the ground, almost as if I'm floating. Whispering, Olin says, "What is the thing that you are unable to live without. Or perhaps, it is not a thing—maybe, it is some emotion."

"Trapped," I mumble. Cool water runs down the sides of my cheeks. "I'm afraid of being trapped."

SEVEN

Blinking, I wake to white walls, white sheets, and a dark-skinned man staring at me, seated in a chair in the corner of my room. He smiles. "You are awake," he says. Standing up, "I will let Olin know," the man adds as he walks past the end of my bed.

"Wait," I say. "Where's Laurence?" The words catch in my throat. The last thought I have of Laurence is his back on the ground with his forehead, curly hair, and sideburns soaked in sweat.

There's a thumping in my chest. Laurence makes me crazy with his ongoing know-it-all arrogance, his dismissive attitude toward me—

"I am here, Jayden," Laurence says. He's in a different bed across from mine.

Laurence's face is pale. Eyes are somewhere else. I yank the sheet up to my chest as my heart races. Coughing, he clears his throat and says, "Almost, better," he says with a snort-cough-chuckle.

"I will get Olin," the man says, shaking his head.

I tap my head with my fingertips and drop my chin. *I can't believe him.* Laurence is always making the stupidest jokes at the most inconvenient times.

"What?" Laurence says, rolling over onto his stomach. His hand drops over the side of his bed.

"Mander's bite," I say.

"What?"

"It's my made-up swear word because I'm not allowed to swear here. And sometimes, I need to say something."

Folding the sheets back, I drop a foot to the floor. The white marble is warm. I wiggle my toes in appreciation for the unexpected warmth. Then, sirens wail in our room! Covering my ears, I try to block out the sound. Our room bursts with heart red light—the walls, marble, and the windows—all of it darken with the color as the sound of scratching on paper continues. Looking around, I see numbers etched onto paper that show 73 and 110/70. The scribbling sound, though, is no competition for the *screeching* from the alarm.

Bending forward, I look up at Laurence. He's laughing. I frown at him. Then he tries to say something. It looks like, *get back to bed!*

I leap back into my bed. The ear-piercing noise stops. The walls, marble, and windows fade back to white.

"We have another one who has tried to escape," Olin says, leaning against the doorway.

Heat flames my cheeks. "I wasn't trying to escape," I say. "I wanted to see if Laurence was okay."

Olin comes over to me and places a hand on my forehead. "Women tend to recover faster." He looks over his shoulder. Laurence is on his belly with his right hand dangling over the mattress. "How are you feeling, my friend?" Olin asks.

"Never better," Laurence quips with a groan.

"If you had not lied—"

"I did not know I was lying," Laurence says.

"I know. Neither of you did." Olin's smile drifts away and is replaced with a grim look of despair. Then, Olin's triumphant grin returns, and he walks to the doorway and says, "You cannot leave until we decide you are well enough to travel." His eyes move back and forth between Laurence and me. Sighing, he says, "I will gather your belongings from your room in Ludswup, as well as your horses, and take them to the foothills of the King's Acres." Leaning forward, he says, "But you must not leave until the doctors and nurses decide you are well enough to go," he says. "Do we have a bargain?"

Sinking into my bed, I tug the sheets up to my chin and give a stiff nod. "Fine," I say.

"Yes," Laurence says. He throws his right hand back onto the bed, grunts when he rolls over onto his back, and mumbles something. The sheets flap and crinkle as he wrestles with them and tries to shake them out over his body.

And Laurence continues to wrestle . . .

"Can I have a less noisy roommate?" I ask Olin.

Olin's cheeks swell, and his nose flares. "I am sorry, we are fully booked." Smiling, he turns and walks out the doorway, his red hair shining.

***

"That is what you look like when you wear boots!" Olin says. "And, cleaned," he adds.

"Yup," I say. Laurence and I spent a day in the hospital, and during that time, Olin had our things sent out for cleaning. I'm still unsteady on my feet. Fog cakes the wheels of my brain. Laurence is at the other end of the hallway, not looking much better. We'd passed a kitchen, and then Laurence doubled back to see about getting a glass of water. Laurence lurches like a car that's lost a wheel on the highway as he creeps toward Olin and me. But we're already on the move and pick up our pace in case Laurence falls over. Again.

Shelves of books line either side of the hallway, floor to ceiling. Scanning the room, I'm still trying to figure out where we are.

I've seen daylight—but I haven't felt the wind on my cheeks or touched the water in a river. We've been too busy with doctors and nurses who have run multiple tests on us to make sure there's been no permanent damage to our organs—our hearts and kidneys were the two they were most concerned about.

Still, I've had a chance to see cooks who patter around kitchens. They were kind and offered us water or tea. The cooks used familiar ingredients I've seen in Canonsland and back home: wheat for bread and vegetables; rudlaw root and yellow berries like Constance uses as a side dish to the main course and the berries to make jam with. (Once Olin felt we were well enough, he turned the alarm off in our room and allowed us to walk around. Escorted, of course.)

We've traveled along so many hallways and tunnels that connect different parts of this place. But there's been no clue if we're north, south, east, or west of Canonsland.

The only thing Olin has said was that we're at Trepid Divide.

I stare up at the bookshelves. Words that make no sense to me are written along the spine—letters from Latin, Greek, or Arabic that I've seen briefly before—while other books are written with numbers, dashes, and other symbols.

Staring at one book, I tilt my head. Squinting, I try to focus on the words, unsure if I'm reading the spine right. Yup, it's what I think it is. Charles Dickens' *A Tale of Two Cities* and *Great Expectations* are there. On the other side, there's a copy of the *Holy Bible* and the *Koran*. Further down, on the fourth shelf is a yellowed copy of Jane Austen's *Emma*. As we walk down the hall, there's a book called, *Forgotten Incantations*, and another called, *The History of Canonsland*.

"You have some books from my world here," I say. I try to hide the suspicion from my voice. I do wonder, though—

"Yes, there are many books. From your world and others," Olin says.

"Are you alright?" I ask Laurence.

His hand rests on a shelf, an attempt to steady himself, I suspect. Right beside his thumb is *Grimm's Complete Fairy Tales*. Covering my mouth, the irony isn't lost on me as to *where I am, what I'm doing, who I'm with* . . .

"What in the name of King Nicholas' do you laugh at?" Laurence's words sting. His face twists.

My ears warm with embarrassment. "Sorry," I say. The

rage in Laurence's voice leaves me flustered, and then my brain hiccups to a stop. I can't begin to explain it to him.

"'Tis the book," Olin says, "the one beside your finger." Reaching over, he grabs the book and flips through it. "These were some of my favorite stories when I was a child." Snapping the book closed, he holds it up and shows it to Laurence. "Fairy Tales—" he says. "—there is a princess who falls into a deep sleep after eating a poisonous apple given to her by an evil stepmother—and a wolf that eats a grandmother—" dimples form in the centers of his cheeks when he smiles. A third one forms in his chin.

"You are a twisted man," Laurence says, watching Olin with a furrowed brow.

"I did not write them," he says. "We are, however, lucky to have acquired them."

"I do not understand. Why do you laugh at a book, Jayden?"

"Seriously?" I snap. Unclasping my hands, I shake them at Laurence. "This world is filled with knights, dragons, wizards . . . Where I come from, that's all stuff from fairy tales."

"Oh," Laurence says with a sniffle, "I thought—"

"I know what you thought," I say, raising one hand. *How dare Laurence think I'm like that?* I say, "I would never laugh at someone so sick."

"Now that we have settled that," Olin says, his eyes shifting between Laurence and me. "Follow me."

We weave our way along more bookshelves. I take in the names of some of the books, all information I'll share with Wyndham when we get to the King's Acres. It'll be something at least to tell him, to see if he's heard about this place. It's unsettling to me that Olin has so much unchecked power here. Although he did say, he's only the Officer. I think of him as Border Security. Still, it's power.

"Where are we?" Laurence says, walking on the other side of Olin.

"I have told you; I cannot share with you that information."

"Can the Winter Dragon find this place?" Laurence says.

"No," Olin says. "The people who are here stay here—with a few exceptions. If you pass the test, you can visit, and it is a place of refuge offered to some if they are lucky to meet one of the few Gate Keepers in the common world. We do not, however, allow visitors to live here."

"We are here," Olin says. Bookshelves, walls, and ceiling have given way to darkness and stars again. Reaching for a rope ladder, Olin tosses it down. "This is where we part."

"Jayden," Olin says, reaching out and shaking my hand. "It was nice to meet you. Thank you for not asking the same questions over and over again." He raises his eyebrows and gives Laurence a once-over.

"You're welcome," I say, fighting the urge to laugh.

"How do we know we are truly at the outskirts of the King's Acres?" Laurence asks. I don't think I've ever seen Laurence be so abrupt with someone. He's always so charming with everyone. It's one of his best traits, and it's only improved with time. "We are in darkness here."

"What choice do we have?" I ask.

"What?" Laurence says.

"We can't stay here. We need to get to the King's Acres. And if Olin were going to kill us, he would have let the fever take us. He's had our clothes washed, he's fed us," I slide my dagger from my sheath and say, "he even gave me my dagger back." Laurence places his hand on his sword. "Yeah," I say, gesturing to his weapon.

"Sorry," Laurence says, "the fever has muddied my judgment."

"Well," Olin says, staring up at a shooting star, "'tis good to ask questions. And I know the fever can diminish one's cognitive skills." Olin's eyes stare up at the darkness. "If I were you two, though, I might want to keep my weapons close by. I have heard rumors that there is unrest in Canonsland and some nations wish for war to settle long overdue debts," he says, his eyes shifting back and forth between Laurence and me.

Laurence's jaw tightens. "There have been others I have helped," Olin says. Unclasping his hands, he raises one hand to us. "They have mentioned they are gathering weapons. I am unable to give names or say where they are from. Just know that some are preparing for a battle. That is a message you may pass to Wyndham."

"Your name is Olin?" Laurence asks.

"Yes."

"Is there a last name?" I ask.

Olin's eyes redden. His dimples return to his cheeks and his chin as his lips purse together. Shaggy red hair tumbles in the wind. "No," he answers as his jawline lengthens. He gives no other details of his life, of who he is. Instead, he looks up to the stars again.

Is he lost, like me? No, he can't be. He knows where he belongs. Still, I want to say something. But if I'm wrong—no, it's none of my business.

"Time to go," Olin says, glancing over at us.

"Thank you," I say, touching Olin's arm.

Olin stares at me and clears his throat. With nothing else to say or do, I look over at Laurence, walk over to the ladder, and climb down the rope with Laurence following me.

***

There's less pain going down than going up. My foot leaves the rope rung, and I step down onto the ground. Laurence is right behind me. Given everything that's happened, I expected something more tumultuous—like being ambushed by hired killers, dropping into the toxic green pit in Vertstone Park, or perhaps arriving in the middle of some battle between the Xyidaks and Trygolish.

The sun shines above us, warming my skin. Blinking, I scan the area we're in. Sure enough, several thousand meters ahead of us are the sixty-foot walls surrounding King Nicholas' primary home, Stock Castle. Smoke rises from chimneys both inside the castle and the town. The smell of horses hangs in the air, except—there are no horses.

"Where are our horses?" I ask Laurence, "and our

things?"

"How would I know?" Laurence says. When I turn around again, the last strings of the knotted ladder fade away until there's nothing there. Laurence's boots stomp the ground as he paces around and cranes his neck, looking behind a single tree we're standing in front of. He's oblivious to the ladder that's disappeared.

On the horizon, horses gallop towards us, and Laurence places his hand on his sword, and I keep my hand close to my concealed dagger. When they're closer, "Laurence!" a man's voice cries. A man finely dressed in a light blue shimmering suede shirt gallops toward us. Smiling, it's Eustace dressed in his clothes that mark him as a diplomat.

"What are you doing?" Laurence says. Watching Laurence, his body careens toward me, and I extend a hand to stop him from tipping over. I rest a hand on his shoulder. "I am alright!" he shouts, pulling away from me.

"Sure," I say.

Jumping from his saddle, Eustace says, "What has happened?"

"Nothing," Laurence grumbles. Waving his hand, he leans forward and then collapses. Eustace grabs him before he hits the ground. "Perhaps, I am not so well, after all," he says.

"We were caught in Ludswup," I say. Is caught the right word? "We needed an escape, and we found one."

"We found your horses and your belongings. Wyndham, Petronilla, Kemena, and I have been scouring these fields for hours," Eustace says.

Weird. Petronilla shouldn't be looking for us. She's in training with Eustace. And yet, she came anyway. Course, Laurence is her Uncle.

"Well, you found us," I say, shoving Laurence's foot into the stirrup of Eustace's horse. "Take Laurence," I say, "he's still feeling the effects of the fever."

Eustace steadies Laurence on top of his horse. He glances over at me as the lines of his face wrap into confusion. "A fever?" he asks.

"It's a long story," I say with a heavy sigh.

Eustace nods and jumps on his horse. "You will be alright?"

Touching my dagger, I nod and say, "I'll be fine."

Eustace's lips tighten, and he says, "Tyson, to the Castle!"

I watch Eustace and Laurence gallop off. Laurence turns around to look behind him, and he nearly slides off the horse. There's grumbling from Eustace and then he leans back, and Tyson stops. Eustace dismounts, and seats himself again, this time behind Laurence, wrapping his arms around his brother. Now with both brothers on the horse again, Tyson ambles towards Stock Castle.

I start to walk. Behind a line of trees, I spin around when the sound of horses' hooves comes from behind me. I recognize the two people immediately—the outline of Wyndham's broad shoulders and Ella's long hair and petite frame. "Jayden?" Wyndham says when he sees me. "Would you like a ride?" he smiles, offering me his hand.

"Sure," I say. I shove my foot into the stirrup and use Wyndham's hand to swing myself up into the saddle behind him.

"Jayden! Jayden!" Petronilla cries from behind us. "There you are!" When she arrives, she extends her hand, and I take it and squeeze it. "We were so worried," she says.

"We're okay," I say, letting go of her hand. She looks around, up to the walls of Stock Castle, and squints.

"Eustace took Laurence because he wasn't feeling well," I say to Ella. "Wyndham," I say, tilting my head over his shoulder so he can see me, "Laurence and I need to share some things with you. Things we've heard."

"Thank goodness," he says. "Abelard, Kemena, and Vik's questioning through cities were fruitless."

I don't have time to tell him we don't have information about the woman because Buckley, the impatient horse he is, throws his head up in the air, snorts, and bites down on the bit. Wyndham releases the reins, and we gallop toward Stock Castle. I turn around and watch Petronilla and Kemena exchange a few words, and then they urge their horses forward and follow us back to Stock Castle.

EIGHT

"You said he is a boy," Wyndham says, "who allows some to enter?"

We're in King Nicholas' Dragon's Den Room that was called The Battle Room a number of years ago. But when King Nicholas took over the Kingdom from his aunt, Queen Hilda, he renamed some of the rooms. The change was meant to be a reflection of the more peaceful times that they'd been lucky enough to enjoy for almost thirty years that started during the Queen's reign.

Leaning back in the wooden chair, I shift under the leather seat and look over at six tapestries of maps. They're hung around the room with names of places stitched into them that once were and are no more—a legacy to the villages and cities that were the casualties of wars that some citizens remember, while many more don't. It's a pleasure of peace that we don't always remember what shouldn't be forgotten. The last words Olin said ring louder in this room.

I say, "No, he's not a boy. He's about the same age as Laurence."

Wyndham stands beside a wall where the entire length of it is nothing but a clock. The handles tick along. Wyndham nods and grabs a chair, and sits down at the table.

"How is it that you escaped without contracting the fever?" Kemena says, leaning her head to the side. Dark eyes stare down at me, down from the other side of the table, and down from her position as a recognized Royal Knight.

I don't know what to say. *Can I tell people that I had a fever if I have no symptoms now? Is it even worth it?*

I decide whether I had a fever or not isn't relevant. And Kemena won't believe me or care. I offer a half-truth, "We were given a test. If we answered *honestly*, we wouldn't get the fever."

"A confession? Under a threat of torture?" Wyndham says.

"No, Olin was only the guard. He didn't cause it. Something else did." I recognize how much faith I'm placing in a stranger's words when I say it out loud. Looking away, I stare at the tapestries again. "Or that's what he said."

"You believed him?" Wyndham asks.

"I know I shouldn't. But yeah, I did. Olin and his people took care of us." Placing a palm on the table in front of me, I trace the outline of a grain of wood under the varnish, wishing I were somewhere else.

Maybe I'm too trusting to be a knight? And if I can't be a knight here, should I even try to be a pilot with the CAF? Maybe the Guidance Counsellor is right—a business career might be the best possibility for someone like me. *Who do I think I am?*

"Us?" Eustace says.

"Yes, when we were sick." Blinking, I notice my blunder.

"You, too, were sick?" Wyndham says.

"Yes," I answer. With a huff at the pointless inquisition, I say, "Listen, I trust Olin. Doctors and nurses there took care of us, they fed us, and they clothed us. Olin even went back to Ludswup to get our stuff from the Inn and our horses. That's why you found our horses and belongings at the outskirts of the King's Acres." Wyndham raises a hand, and I lift mine to him. I'm not done talking yet. "Olin says some nations are accumulating weapons, and they want war. He couldn't give us names to his sources or where it's going to start," I run my fingers through my hair and add, "but he was convinced it's going to happen."

The room is silent. All I can hear is the deafening tick-tock of the clock.

"So, you lied to us?" Kemena says.

"Kemena!" Abelard barks.

Kemena's accusation makes my ears warm, and my eyes sting. My mind is a chalkboard that's been wiped clean. I can't remember what I told everyone when Wyndham asked the question about the fever.

Wyndham, Kemena, Eustace, and King Nicholas stare at me. Abelard's cheeks are flushed red. Kemena's nose is in the air as she waits for me to answer. *She's waiting for me to agree with her.* Glancing around the table, I notice Eustace looks away now. But the person whose opinion of me I care the most about is Wyndham, and he's unreadable. He's sitting there . . . waiting, too.

Leaning back in his chair, King Nicholas sits there, his eyes resting on me, making me squirm in my chair. *What have I done wrong?*

"Jayden never lied. She provided details about how they must answer the question," the King says. "She said you must answer honestly to gain access to Olin's world so that a fever would not befall the speaker. She never said she was spared from the punishment."

"How did I miss that?" Eustace says, frowning.

The King unclasps his hands and says, "If it is a new idea, something that you have never heard before, you will miss such subtle words. But I have been to where Laurence and Jayden went," the King says.

"Tell me," King Nicholas's face tightens, "do you remember the question?"

"Yes," I say.

"Please tell the room," the King says.

"What is it you most fear?" King Nicholas and I say together.

"The question has not changed," the King says, leaning forward, looking away. Silence descends in the room except for the odd squeak because someone shifts in their chair, sniffling, and the occasional cough. "When I was there as a young man, it was not a boy with red hair that greeted visitors—it was a young woman, red-eyed, red-haired. Her name was Royse," he says, his voice lowering.

King Nicholas looks around the table. Wyndham and Abelard frown, Kemena's head's raised, and Eustace gapes at the King. Taking a cue from all of them, I snap my mouth closed and rest my hands on the table.

"How is it that we have not heard of this before?" Wyndham asks. His voice is harsh, harsher than I've ever heard him say anything to the King before. My eyes widen at Eustace, seated beside me. He leans closer to me, leans forward, and doesn't look at the King or Wyndham.

"I am under no obligation to share all the details of my life with anyone," the King says, his voice even, his eyes locked on Wyndham.

Wyndham squints at him, cups his hands together, rolling his thumbs around each other, and says, "You are right, my King. Please forgive me. I have forgotten my place at this table."

King Nicholas nods. "It was a long time ago, and it has borne no relevancy up to this point."

"We will return to Ludswup," Kemena interrupts. "Jayden and Laurence should be able to identify the Gate Keeper. He will allow us to pass, and then we will interrogate the man, Olin, about who is accumulating weapons," she says, staring at the King.

"No," the King says, "you will not. Only if we have no other options will we try to question the citizens of Ludswup, find the Gate Keeper, and Olin. I have made a promise to the people of Ludswup that I would allow them as much autonomy as possible." Sighing, the King says, "Besides—the people of Ludswup do not care for knights. They will not cooperate with you, as Laurence's experience has proven.

And Olin has committed no crime. In truth, he provided us with information when it was not required."

"There were two other men," I offer, "the elderly man's son and another guy."

"How do you know the connection between the younger man and the older man?" Eustace says.

"The grey-haired guy told us it was his son. I'd—" clearing my throat, I try to sort my thoughts out. I know my actions of placing a dagger to a senior's throat might not be viewed in the best light.

"Jayden? What did you do?" Wyndham asks, raising a questioning brow.

I slouch down in my seat, bite my lip, and run a hand along the edge of the table. *Well, I wanted to be a knight.* That means taking responsibility for my actions. Whatever those actions might be: good, wrong, or something in-between. Sitting taller, I say, "Laurence went through a trap door, and I followed him, and when I got there, Laurence was being beaten by a man, and there were two other men in the room, too. So, I used my dagger and took the older man hostage so we could ask them some questions about the woman and Edric." Taking a breath in, I say, "I was just trying to help Laurence." I look around at the completely unreadable faces, except for Wyndham, who doesn't look happy. I swallow hard. "We managed to escape running through tunnels with the man's father. But the other two men were right behind us. The man's father told us his son had some charges against him issued by knights."

I glance over at Abelard and Kemena, who only blink at each other and say nothing. "The father also said he was the son's last surviving family member." Wyndham's Adam's apple moves with a gulp. I wiggle in my seat and hold the armrest to stop myself from slinking back down. "His son's wife died a few months earlier of an illness, and then his only son was killed near Mt. Lieuschanean by Xyidak thieves. And since all that happened, the grey-haired man said his son had become angrier and unpredictable. His son had never killed anyone, but given everything that had happened in the last few months—the father didn't know what his son would do if he caught up to us. So, he opened the gate to Trepid Divide. Or that's what Olin called it."

"Why was his son near Mt. Lieuschanean?" Abelard asks.

"He didn't say."

"I think we have our lead," the King says, leaning back in his chair. "Abelard and Kemena, go through our records and see if you can find a register for the death of a man killed near Mt. Lieuschanean who was from Ludswup over the last few months. Hopefully, they filed something with our records. Afterward, return to the Trygolish and Xyidak borders with the other knights and soldiers to maintain peace. If war is coming, I guess that it will begin there."

"Do you believe that it will happen?" Eustace says.

"I hope not. But it feels like the time is ripe," King Nicholas says. "There are some parts that are stable now, such as Ikansterup. Other parts such as Trygolish and Xyidak—skirmishes over land, water, and minerals have plagued that part of our world for decades, and now they are becoming more frequent. I hope it is not true. But I know war does not happen overnight. Instead, it slithers across towns, villages, and cities, takes hold of minds, and people arm themselves. Before you know it, the world is on fire."

"Wyndham, Laurence, Eustace—you have friendships in Ikansterup. Go there and see if anyone heard any news of a murder near their city and if you can gather more details about the circumstances of the man's death. Hopefully, Kemena and Abelard will be able to supply you with the man's name before you leave." Staring at me, the King says, "Jayden, I heard your mother was injured. Are you able to stay much longer?"

"I don't know," I say, looking over at Wyndham.

"Yes," he answers. "Jayden has time." Shifting in his chair, he says, "I have taken the liberty to check in on Jayden's home, and no one yet knows she is missing," Wyndham says.

"Do you wish to help?" the King says.

"Yes," I croak. Great, now my voice decides to fail me?

"Then go with Wyndham and the others," the King says. "Laurence told me briefly what you did for him—how you found him and left your sword in your room and armed only with a dagger surprised those who attacked him and pretended to be—" the King pauses, "no more. You were resourceful," the King says as he glances at me. "I understand you took a person as a prisoner so that you could escape—while we prefer other methods be exhausted first, I understand your choices. I do not know if there were other options. But I would ask that you review the situation with the help of the more senior knights and see if there was some other way. Given the circumstances, though, you did well, Jayden."

Don't cry. Don't cry. Don't cry.

I nod once, and my cheeks warm. "Thank you, King Nicholas," I say as we all stand.

Wyndham flaps a hand in front of me. "Oh!" I say. Hastily, I bend forward in the King's direction.

King Nicholas nods. Hidden underneath his black-grey beard, there might be a smile there.

"Before everyone leaves, who has a sketch of the woman?" the King asks.

"I do," Abelard says, pulling the paper from his pocket, unfolding it, and handing it to the King. "Thank you," the King says. He takes the sketch out, places it in front of him, and frowns. "Wyndham, a moment?" the King says, glimpsing at him.

"I'll take Jayden to see Dr. Eastwood," Eustace says. "I need to check on Laurence. That way, the good Doctor can look her over as well."

"I'm fine," I say, standing taller.

"'Tis' an order," Wyndham says, his eyes locking on me.

***

My cloak covers my arms, blocking out the wind that's picked up. I tug at it as we pass a marble statue of Enisseny and Wyndham in the middle of the courtyard.

"He does not like it," Eustace says as we pass it.

Smiling, I say, "Yeah, I know."

"The King, he wished to do something for Wyndham and Enisseny—for their long service to King Wimarc, Queen Hilda, and his loyalty to his Crown."

"I think that's the problem," I say reluctantly. Turning around, I stare at the marble features of the lined face of stoic Wyndham with his eyes that look below him as he sits on top of Enisseny. The dragon's wings are extended as if they're in flight. It's not the dragon of war that I saw in Ikansterup that caused the ground to shake and the air to vibrate, the dragon who hates death at the hands of others—instead, it's the peaceful dragon who enjoys games, children, and soars above Canonsland making sure his world is safe.

Eustace stands beside me. His features are swept clean of any indication of how he's feeling. "How old is Wyndham?" I ask.

"I do not know for certain," Eustace says, mesmerized with the sculpture, too. "I would guess him to be somewhere in the mark of two hundred and twenty, though."

"When I saw him," my words break off, remembering his wound, the blood, "after he was injured, he had a picture of a woman on a table, near his bed, in his room."

"Yes," Eustace says, turning to me. "'Tis Wyndham's wife. He said she has been gone for many years." Eustace stares at the carved outline of Wyndham and Enisseny, clears his throat, and says, "Wyndham did not want to bring the photos when he first came to live with us as he thought we would feel less important," Eustace says, shaking his head. "He has only reclaimed those items from the King in the last few months." There's silence between us. "We should go," Eustace says.

We walk faster, passing vendors that sell vegetables and fruit on the inside of the castle. Stone and wooden buildings are inside the castle walls; cafes where knights, counselors, and diplomats can find porridge or eggs and lentils for breakfast, brandy cauliflower soup, and kidney stews with fresh bread for lunch. Bakeries are also inside the walls that offer bitter chocolate, marmalade cookies, rice, rye, and sorghum bread.

After we're through the gates, we walk along cobblestone where shops sell clothes and boots, and there are tack stores where you can find bridles and saddles, furniture can be ordered, and wood purchased to build a home.

"Eustace," a gruff man says, "how is young Laurence?"

"He is nearly recovered," Eustace says. "Jayden and I are on our way to visit Dr. Eastwood as we speak."

"Glad to hear it!"

I don't know the man, his position, or his title. He's dressed in tweed pants and a white shirt. A black hat rests on top of his head, and he tips it in Eustace's direction before he leaves. Eustace has lived here a long time, is well-liked, and is well-known by wealthy businessmen, diplomats, knights, soldiers, and farmers.

As a drifter in and out of two worlds, people here don't know who I am.

Further along, the road turns to dust as we pass sunflower fields, yellow berry fields, cornfields, apple trees, crispy trees, and whatnot orchards. Bluebell flowers are everywhere, and the soil changes from black to green. "Will you consider what the King said?" Eustace asks.

"What?" I say.

Stepping back, Eustace says, "How you might have done things differently in helping, Laurence?"

Placing my hand on my belt, I stop. "I don't know," I say. "I don't see how there was another way. Besides, it worked. No one got hurt. And Laurence and I escaped."

"Only because of the man's father."

"We might have found another way out."

"Perhaps you would have. But you might not have. Then, what would you have done?"

"I don't have time to think about that now," I say. I take long strides towards the stone house by Gateside River that's a short distance from Dr. Eastwood's home.

"Jayden," Eustace says as he straightens his collar. "You are not arrogant," he says, "like Laurence or Edric. Your ability to care about others is one of your finest gifts. Do not let your mother's accident and Kemena's unrelenting bullying of you change what makes up the best part of you."

Eustace has never said something like that to me before. It's usually Wyndham who calls me out on bad behavior. Eustace walks toward me, and once he's in front of me, he looks down at the stone house that shines in the setting sun. A white wing extends, and then I see Enisseny raise his head as he stands and watches Eustace and me.

"You need to consider if there was another way to help Laurence. Look at your emotions at the time and why you behaved the way you did. Were you methodical in your planning? Or were you blinded by something else? Perhaps," he frowns at me, "there was no other way. Then again, if the situation had been handled more calmly, if you had said other things, perhaps more options may have been available to you."

With that, Eustace stumbles down the hill. Tightening my lips, there are so many things I want to say.

How dare you? You weren't there. You don't know what it was like. You would have done the same thing if it had been—

My mouth opens, and I shift from one foot to the other. *If it had been your mother . . .* I gulp in the fresh air and watch Eustace stride down the road to Dr. Eastwood and Dr. Wretchell's house.

"Come along, Jayden. Dr. Eastwood waits for us!"

I gape at the thin outline of Eustace, who takes quick steps across the pathway, grabbing at long grass as he walks down the hill. Looking back at Stock Castle, the flag flaps, and I wonder if Kemena and Abelard have found any record of the man who was killed near Ikansterup.

"Jayden!" standing in front of the door now, Eustace waves to me, so I sprint down the hill to him.

NINE

Thomas Catcher was his name. He was killed more than three months ago near Mt. Lieuschanean. Abelard found the report that was filed by Ikansterup soldiers.

Riding Enisseny, we veer right over Mt. Lieuschanean when the Tower comes into view. Enisseny slows down as we approach, flaps his wings backward, and we descend in the meadows near the Tower where Wyndham and Osgoode were imprisoned the first time I came to Canonsland.

In the meadow, two men sit on horses and hold the reins of four more horses.

As I'm the person seated at the back, I'm also the first to dismount Enisseny. Swinging one foot over the side, I grip Enisseny's fur and dangle both feet over his stomach as I try to hold on, in the hopes this will be one of the few times I won't land on my butt. My hands filled with his white fur, Enisseny twists his neck around, and his brown eyes blink at me in the setting sun.

"Jayden, with haste!" Laurence barks. "There are others who are waiting!"

"Oops, sorry," I say to Enisseny. I don't care what Laurence said. What bothers me is that it looks like Enisseny's in pain. "Mander's bite!" I cry as my fingers release the dragon's fur.

"Oof!" I grunt as I slip, slide, and spin down the length of the dragon's body.

"Ow!" I cry when my head knocks against something hard, and I crash to a stop. Enisseny's nose is the first thing I see. And it nearly touches mine. His enormous eyes flutter, and I'm not sure, but I think those lips might be a smile.

The sky is above Enisseny's head. Wyndham and Eustace stare down at me, laughing.

Laurence's head is turned in the opposite direction. "I'm upside down," I mumble. I nearly landed on my head.

Stretching out a hand, I touch the thing to my right and look over. It's Enisseny's tail that's stopped me. "Thanks," I say to Enisseny. The dragon's cold breath warms, and within a few seconds, it smells like—I cover my nose—a skunk that's been hit by a truck and has been cooking under a sizzling sun. Curling my lips, I wave a hand in front of my face, and say, "You ever heard of a toothbrush?" Rolling over on my stomach, I flop over Enisseny's tail and drop to the ground.

Well, it starts off on my feet. Until I crumple to the earth. Butt first.

I sit there with my hands on my knees and watch Eustace, Laurence, and Wyndham all dismount without incident. Yeah, wobbly flight legs constantly plague me.

Throwing a hand in my direction, Laurence says, "As usual!" as he turns his back to me and trudges toward Gamel and Henry, thanking them for the horses, and asking them how things are at Ikansterup. Eustace pauses in my direction and gives me a thin line of a smile before joining Laurence, Gamel, and Henry.

"Jayden?" a raspy voice says. Wyndham's leathered glove is outstretched with specks of leather that's fraying and strings from stitching that have come undone. "Jayden . . . ," Wyndham says again, "would you like a hand?"

"No. It's okay," I say. I push myself up, ignoring Wyndham's hand.

We walk side by side, down the hill toward the four men there. From a distance, I hear the odd word about *crops, marriages, births, and illnesses.*

"Did you hear about Lavendria and Kitt?" Henry says to Laurence. Laurence shakes his head, and Henry says, "They are to be married."

"Jayden and I will meet you back in Ikansterup," Wyndham says. "There is something we must do first."

"Where are you going?" Laurence asks.

"Do not fret, Laurence. I will return in time for the Council Meeting tonight."

Weird. Squinting, I look up at Laurence, seated on his horse. I don't think in all the years I've known Laurence, he's ever asked Wyndham where he's going. We all know that Wyndham only shares what he wants to.

"I will come, too," Laurence says.

"You are not invited," Wyndham says, tilting his head with a frown.

Holding the reins of the horse Henry gave me, I squeeze them tighter. Gulping, my stomach curdles like milk left on the stove too long. *Wyndham's going to send me back home because I can't dismount Enisseny properly?*

No. Wyndham has a better reason than that. *He's going to tell me I'm not cut out to be a knight because I took that man's father as a hostage.*

"You will tell us where you are going," Laurence says.

"I will not. Remember, I am the more senior here—both in rank and in age."

"I will follow you, then," Laurence says.

"The'y're tree uf us," Gamel says, "Wee cun bind thee, and force yee to cum with us . . ."

"You would not. I am a knight."

"I dunn't carrrre," Gamel says. His lined face scrunches as he winks at Wyndham and me.

I lower my head and run a hand across the horse's smooth hair to hide my smile.

"Come, Jayden," Wyndham says. He spins his horse

around the other side of mine so that we can walk side by side. "We have things to do. They will take care of Laurence if he does not follow orders." Walking away, Wyndham glances over his shoulder at Laurence as we cross back over the same meadows, wildflowers, and newly planted trees on the outskirts of the Tower that we just passed.

As we approach, I stare at the sunken roof that looks like something has punched it from the top down. When I saw it the first time, I thought it was on the verge of collapsing. Now stones have shifted more with each year that passes, and the northern wall bulges. The Tower is scheduled to be torn down as it's a reminder of prisoners who died there that were sometimes innocent—or so the Ikans said. All that happened a long time ago, though, before I came here and before both Wyndham and Osgoode were prisoners there. It's one of the many projects that are part of the reconstruction of Ikansterup that they haven't got around to finishing yet.

I look back over my shoulder to see if Laurence has kept his word and if he's following us. He's not, though. Laurence just sits there on top of his horse, watching us. Eustace takes a hand and slaps Laurence's knee, and he says something to him. Then the four horses step forward, and the saddles shift from side to side as they move in the opposite direction.

"Leave it to the diplomat to convince his younger brother to do as he is told," Wyndham says. Wyndham's face twists at the group of men, a look I know well. It's the face when Wyndham is questioning something. Hands on his hips, without looking at me, he says, "'Tis odd for Laurence to behave in such a way, is it not?"

If I say, *Yeah, I noticed that too. What's up with him?* It might be considered gossiping, which I know Wyndham frowns on. And if I say, *I hadn't noticed,* it would be a lie. With the chances of becoming a knight seeming to diminish minute by minute, I decide not to say anything.

Wyndham's cape flaps with the northern wind, and his long hair follows the rhythm of the cape. I take a step back from Wyndham. For the first time in my life, I'm not sure if I should be standing next to him, in this world.

We watch the horses' necks lengthen as they struggle up the side of the steep hill. Soon, they'll cross over the bridge to Ikansterup Castle.

There's no Lord in these parts. Instead, Ikansterup Castle houses the leaders of the Ikans. Elected officials who represent the Ikans provide updates to the King on the progress made in the city and raise any concerns with the King where they might require additional help.

"I have arranged for you to visit with your mother," Wyndham says. His gaze only breaks when we no longer see Gamel, Henry, Laurence, and Eustace.

Gulping, my heart and stomach sink, and I say, "You're sending me home." *Face it, head-on, Jayden.* I stare down at Wyndham's horse's legs. Taking a breath in, I look up and meet Wyndham's eyes as I wait for his answer.

"No," frowning, Wyndham says. "You must speak with your mother in case locating the woman takes longer than expected."

***

Wyndham, Enisseny, and I stand in front of the concave Tower that's threaded with flowers through the stones. Enisseny's breath is cold over my shoulder. I've come to know the white circles well, and they circle in front of us and drift toward the protruding brick before they spin around and form an image. This is all similar to what I've seen at home, through my mirror. This location, however, is new.

Slowly, the white dots sprinkle around from Enisseny's breath and peel back layers of the wall as if it were an orange. In front of us now are white walls with Mom sitting upright in bed. She stares at me.

I hold onto the reins of my horse and whisper, "Mom?"

I saw her today (was it today?) with Dad, and it didn't bother me. Now though, the view of her head stapled up and dry blood still caked along the side of her face with the blend of darkness and light gives her room a grey tone—and Mom seems paler and weaker than ever before.

85

Placing a finger to her lips, she says, "Shh," as she moves her fingers toward her and encourages me to come forward through the wall.

Mom can see me?

No, she can't see me. She can't see Wyndham. So, she wouldn't be able to see me here, in Canonsland, right?

Wyndham says, "I will take the reins of your horse." I twist my face at him as I try to process what's happening. Numb, I let the reins slide through my fingers. "She asked that I not tell you," Wyndham says. "She thought Canonsland would be good for you. And it would be good for you to have your own adventures, your own secrets." A small smile crosses his lips. One eyebrow rises as he stares at Mom and whispers, "Secret adventures, she always asked me to share with her after," he chortles. His eyebrows, his lips, the lines in his face fall when he turns to me again. "You must speak with her," Wyndham says.

Snapping my mouth closed, I stand there. Mom flaps her hands at me, and with a louder voice, she says, "Jayden?" In between all the movement and words, she glimpses at the door to her hospital room.

Even though I'm angry with both of them, I step through the peeled-back wall. When I do, I stand next to Mom's hospital bed. Mom grabs my hand as her eyes fill with tears.

"Mom?" I say, grinding my teeth. I try to hold back my own waterworks of frustration.

And I wait for her to say something and give me some explanation because she owes me one.

Yes—she owes me one.

TEN

"How long have you been able to see Wyndham and the dragon?" The words quake in my voice. But I guess it's better than yelling at Mom in the hospital.

Wiggling in her bed, Mom grabs the pillow from behind her, shakes it to fluff it, and places it back behind her back. "These beds really aren't comfortable," she says as she smooths out the sheets that cover her legs. Linking her fingers together, she sighs and says, "Since I was first diagnosed with cancer. So, what's it been? Five years?"

"Why didn't you tell me?" I say, taking a seat in the chair next to her bed. "All these years, I've been doing this, and every time I came back with a bump or scrape, I had to make up some story about them. I could have just told you the truth," I close my hands into fists. I know this isn't the place to have this conversation with Mom. She needs her rest, I know.

Still, I need answers. My cheeks blister with warmth as I fight to keep the anger out of my voice.

Mom's nostrils widen, and she giggles. "It's a good thing you've always been a clumsy kid. You always had a way out." Mom tugs at her sheets, and I know she's buying time to answer my question. It's her way—it's our family's way. We make jokes to cool tempers. That way, if you're mad about something, if you laugh, you can't possibly still be as angry as you were.

You wanna bet?

"Mom?" Leaning forward, my elbows on my knees, I lock my fingers together. I watch Mom, and I wait. Wait for her answer or to give me some explanation. All this time, I've been straddling two worlds alone. Okay, there was Dr. Eastwood, but he spent the majority of his time in Canonsland. And now, Dr. Eastwood calls the King's Acres with his wife, Dr. Wretchell, his home. So now, it's just me. Or, so I thought.

Some days, I wondered whether Canonsland was real or not—whether I'd let my imagination run away with me, and I was only galloping in nearby woods *pretending* I had friends named Wyndham and Enisseny. It's hard for me to say a place never existed, though, when I've learned so much there.

Mom brushes a hand across her stapled head. Remorse consumes me. Pressuring her now to tell me why she lied to me—I shake my head, "Never mind, Mom," I say. "It doesn't matter."

Hidden under her sheet, Mom's legs move like lumps. The motion reminds me of Bob when he was a puppy and how he would hide under the camouflage of orange, red, yellow, and brown dead leaves and wiggle closer to Mom and me as we raked them up. Then his head would burst out, tongue hanging to the side, ears perked up, grinning like a fool as Mom, and I laughed.

"I wanted you to have adventures. You've had to grow up so quickly." Shaking her head, sitting up taller in her bed, she bites her lower lip, looking out the window where rain streams down the glass pane. Streetlights in the hospital parking lot shed light on the parked cars. A lone person walks to their car, the headlights *flash* on, and the person gets into their vehicle. "Your father and I, we can't send you to different cities. Wyndham could give you adventure. He could show you things—and how not to be afraid."

"I still get scared, Mom." My chest tightens as I squeeze my hands tighter together.

"I know Jayden." She tilts her head and says, "Don't be ashamed of your fear. Whenever you do something new that you've never done before, there's a risk that things won't work out. That's alright. Just do your best."

"No, you don't understand," I place my hands on the wooden armrest of the reclining chair, blinking around the room at the pale walls. There's really nothing to see. Mom's lucky because she doesn't even have a roommate. That would make it more difficult for us to talk. But it would also give me a distraction, something else to concentrate on versus this conversation. "There are other things I'm afraid of too," I drag out the last word and peer up at Mom.

"I know, honey. Me too," Mom says, running a hand across her cheek while her eyes gloss over. Waving her hand, she laughs, leans in, and says, "It's the elephant in the room," as she extends her hand to mine. I lift my chair, making sure it doesn't drag, squeak, or thump when I place it back down. Sitting closer, I take Mom's hand and hold it in mine. "When I was growing up, it was only my mother and me. I never knew my dad. And your Grandma Nettie—" she pauses and says, "—she did the best she could. But she had to work two jobs to pay the bills. So, I never had the chance to go on school trips to museums because my mother never had the extra money. And forget about going on a ski trip." Mom's nose crinkles, her face twists, and she says, "I wanted more for you."

Mom's rarely spoken about her childhood. What I remember about Grandma Nettie were snuggles and cookies. Then she came to live with us, and I got kicked out of my room so she could sleep there. I was young, probably not even six years old. Grandma Nettie and Mom would come back from wherever they went, and grandma came back twice as tired and sick than when she'd left.

Grandma died a couple of months after she arrived. Mom

told me she got pneumonia, and I never forgot the word. What also stuck with me, too, was the guilt. I finally got away from the lumpy downstairs couch and got my room back with the Ariel lamp from *The Little Mermaid* that we'd found at a garage sale and the stars that Mom and Dad had just put up on my ceiling that glowed in the dark. Every time I looked up at those stars after Grandma died, I had a hard time sleeping. I told Mom and Dad the stars kept me up, and I didn't like them. So, within a week, they removed them and repainted my ceiling. "Do you remember your Grandma Nettie?" Mom says.

"Yeah, not a lot, though. I kind of remember her face and the sound of her voice." When grandma first died, I could see every line of Grandma's face clearly, like when she came over to babysit when Mom and Dad went out, and she tucked me into bed and pulled the sheets tight around me. With time though, the memory has faded. I now struggle to recall certain features. Grandma's eyes were brown-green. Or were they more green-brown? Smiling, I add, "I remember her laugh really well."

Mom grins, "Yes, your grandmother never let things get her down," she says. "Your father and my mom got along so well," Mom adds, laughing.

There are beeps, then the squeak of sneakers walking down the hallway, and voices that sound close by. Mom and I clasp our hands tighter, and we wait.

I scan the clothes I'm wearing—the knee-high boots that I've left a mud trail on the hospital floor, my black trousers, and the brown tunic. Not to mention the dagger tied to my thigh and the belt with my sword in it. If I get caught, what possible explanation would I give for how I'm dressed? School play?

The sound of footsteps and voices becomes more distant. "Are we okay?" Mom says, squeezing my hand. Resting on her elbow, she leans toward me and to our knotted hands.

Uncomfortably, I lean back and say, "Yeah."

We are okay. It's true. Mostly.

Wyndham reappears in the wall with his mouth slightly open and his face set. I know that look—there's some uncertainty written in his face as he looks out over the hill that leads to Ikansterup.

"You should go, Jayden," Mom says as she settles herself into the center of her bed again. "After all, adventure awaits you!"

"Okay, Mom," I say. Hesitating, I turn back around. It was hard before when I believed that Mom couldn't see Enisseny and Wyndham. Now though, I wonder—should I tell her about what Olin said? If she knew I was in danger, would she still let me go? "Do you worry about me?" I ask cautiously.

"Of course, I worry about you," Mom says. Her lips pinch together. Staring at me, she says, "I wanted to tell you before that you weren't allowed to go anymore. Especially when you came back the first time all banged up. But I would have to admit that I knew. And you came back so much more confident, so sure of yourself, not afraid of heights—how could I take that away from you?"

I look over at Mom's side table, the curtain, the whiteboard that's in front of her bed. "So, Wyndham told you all about it?" waiting, I keep my eyes on her whiteboard with a time of three o'clock written there. Is that Mom's discharge time? I need to remember to ask her.

"I'm sure he didn't tell me everything," Mom says, squinting at me. "All I know is that I wouldn't be here today if you hadn't jumped in and pulled me from the river."

"You wouldn't have fallen into the river if I didn't go to Canonsland." Glimpsing over at Wyndham, he watches me in the wall with his arms folded, and he looks down.

"Sure," Mom admits with a small smile. "But something else might have happened to me." She takes a deep breath in and says, "Besides, Wyndham's managed to keep you," laughing, she glimpses at Wyndham and says, "*mostly* safe." Peering up at Mom, Wyndham smiles. "As well, if you're really thinking about joining the CAF, then training with Wyndham to become a knight may help you pass any physical test." She stares at me and says, "This might be a good test as well, to see if working in the military is something you want to do." Mom's mouth is a line. Rolling her eyes, she adds, "Yes, I know about your training to be a knight."

"Jayden," Wyndham says, "we must go. Someone is coming."

"Does Dad know, too?" I say quickly.

"Oh, no!" she says, laughing. "I'm pretty sure your father can't see Wyndham. I've tested him. He's failed." Mom's eyes and nose scrunch together. I shake my head and smile.

"Jayden," Wyndham's outstretched hand is extended and pokes through the wall.

"Oh, that's cool!" Mom says, just a little too loud.

"Lisa?" someone says from the other side of the curtain. "Did you say something?" there's the squeak of shoes shifting on the tiled floors. Mom covers her mouth, shakes her head. She waves her hand at me and points in the direction of the wall to Wyndham as the squeaking shoes get louder.

"Bye, Mom," I whisper. Leaning in, I give Mom a kiss on the cheek.

She plants a kiss on my cheek and gives me a quick squeeze of a hug, and whispers, "Please, be careful." I nod.

I grab the worn black glove that's in front of me. Enisseny's head faces me. And it's through the dragon's breath of ice crystals, circling Wyndham's extended hand that I link my fingers together with the old knight while I stare at Enisseny when my feet cross back into Canonsland.

Staring up the hill, there's a lone rider galloping toward us. "Who's coming?" I ask. Glancing over my shoulder, the wall folds closed like wrapping paper over a gift. Before it does, though, there's a man in blue scrubs who stands next to Mom's bed and stares at me through the wall. His mouth and eyes are wide, eyebrows are crumpled. Placing his fingers to his eyes, he massages them for several seconds. Blinking, he stares up again. I can still see him. So, he most likely can still see us.

Mom and the man fade, and I place a hand on the wall.

What am I doing? Trying to hold on to my mother from Canonsland? I can still see her. Her head's tilted, her words are quiet, and I hear Mom say, "What's wrong?"

Staring at us, the nurse shakes his head, and the wall closes. There's no one in the wall anymore. But I hear a man's voice say, "I thought I saw something. Man, I really need to stop drinking so much coffee."

There's the rustle of leaves on the nearby trees from the wind, the sound of birds singing their evening song overhead, frogs croak in streams nearby, and the two white moons hang high in the sky. Light is fading. The sound of horses' hooves pounding the ground grows louder.

"I told you," Wyndham says, "you were not invited!" he shouts. Wyndham spins around, sighs at me, his hands on his hips, and his pinky finger taps on one side.

Laurence yanks on the reins, his breathing labored. His horse skids to a stop in front of us.

I touch the bridle. The stallion's coat shines with sweat. And the animal's breath is warm with the scent of hay and oats. I rub the center of the horse's head and whisper, "Easy." When I glance up at Laurence, his face shines pale like the two white moons overhead. "What is it?" I whisper as I pass a hand over the horse's forehead and lay my palm flat against it. My hand trembles. I don't know why.

"Laurence?" Wyndham says, standing in front of Laurence now. His hands hang limply at his side, waiting like me, for some explanation. Gone is any angry look from Wyndham.

Licking his lips, Laurence says, "We have received a message from the King through the blue raven." Laurence stutters, shakes his head, "Rumbling Town—" he croaks, "— 'tis under attack!"

Enisseny shrieks and his wings extend as he stomps and blows cold air against the Tower, and an icy layer forms against the bulging wall. The dragon's neck lengthens, and he releases another piercing screech. I've heard this sound only a few times before, and it always makes my spine tingle.

"Laurence, ride with me on Enisseny!" Wyndham shouts

over his shoulder as he sprints toward Enisseny. Several hundred men and women from Ikansterup gallop down the hill on horseback with mud flying up behind them.

I hold Laurence's horse's reins. I spin back and forth between the troops who are charging down the hill and Wyndham, my hands shaking as I tighten my grip on the leather reins. "Where do you want me?" I ask Wyndham.

"Ride with the Ikansterup soldiers!" Wyndham shouts as Laurence jumps on Enisseny's foot and climbs up on the dragon. I shove my foot into the stirrup and swing myself up onto the saddle of the horse that Gamel had given me to ride and hold onto the reins of Wyndham and Laurence's horses.

"Wyndham!" Eustace shouts, leading the Ikansterup riders. "My brother, Idonea, my sister, Osgoode, the children—" struggling to breathe, he races toward Wyndham and Laurence, "—my family!" he cries. I run along with Eustace's horse as he pulls back on the reins and tumbles off as I tug at the reins, and his stallion comes to a stop. "I wish to go with you!"

Wyndham shakes his head. "You are unarmed!"

"I wul go!" Gamel says, leaping off his horse, his sword tucked into his belt. "I wul fight fur yur f'mly!"

"Huw meny cun the drugn take?" someone asks in the crowd.

"Up to ten," Wyndham shouts.

"Thee best shuld go!" Gamel hollers. "But He'ra, you stay an leed the rest of our troops in my absence!" I see a female Ikansterup soldier nod. And then Gamel lists names, some I know, others I don't, and men and women begin to step forward. Enisseny lifts them with his head, and they take a seat behind Wyndham.

I hate not being a full knight! Constance, Osgoode, their children, Alwyn, Idonea—they're all at risk and because I'm not a knight yet, I can't go and fight. Biting my lower lip, I look over at Henry because Gamel's called his name. He rolls his eyes, jumps off his horse, and says, "Wait for me!"

I nod. Henry can always be counted on to do the right

thing. *He swore he'd never ride on Enisseny.* I watch as he stands in front of Enisseny. Hands at his side, he says, "Would you mind giving an old man a lift?" Enisseny answers by shoving him up with his head onto his back and some of the other Ikansterup soldiers help him take a seat.

"Eustace," I say. "We should check the exit route."

"Yes, yes, of course!" he says, flipping from a deflated look to jumping back onto his horse. "Jayden, ride with me!" Eustace says as he gallops toward Wyndham. Holding the reins to Wyndham and Laurence's horses, an Ikansterup soldier takes the reins from my hand, and I let my horse chase Eustace.

"Wyndham!" Eustace says. "We will ask Hera to split the Ikansterup soldiers. We will send half of them to the entrance of the city of Rumbling Town, and the other half will head to the opening of the Exit Route."

"Yes, very good," Wyndham says. "It has never been used." With the last of the Ikansterup soldiers loaded on Enisseny, Wyndham says, "I do hope Constance and Osgoode remembered to take the people there." His words are reluctant, remorseful, and almost said as an afterthought.

"Everyone, grab the person who is in front of you. And hold on tight! Enisseny, GO!" Wyndham shouts. Enisseny's eyes glow red, he runs, his white wings extend, and he screams in the direction of Rumbling Town.

"Let us go!" Eustace says, clicking his tongue and shaking the reins threaded through his fingers.

"Yes!" I say with a nod. But Eustace doesn't see me because he's already gone. My horse is eager to follow so, I squeeze my heels into the sides of the stallion, give him his head so he knows he can run as fast as he wants to, and we gallop behind Eustace before we turn south toward Rumbling Town.

ELEVEN

"Easy!" Eustace says, pulling the reins back on his horse. The stallion kicks dirt as it twists to a stop. Dark smoke billows and rises above a town as flames burst from buildings. From our spot, I know, it's Rumbling Town. Breathing heavily, I watch as white lightning blasts from the air. But it's not lightning—because long wings stretch out, and Enisseny's neck extends as he drives straight into a cluster of stone buildings, and he screeches before he disappears below the walls.

Thunder erupts. And even from where we're standing, the ground shakes beneath our horses' hooves.

As quickly as the white dragon descended, he ascends with the same thunderbolt speed. My jaw's locked. I fight the hate, the rage, and the tears. Blinking, I glance over at Eustace. The reins for his horse are threaded through his fingers. He sits there, turns to me, and then looks back out in the direction of Rumbling Town—his childhood home.

"Eust'ce," Hera says, a young soldier with the Ikans who only became a soldier a year or two ago. I guess her to be my age, but unlike me, Hera is tall and stands about six feet, and her arms bulge from under her armor. She's also the second in command under Gamel.

Hera's dark skin shines, her green eyes glow as she flashes them in my direction. Her face is smooth of lines from age. Still, she doesn't need help with wrinkles that show her fury because it's evident enough in her eyes.

"Eustace, the entrance is this way," I say. I sometimes have zero navigational skills, but for some reason, I never have a problem finding the way to the door for the tunnel that's part of the exit route from the center of Rumbling Town.

I place a hand on Eustace's elbow, and he jolts.

He nods and mumbles, "Yes, yes." His words are distant, his eyes rest on the brush surrounding us, and he makes no effort to move. Eustace's pale face, his shaking hands, the way he licks his lips—all are indicators he's suffering from shock.

"Eustace," I say again. I tug at the fabric of his shirt by his elbow. If I were to wake someone when they're being chased by a headless killer while asleep, I would do it gently, so they're not startled awake amid the horror.

"Yes! Let us go!" he says, clicking his tongue as he urges his horse forward. His horse shifts and then moves toward the downward slope, and steps gingerly over rock, and slides down a slick of mud as Eustace coos, "Easy girl," in her ear while leaning back in his saddle.

"Jayd'n, lean back," Hera says.

Lengthening my body, I throw my words behind me and say, "Thanks." I'd noticed the faster pace from my horse, but I hadn't corrected my posture. The stallion slows, and he trudges along more carefully. Too much momentum, and I would have killed us both. I force any thought of worst-case scenarios from my mind. Right now, I know I need to stay focused.

We cross Rocky River on horseback. When we're on the other side, we dismount, tie the horses together and leave them with a few of the Ikansterup soldiers. Long vines are draped across the mountain. We use them as ropes to pull ourselves up the side of it. Eustace stops partway up.

I climb up beside him. "Are you okay?" I ask.

"Yes, yes," he says, gazing at the rising sun, choking on his words. His breath is short and raspy.

"Please," he says, glancing up ahead. "I will be right behind you."

Hera nods. I take the lead, hooking my foot into rocks, holding on tighter to the thick vines that burn my wrists. I quicken my pace, scaling the side of the mountain faster. There are birds, ants, caterpillars, and butterflies that emerge from cracks in the rocks. I barely notice them as I race up the side of the mountain. I find a ledge, and there—there is the wooden door.

I touch the door with my hand.

"Eeek!" I snap my hand back at the sound when a hairy hand slaps me.

Clutching my chest, I run a hand over my forehead and say, "Buddy, you scared me!" I hiss.

"What, what is it?" Eustace asks from about twenty feet down.

Shaking my head, looking down at him, I say, "It's one of those hairy, slow-moving things."

"A wanderer?" Eustace says. I nod. Eustace, clutching the vines, looks at Hera, huffs, and turns back to me, and says, "They are harmless."

"I know," I mutter, "he surprised me." I place a hand on the door again.

"Eeek!" the wanderer screeches, slapping my hand a second time.

"Knock it off!" I growl as I place it back on the door. His dark eyes stare at me, and his head tilts. His three hairy fingers poke at my hand. But I won't move it. "Stop it," I snarl as it tries to lift my fingers from the latch. My ears and cheeks flame. If Alwyn and his family are on the other side of the door, why haven't they heard me yet, and opened it? Emma, and Hugo—they're just children . . . I slap the hand of the wanderer. "There. Now you know how it feels!"

"Are you fighting with that creature?" Eustace's

incredulous voice says from behind me.

His assumption irritates me. "Yes," I say. "Nice of you to make it," I whisper.

"We all have our strengths," Eustace says, "and weaknesses," he concludes, looking down at me.

Hera stares at me. My face burns. Eustace never says stuff like that to me. I want to make excuses for him—he's short-tempered because his family is either behind that door or they're still in Rumbling Town. And if they're in Rumbling Town—Osgoode lost his whole family the first time I came here because of—

Shaking my head, *rely on fact, Jayden,* Wyndham's words come back to me. Eustace watches me. Nodding, I know I have weaknesses: my height and size, math and science in school. "I know," I mutter, glancing out to the horizon.

Sighing, Eustace places a hand on my shoulder and says, "'Tis nothing to be ashamed of." Letting go of my shoulder, he grabs the handle for the door and says, "Now, about this door . . ."

"Eek!" the wanderer cries, snapping his mouth over Eustace's hand.

"Ow! You wretched beast!" Eustace whispers as he yanks his hand from the animal's mouth and covers it with the other hand.

I cover my hand over my mouth, gasping. The wanderers are harmless—everyone knows that! I've never heard of one biting a person, and I worry that rabies might be a problem, just like at home, which turns a gentle animal into a snapper. But in all my travels in Canonsland, I've never heard of rabies being a problem here.

"Are you alright, Eustace?" I say. I grab his hand and see blood dripping from a dozen perfect circular holes.

"Yes," Eustace says, pulling his hand away. The wanderer tilts his head at us again and—*wanders off.*

A blue raven appears. It flutters near us, circles us, hovers for several seconds in front of us, and then flies off into the clouds.

The wanderer is back. Eustace covers his eyelids with his hands and hangs his head.

"Wh't is goin on?" an Ikansterup soldier asks quietly as he hangs from the vines.

Rolling my eyes, I say, "We're having problems opening the door!" Hera looks away, smiling. "I saw that," I whisper. She places a hand over her mouth and snorts. When Hera removes her hand, her lips are a solid line again.

When I look over at the wanderer, he's got an open-mouthed brown tooth grin. And in his three fingers, he holds a key. Eustace frowns at him. Then he yanks the key from the creature's fingers, and the animal turns, glimpses back at us once, before scrambling down the hillside using the vines.

Eustace stares at the key. "We weren't told of any key?" he mutters, placing the key in the lock, it *clicks*, and it *creaks* open.

"I wonder if Enisseny had something to do with that?" I whisper to no one. Sliding my sword out, I touch Eustace's arm and say, "Eustace, get behind me," and I step in front of him. Hera comes up behind me. Placing a finger to my mouth, I point at three male soldiers to a spot in front of Eustace, and they take their position in front of him. Five more soldiers remain behind Eustace. As a diplomat with the King, Eustace's life is always in danger. It's part of the reason why there's always an escort with him. Even though Canonsland has been relatively peaceful over the last few years, diplomats have still been killed. And Eustace, unfortunately, still wears the clothes that identify his position in the King's court.

Stepping into the cave, I blink a few times, giving my eyes time to adjust to the darkness. Grasping the grip of my sword, it slides through my fingers because of sweat on my hands. I try to steady my breathing as I've been taught and relax into the situation. *Jayden, remain calm. If you do not, you will lose the ability to think and react. Be alert. But you must not let your emotions control your sword.*

Sounds good, in theory, Wyndham.

I place both hands on the sword with one at the grip, the

other near the pommel, to steady it. Hera and I move forward, hiding behind rocks, peering around corners while the others follow our lead. Moving forward, further in, there's a dim-lit room.

Hera glances up as she's closer. Using two fingers, she points them at her eyelids and shakes her head from side to side. Looking around, there's no other way to see who's in the room. But one part of the cave is narrower, where large molded rocks come together. If someone's small enough, they can squeeze into the space and see who's in there.

I return my sword to my belt and crouch down to fit under the low-hanging jagged rocks. Raising my head, I peer into the room.

Alwyn's there, and he sits on a wooden bench and leans against the wall. Hugo's there too and sits on his lap with his head against his Uncle's shoulder. Idonea is beside him and holds Emma. The little girl's back is toward me, her arms wrapped around her aunt's neck, and her small face rests against Idonea's chest.

Nausea and rage wash over me. To see Emma reduced to an inconsolable uncertain child when she's been so confident up to now—

I close my hands, and stare down at the rock and dust, and work my way out of my hiding spot.

Stepping out of the area, I nod and raise my hand to everyone to stop moving. Once I'm out and come around the corner, I say, "Alwyn?" When he looks up at me, lines bunch at the corners of his eyes while Hugo and Emma stare at me. Alwyn's eyes are uncertain, holding no trace of recognition.

Turning around, I raise a hand to Eustace, encouraging him to come forward. "Eustace is here," I say as Eustace steps into the room lit by only a couple of lanterns.

"Brother!" Alwyn says, his voice cracking. Alwyn picks up Hugo, cheeks turning pink, and walks toward Eustace, who leans against a wall. Before Alwyn gets to him, Eustace meets him, and the two brothers embrace.

"Jayden!" Emma cries as she leaps from Idonea's lap and

wraps her hands around my leg.

"Shhh!!!' Idonea whispers, placing a finger to her lips and jumping to her feet.

Running a hand over Emma's head, I say, "Are you alright?"

Now that I'm closer, I see black soot on Idonea's cheeks, nose, and forehead. "Yes," she says, raising her chin.

Several hundred people are in the room—shopkeepers, some of the vendors Laurence and I passed when we left a few days ago, and Walter, the cook from Isons-Lydric Castle. The people don't say anything—instead, they sit there, eyes wide, staring at us.

Mrs. Cramwell, a recent widower, sits beside her daughter, a red-haired young woman highly sought after by many young men in town because she's thin, tall, and her eyes are the color of the ocean from my realm. Her best feature? She's also kind.

When she looks at me, her face falls, and she sobs softly. Her mother wraps her arms around her daughter and pulls her to her shoulder.

I scan the gathered faces, searching. *Where are they?* *They wouldn't . . .*

I stare at Hugo, who has his hand in Alwyn's. I peer down at Emma, who stares up at me, still clutching my leg.

"She's not here," Idonea says, wiping her hand across her nose, "and neither is Osgoode." She places a hand to her mouth. I gulp, forcing the tears back. "Emma, love, come here," Idonea says, extending her hand to the little blonde-haired girl.

Now what?

"The best course would be to stay here," Eustace says. "We should place a couple of soldiers, hidden out of sight so that they can warn us should any trouble come our way." I step back from the group and see that Emma and Hugo sit beside Idonea again with Mrs. Cramwell on the other side, who's whispering something to Emma.

Hera watches me. One of the great things about being

short is that you can slip away unnoticed.

"Jayden," Eustace says, turning to me. "Stop moving." Lifting my chin, I wait for my next opportunity. Rolling his eyes, he says, "I will send you to Rumbling Town to help the others. But you will not go alone."

My eyes flutter with relief. "Hera, choose three soldiers. We will need two to hide in the trees, and one should be positioned on the inside of the door. You know your men well, so 'tis best that you decide. After," he says, facing me, "go with Jayden to Rumbling Town. To fight," he sighs, "or to tell us when it is safe to return. We will wait here until you return." Silence follows. "For a day, maybe two, and if you do not return . . . ," Eustace's head's bowed, and when he looks up again, he says, ". . . we will send another soldier."

Hera names off her three soldiers and leaves another in charge should we not return. I start to go back through the way we came, "Jayden," Eustace says, "you may travel through the tunnels."

Placing a hand on the rock, I bite my lip. To disagree in public is never acceptable. Given Eustace's position and my lack of it, he outranks me. Choosing my words carefully, I don't stop myself, though. "As far as we know, those who are attacking—"

"They are Xyidaks," Alwyn says.

I lean against the rock. *The King said if war came, that it would start with the Xyidaks and Trygolish.* Abelard, Kemena, and the other knights were there to make sure the skirmishes didn't escalate. How could the Xyidaks have slipped by the knights and soldiers?

Sighing, I continue, "—they don't know about the tunnels. If we pop up out of nowhere and look like we haven't been fighting for hours, the Xyidaks might get suspicious."

Eustace steps back. Tilting his head, he places his hands on his hips and says, "Yes, you are right. Go," he adds, "and be careful."

"Okay," I say. Before we leave the tunnel, Hera instructs two soldiers to hide in the trees, and another one is assigned to the inside door of the tunnel. Hera leaves a fourth soldier, Elliam, in charge in her absence.

When we get to the vines, I grab hold of several and climb down the mountain. I'm careful not to make too much noise, though, as I don't want to alert anyone to our presence.

As I climb down, I look up, and Hera's right there.

TWELVE

"Faster!" I shout.

As we climb over the meadows, Enisseny stands at the front of Rumbling Town's walls. I pull back on the reins and say, "Easy."

Enisseny's coat's no longer white—instead, it's grey from the black ash gathered on it. The wall surrounding Rumbling Town has been split into parts with stones and rocks scattered around. Some buildings are crumbling, bent, and blown apart while orange flames burst through windows and doors of other buildings. Enisseny rises into the air with his grey wings flapping and disappears into the center of town. I see only part of his nose, and his eye as his head moves behind the outline of a two-story building, and then the flames are extinguished.

I urge my stallion forward, and it whinnies from the flames and smoke, his neck twisting, his eyes wide with fear. Running a hand along his neck, I say, "It's okay." Hera and her horse walk beside us, Hera's face twisting, and her eyes glisten. I cover my nose with my hand—in the air, there's the smell of burning wood, ash, and flesh. Nausea washes over me as my stomach tightens. I turn to Hera and try to say something, but I can't summon any words. Instead, I look back at the view in front of me.

"Gamel!" Hera shouts. Her horse's head swivels in the direction of her Captain, who's seated under what remains of the blue weeping willow tree. Limbs from the tree are twisted, splintered, snapped off, and scattered along the muddy ground with blue leaves that still cling to the fallen branches.

"Can you take my horse, Hera?" I say before she gets too far away. Hera nods, and I dismount, hand her the reins, and say, "Thanks." Slowly, I walk the ruins of Rumbling Town.

Passing through the remains of the town's outer wall, I hear, "Jayden?" from behind me.

Turning around, Laurence's clothes are sprinkled with red-brown-black. Sweat hangs around his neck and under his arms. His cheeks are flushed and dusted with black ash. His brow crinkles at me, and snakes of red veins are through his eyes, and his dark hair is caked close to his face.

My hands form fists at my sides as my skin tingles. "Where's Constance?" I say.

"I am here," her voice, quiet, worn, comes from behind me. Coughing, her clothes stained with blood, she has a woman's arm across her shoulder, and Constance's other hand is around the woman's waist.

Running over, I say, "Let me help," and I place my shoulder under the woman.

"Thank you, Jayden," the woman says.

I blink once and then, a second time. *Ms. Gracie. Yes, I know her.* Constance squeezes my arm gently as tears swell in her eyes.

I turn away.

I wasn't here. I didn't help.

I want to ask if Wyndham's, okay? Where's Osgoode? Did all of the Ikan soldiers make it? Including Henry, who never wanted to fly on Enisseny?

Looking around, I don't see anyone I recognize. A man wearing an apron sits in front of a building, a hand on his forehead, his eyes staring at the road where bodies litter the streets, twisted at odd angles, blank stares from men, women, and children. Clothes, rocks, and splintered glass from windows are everywhere.

I turn away and focus on the cobblestone road. When I look down, I see Ms. Gracie's leg is bent, and blood soaks through the fabric tied around it.

Several Xyidaks walk by, surrounded by Ikansterup soldiers, arms tied with ropes. Enisseny blows cold air onto a fire that sprouts from the top of a building. Smoke billows above, with ash. The building continues to smolder even with the dragon's cold breath.

"We'll take her," one Ikansterup soldier says, who's with another, and they both carry a stretcher. They help Ms. Gracie onto it and lift her up and take her to Isons-Lydric Castle.

I stare at it. The door is missing. Several windows have been broken, and one section is now rubble. Of all the buildings, though, it seems to be the one that's fared the best.

Constance puts her arm around my shoulder, pulls me close, and plants a kiss on my forehead. "I am glad you are safe," she says.

Shaking my head, I say, "I should've been here."

"What would you have done?" she asks, tilting her head. *I would have fought to protect Rumbling Town. Maybe I could have made a difference.* "You are not fully trained. We have lost—" her voice cracks, lower lip trembles, she brings me close to her, and wraps her arms around me, and says, "—many good men and women."

"Osgoode?" I say, covering my mouth with my hand.

"No, no," Constance says, pulling me away. "He was injured in battle. The doctors, however, say they are confident my husband will recover." She keeps her hands on my cheeks, brushing tears away with her fingers until no more fall.

"Jayden," Wyndham says.

"Wyndham!" I say. Running over, I wrap my arms around him and say, "You're okay!"

"Yes, of course," he says. "Eustace?" he asks.

Pulling back, I say, "Yes, he's with Alwyn. They're all safe."

"Good, good," Wyndham says, looking around. The lines in his face are heavy. He looks over at a building that smolders and a man that lies in the street. Bricks are in mounds where buildings were, and other stones are on sidewalks as if someone has thrown them. Wood, glass, a blue shirt, a child's doll that's missing the head, a purple silk dress, corn, berries, and canned food are everywhere. Wyndham's face falls.

"Wyndham?" I say. "Are you alright?"

"Yes, yes," he says, patting me on the shoulder.

"What should we do?" I ask.

Wyndham places a gloved finger to the corner of one eye. Then he kneels and bends his head to what's left of the road. I stand there, not sure if I should say something.

He looks up at me. Then he stands, looks around, nods, and says, "We build—again."

***

Gamel and Constance have left to go to the tunnel to tell the others it's safe to return to Rumbling Town. While Gamel is gone, Hera's in charge, and she's sent some of the Ikansterup soldiers back to her city so that more troops, wagons, and supplies can be sent to Rumbling Town. Wyndham, Enisseny, and Henry move between buildings and make sure all the fires are out. The last thing we need is for something to spark in the middle of the night.

I tighten my grip on a lead of a horse as I touch a woman's elbow. Leaning to the side, I offer her my shoulder as she slides her foot into a stirrup and mounts the horse I'm holding. Once seated, she stares off at nothing. Most of the seriously injured are at Isons-Lydric Castle, where teams of nurses and doctors and others from nearby villages like Wringing Sound Station care for them—including Osgoode. This woman that sits on the horse, though, isn't injured—not physically, anyway.

"Madam," a young Ikansterup soldier says. "Are you well

enough to travel?" he says softly.

She hums. I glance past the saddle horn, over to the soldier, and see his mouth is a single line. "Yes," she murmurs. I look up at her and notice her chin sticking out. Her eyelids flutter. Then her shoulders roll back, and she straightens her posture in the saddle. More firmly, she nods and says, "Yes, yes," and then her horse moves forward, following the other people in Rumbling Town who will stay in Ikansterup until some of the debris is cleared.

A peace treaty of sorts, or partnership if you will, is in place between Rumbling Town and Ikansterup, where the cities have agreed to help each other in conflict, whether that's through war or natural disaster. But the agreement also allows for support—to provide food and shelter to displaced citizens and resettlement at either city should the person or family wish to relocate. This woman is already familiar with Ikansterup—she came from there. Now that her husband has been killed—I was at their wedding even though right now, I can't remember her name. I watch her horse amble through the dilapidated stone wall, and she disappears through it.

"Jayden, we must talk," Laurence says, "in private." He grabs me by the elbow and drags me toward the Isons-Lydric Castle.

My heels slide against the dirt as I squint at him. "What are you doing?" I snap.

"I need to speak with you!" Laurence shouts.

"Yeah, well, you don't need to drag me along like an animal on a rope!" I say, yanking my elbow free.

Laurence's face reddens, his mouth opens. From behind us, "Laurence," Wyndham's voice booms. It's not angry, more like reserved and sad. Loud enough, though, that we both hear him. "Do not ever force someone to come with you. Always ask," Wyndham says, sighing.

"Still, Jayden," Wyndham whispers, glancing around, "consider Laurence's situation and those of the people of Rumbling Town." Looking around, I notice some have stopped doing whatever they were working on, their heads slightly bent, tilted toward us. Others focus on whatever task is before them, their eyes glancing over at me every so often.

"Sorry," I say to Wyndham.

Wyndham squeezes my arm once, walks past me, and says nothing else.

Laurence paces back and forth. I fight the urge to roll my eyes because nothing bugs me more than apologizing to him. I say, "Sorry, Laurence."

"As you should be," Laurence says. His head's bent, and his eyes are filled with rage. His fingers flick at his sides.

Wyndham's eyebrow arches, he takes a step forward, and his mouth is poised to say something. I place a hand on his arm and shake my head.

"I believe I know who is responsible," Laurence says.

"'Tis the Xyidaks," Wyndham says, sighing and waving his hand in the direction of prisoners passing us.

"No," Laurence says. "I do believe someone else is involved."

"Who?" Wyndham asks. His face twisting, he waits for Laurence's answer.

Looking away, Laurence says, "Jayden and I must speak in private."

Wyndham looks over at me. I shrug, shake my head, and say, "I have no idea what he's talking about."

"If you know something else," Wyndham says, rubbing his forehead with a hand, "you will tell me." Laurence's head is bent. Scanning the area, Wyndham watches men and women carry out food from their flattened homes, pull clothes from the rubble, and try to salvage what they can. "You are right, in one way. We should speak in private. Let us go to our home," Wyndham says. Laurence opens his mouth to say something, and Wyndham glares at him while raising a finger.

Laurence snaps his mouth closed. Then we head toward Isons-Lydric Castle in silence.

THIRTEEN

Tossing a log on the fire in Wyndham's study, I see books piled high on Wyndham's desk on the *History of Swordsmanship*, R.H. Price's, *Changing Boundaries*, Margaret Ryholms, *A History of the Monarchy*, and Jacob Potwell's, *Ikansterup's Sleepy Time Stories*. Wyndham would often put Hugo and Emma to bed, and he'd read them a story from the collection. Although the books piled on his desk were scattered on the floor when we first arrived.

I wince at the thought of Emma and Hugo—and I wonder if Constance will bring them here or if she'll send them to Ikansterup.

"I believe Olin had some part to play in this," the sound of Laurence's voice interrupts my thoughts. Laurence and Wyndham are seated across from one another in oversized leather chairs in front of the fireplace. Wyndham stares at Laurence. Standing, my fingers flick at my sides, and I squint at Laurence.

Did Laurence hear something during the battle? Did a Xyidak share this piece of information with him? Or was it something he heard when he was at Ikansterup?

Laurence's hands rest on his knees, and he says, "I have spoken to Ms. Sidespot and Ched Kiting—they, with others, say the Xyidaks were looking for you, Father."

Wyndham runs a hand over the leathered armrest. "There are many who search for Enisseny and me, who wish to do us harm . . . ."

"No," Laurence says. Shifting in his seat, the leather squeaks under his weight, and he says, "They were looking for you, not Enisseny."

"Well," Wyndham sighs and says, "I have not always been at my best." Nodding, he says, "I have made mistakes, and I am certain some wish to repay me for past decisions."

Hands behind me, I'm leaning against the wall. I shouldn't interrupt, and I know it. But I can't help myself. "No," I say. "You haven't done anything wrong. What could the Xyidaks possibly have against you?"

Wyndham twists his head toward me and says, "Live long enough, and you too might make decisions that you one day live to regret. And I have had many years to make missteps." Wyndham's eyes redden. I want to say that it's because he's tired, or that it's late, or maybe it's from all the smoke. "Still," his chest rises, falls, as he runs his hand over the armrest some more. Shaking his head, he says, "If there is some truth to this, then I have placed the people of Rumbling Town in danger.

As for the question you asked, Jayden, I do not know what I may have done to the Xyidaks to bring such destruction to Rumbling Town."

"No," Laurence says, shaking his head.

"I don't get it. What exactly did Ms. Sidespot and Ched Kiting say?" I face Laurence and cross my arms in front of me and step away from the wall.

"They said the Xyidaks wished to know where Wyndham lived. Which building was his, and when they refused to answer, they set their homes ablaze."

"Yes, but why were they looking for him? What did they want? To kill him?"

"I do not know!" Laurence says, throwing his head against the bulky brown leather backing of the chair. "Perhaps it has something to do with my confession to Olin," he says.

"How can your confession to Olin cause the Xyidaks to hunt Wyndham? That doesn't make any sense."

"Why do you have such affection for him?" Laurence asks, frowning.

Heat rises on my face as I spin to face him. "What do you mean?"

"You understand what I say." Laurence's jaw lengthens as he straightens up in the chair.

Rubbing my nose, I shake my head and say, "I liked him, sure. But not in the way you think. Olin took care of us when we were sick, gave us a place to hide, and returned us to the King's Acres. And he did it all and asked for nothing in return."

"Olin was kind—by causing a fever to overrun us?"

"He didn't do that!" I say, snapping. "It was someone else. Or something else."

"What was your confession to him?" Wyndham asks, watching Laurence.

Laurence slouches and sweeps his fingers over a cut on his other hand. Sitting up taller, he shifts in his seat and glances over at me and back to Wyndham. "It was about you."

Sighing, Wyndham says, "And what specifically?"

"That I was afraid something might happen to you." Laurence's voice is small. Gone is the arrogant man I've known since I first came to Canonsland. Laurence's eyes are locked on the stone floor. He won't look at Wyndham or me.

"I would hope," Wyndham says, with a crooked smile, "there would be some concern."

"'Tis the thing I fear the most," Laurence whispers.

"Well, I would hope to make at least the top of the list," Wyndham says. "Do not fret, my boy. That would not be the reason they came to Rumbling Town. Unless there is some unknown power you wield where you might be able to be convinced to help them so that they can win the conflict on the Xyidak-Trygolish border." Looking over at me, Wyndham says, "But I know you well enough to say, I do not believe you possess mystical powers."

"They most likely came for you because of your connection with Enisseny." Alright, I'm stepping out on a crumbling ledge here, and I know it. I know I shouldn't make assumptions. But I don't care.

"Do not speculate, Jayden. We must always deal in facts."

"Right, because that's what you and Laurence just did?"

Wyndham scratches his forehead, his head teeters up and down, and he says, "You are right."

"Of course, I am," I say. "So, we're going to leave Olin alone, then?"

Wyndham's hands are folded together. He stares at the fire as it burns orange in the fireplace, and the wood crackles. "I do not think Olin is responsible for what has happened in Rumbling Town. However, he might have played some part in this that he might not have known." Placing a hand to his mouth, Wyndham says, "Jayden, would you consider returning to Ludswup to see if you might find Olin?" Raising his hand, he waves it and says, "You do not need to hide your intentions from him. If you find him, be truthful about what has transpired here and see if he has shared the knowledge he had with another person."

My heart thumps. Rubbing my hands together, I say, "You said, you didn't think Olin played a part in this. But do you think he unintentionally did?" Looking over at Laurence, his face flushes, and he visibly squirms.

"Yes, possibly—" Wyndham looks between Laurence and me. "The woman we search for, her name is Nesta."

I step forward and look down at Laurence. When did we get that information? *Wyndham was with me, and then, as far as I know, he left to come to protect Rumbling Town.* "What?" I say. Laurence leans forward in his chair, but otherwise, there's no movement from him as he gapes at Wyndham. *Okay, so Laurence didn't know either.* "Where did that information come from? From my understanding, Kemena, Abelard, and Vik didn't find anything when they asked at the other cities. And neither did Laurence and me when we passed through the towns and villages."

"The information I share with you must stay within these walls," Wyndham says, sighing. "Before the King married Queen Mitra, he had a relationship with another woman named Royce. Royce was the guard of Trepid Divide, and Nesta was a close friend. After our meeting, when you both returned and told us of Olin, King Nicholas looked at the sketch again and recognized the young woman as the older woman in the picture." Wyndham runs a hand through his beard, "You both did well in describing Olin, and that would make him the right age at which Royce and the King parted ways when Royce informed him she carried his child. That is how the King knew of the place and the question that is asked. The relationship between King Nicholas and Royce ended shortly after." Wyndham's eyes switch back and forth between Laurence and me. "We cannot be certain, though, which is why I ask this conversation remain within these walls—'tis speculation."

"So, what, the King decided to toss Royce aside after she got pregnant? He decided she wasn't good enough?" I keep my voice calm, but it shakes on the last word.

"Based on what evidence do you make such an accusation toward King Nicholas?" Wyndham demands.

Biting my lower lip, I shift uncomfortably. Clearing my throat, I say, "In my world, sometimes, even today, marriages are frowned on if you're not wealthy enough. If you're from different—" I stare down at the area rug with clumps of mud on it as I search for the right word. Then it comes to me, "—social classes." A lump forms in my throat. I cough again, clearing it.

Daddy's slouched forward posture haunts me. *I'm seated at the dinner table, and I blurt out to the stranger how Mom ran out of butter and milk and made the sauce for the pasta with water.*

Straightening, I raise my head and stare at a photo of Wyndham holding Emma and Hugo's hands taken in the fields behind Lydric-Isons Castle. Emma's hand is raised as she clutches a sunflower up to Wyndham's nose. "And it's not just relationships. It affects the friends you have, the jobs you can get," I sniffle, "even the education you're allowed to pursue. For women, it just adds another barrier."

"Ah," Wyndham says, "yes, it happens here, in Canonsland, as well."

There's silence. Blinking, I look at Wyndham and run a hand across my wet cheek before anyone notices. "King Nicholas loved Royce. He wished to marry her. She rejected him."

Okay. I got nothing now as a defense for this woman, Royce. *Was Nesta really her best friend?*

"Jayden, what do you say? Will you go to see if you might once again gain a meeting with Olin? The King has left the decision to me when, and if, someone should return to Ludswup. And given the destruction of Rumbling Town now, it seems war may be imminent. So, I believe the time to return is now."

"Yes," I say, taking a deep breath in. I can't believe Wyndham still trusts me—even with everything I accused King Nicholas of and even though I messed up in Ludswup the first time.

"Very good. I'll leave it to you to decide who you wish to accompany you."

Hesitating, I say, "Can I take Hera?"

"Wait, why is Jayden being sent to Ludswup?" Laurence says.

Wyndham raises his eyebrows and says, "You are not very good at subtle—and the way you convicted Olin without any evidence, I suspect Olin would be hesitant to share much with someone who may have been—how shall we say?—hostile on the first meeting?"

"You cannot take Hera," Laurence says, turning to me.

"Why?" I say, taking a step back.

"She has never been to Ludswup. You will both be lost forever."

Rolling my eyes, I shake my head and say, "She's a strong fighter, she's good at reading a map, and she has a sense of direction. I know too, she also has my back. As well, the people of Ludswup have never seen her before. I think she'd be good at blending in with the locals."

Laurence clears his throat and says, "I have some of those qualities. I am a good fighter, and I know how to travel to Ludswup *without* a map," he says, tilting his head while watching me. He shifts his gaze to the area rug that's a picture of the cave in Mt. Lieuschanean portraying a cross-section of what you would see there; the trees, the light, the red, blue, orange flowers. The two white moons shine above the view of the cave. It was a gift to Wyndham from the people of Ikansterup. "I, too, have your back," Laurence adds, craning his neck in my direction, "and I can—how did you say it? Blend in, if I must. As well, Hera is Gamel's second-in-command. He needs her."

Wyndham's hand is on his mouth, and his eyes rest on me. Sighing, I say, "What do you think?" I ask Wyndham.

"Hm?" He reaches down and fusses with the buckle of his boot. "It is not for me to decide. The decision rests with you," he says, looking up at me.

I scratch the side of my leg. *Well, that's a lot of responsibility to place on a sixteen-year-old.* Raising my chin, I try to keep my hands relaxed at my sides. *Couldn't he give me a smaller task? You know, like overseeing the reconstruction of Rumbling Town or something?*

Yeah, that wouldn't work either. As hard as I try, I'm not good at math. So, a career in architecture is out of the question for me, too.

"Fine," I say, "Laurence, would you mind coming with me to—"

"Your enthusiasm for me warms the heart," Laurence says, his lips curling into a smile.

"No," I say, "that's not the reason I wanted Hera to come." Laurence is covered in mud, his face is pale, yet his eyes are kind, tired, and playful. Remorse consumes me. I shift. I never meant to offend him or hurt him, especially given everything that's happened to his home and family in the last few hours.

"I know how I am at times. Arrogant, abrupt, forgetful in manners . . ."

"Well, at least you're not someone who sails away with their emotions," I say, running a hand across my forehead.

"We are all imperfect," Wyndham says. "What matters is that we learn something from the events we have lived through." Standing up, Wyndham taps Laurence on the knee and says, "On that note, you will need to find a change of clothes. Those who reside in Ludswup do not care for knights as your last visit there proved."

"Yes," Laurence says. "I will speak with Constance to see if I might borrow some clothes from Osgoode as I do not have much that remains here."

"That is a good plan. But please, do not share this conversation with your sister. The less who know of your travels to Ludswup, the safer I believe you will both be."

"Constance has returned?" I ask.

"Yes," Laurence says. "Emma and Hugo do not wish to go to Ikansterup. They want to help." I smile and laugh. "But Constance was firm. She asked them to be brave and go with Idonea in the morning and stay at Ikansterup until some things can be sorted out here."

"The children are so much like their parents—they are remarkable," Wyndham says, staring at the floor. When he looks up, he smiles at me.

"Be prepared to leave at dawn," Wyndham says, standing, and Laurence stands, too.

Walking to the door together, I ask, "And what's next?"

"The King is sending troops to help us rebuild Rumbling Town and to protect it. Other knights and soldiers will go to Ikansterup as there is a concern now that the Xyidaks may retaliate against Ikansterup because they helped defend Rumbling Town. Hopefully, Ikan reinforcements will arrive tomorrow as Hera requested them earlier today. We know some of the Xyidak soldiers escaped, so they may have fled back to their borders. I will wait here until the King's soldiers arrive, and then I will travel to the King's Acres." Sighing, Wyndham says, "I fear we are falling behind, always making a move too late. Fighting a defense when perhaps—" Wyndham holds his knuckles to his lips and says, "we need to fight an offense. Meet me at the King's Acres with what information you gain from Olin if you find him. After two days, leave Ludswup and return to the King's Acres if you are not successful. Either way, I believe our next step will be to head to the border of Xyidak and Trygolish. The Xyidaks are responsible for what has happened at Rumbling Town, and both Enisseny and I were injured there, and that was the last place I saw Edric before he went missing. It seems the best place to begin if Olin is unable to shed light on where we might find Nesta."

Wyndham opens the door to the study, and the wind howls through a broken window in the hallway. It stops us for a moment. Then we separate. I know what I need to do— I need to gather some supplies for our return to Ludswup, pack, bathe, and get some rest.

Yes, sleep. I really must sleep soon.

FOURTEEN

Hera and I walk along an alleyway in silence. Or at least, it was an alleyway—now only one side has buildings, and on the other side, there's nothing more than heaps of rubble and dust. Holding a bag filled with bread Constance gave me, I throw it over my shoulder and walk up to another door.

Lights flicker inside a building, one of the few that's still on. I'm already packed, and I'm ready to leave with Laurence at dawn. I'm sure I haven't slept in days based on Canonsland time, but I'm not tired. So, when Constance asked if I could help, of course, I said yes.

Hera towers over me. Her eyes fill with water as she stares at the road, still stained with crimson, littered with broken glass, dust, rocks, clothes, pots and pans, and children's toys. Hera makes a fist and knocks on the door. "Ikanst'p Sold'r, we wish to speak with thee Mast'r of thee h'ous."

The door creaks open. A woman with long black hair holds a child on her hip and says, "I am the master of this house."

Hera steps back. Many Ikansterup soldiers still hesitate to speak to the residents of Rumbling Town, given the Ikans were outcasts in Canonsland. They were blamed for destroying their land, characterized as a warring group when all they wanted was to have a roof over their heads. They wandered for hundreds of years with no place to call home. Not one town or village would allow them to resettle on their land. At times, they were starving. Then Lord Fulke and Droart happened, and the people of Canonsland learned what happens when you turn your back on others. Hera would have been about my age when all that happened. I don't know if that's the reason for sure why Hera doesn't say anything to the woman. But she doesn't.

"Hi," I say, "I'm Jayden."

Switching the child to the other hip, the child leans her head against the space between her mother's shoulder and neck. Both are dressed in their coats and boots.

"I know who you are," she says in a tired drawl. "What can I do for you?"

"Constance asked us to check to make sure everyone's okay for the evening—that everyone has food and somewhere to sleep."

"We have somewhere to sleep," she says.

"We have bread," Hera says as she reaches a hand into the bag and pulls out a loaf. "Would you like some?" she asks.

The woman stares at her child, and then she faces us again. Reaching over, she takes the bread from Hera, gives her the outline of a smile while saying, "Thanks." Her cheeks pulse a few times. "They were looking for Wyndham," she says.

"Yes, we heard." My role tonight isn't to gather information. I'm only here to check on them. Still, she brought it up, not me. "Did they say why they wanted him?"

"We hid. The Xyidaks did not see us."

Hera leans against the stone building as she faces me and drags a hand across her cheek. "You stayed while they were in your house?" I ask.

"Yes," she whispers. "My child is very good. Never cries. She listens to me, always has. I told her, shhh," the woman holds a finger up to her mouth and faces the little girl, and I watch as the child's mouth tightens and closes. Placing a kiss on the child's cheek, she says, "She never gurgled, never cried."

"Wow," I say, "what a good girl." Waving at the child, the little girl sticks out her pudgy fingers and imitates me, waving back. "What's her name?"

"Iyanta," the woman replies. Her eyes dart along the dark streets, looking for something. "Wyndham—they did not care if they found him or not. The Xyidaks," she glances over at Hera and says, "were told to destroy Rumbling Town—" her voice and eyebrows rise, and she says, "—to burn it to the ground." Her words disappear like shadows devoured by light. "They did it because they were told to do it."

"By whom?" I say. Hera's head snaps in the direction of the woman. "I did not hear the name," she says. "I am sorry. Please tell Wyndham—there are some in Town who blame him and wish him and Enisseny to leave." Sighing, she says, "I know they have been our protectors. I do not wish them to leave. Good nite," she says, and takes a step backward and moves to close the door.

"Wait!" I say. "Uh, is there anyone who can help you? It's cold tonight and," leaning to the side, I add, "and your fireplace isn't lit."

"I prefer to stay in my home," she says.

"Can we come in and see if we can get the fireplace working?" My hand rests on the wooden door. Not too hard, though. I understand she's probably tired and frightened. I want her to know she has a choice. At the same time, I need to make sure she knows we're willing to help. There's a chill in the air, enough for white wisps of air to come out of our mouths when we talk.

Her head rocks to the side, and she says, "Are there not others you need to tend to?"

"We'll keep going when we're done. But there are other soldiers out too. So, we have a few minutes to see what we can do for you."

"I would appreciate it," she says, swinging the door open.

***

I walk the hallway in Isons-Lydric castle and head in the direction of the room I shared with Ella and see the windows have been boarded up. Constance said Petronilla left shortly after Laurence and I went to enquire at the other smaller towns on our way to the King's Acres, and I'd just missed her. But I told her I'd seen Petronilla when Laurence and I returned to Stock Castle. I'm glad Petronilla wasn't here to see her home in ruins.

"Jayden?" a low voice whispers from behind me.

"Yes," I say, facing Laurence. He stands there in the same clothes from the battle, his curly hair now dry of sweat. But the thick, pungent odor of salty meat and cheese oozes from his pores.

"You were to sleep before we left. We have only a few hours now before daylight."

"Really? You haven't even showered yet," I say, covering my hand over my nose.

Laurence's left eyebrow rises, and he says, "Neither have you." His eyes glimpse down to my chest, arms, and legs. When I passed a mirror, I saw my crooked ponytail and my hair bulged on top of my head. I didn't care then. Now, trying to be cool, I slide the elastic out, and my greasy hair falls to my elbows. Twisting my neck to the side, I take a whiff of my armpit. "Oh, I really need to bathe," I mutter. The smell of onions and garlic clings to my linen shirt.

"My sister, she assigned you chores?"

I rub my nose with my thumb and laugh. "Yes. I didn't know what to say."

"I, too, faced the same dilemma. Constance asked me to board up some windows and tend to the horses. What could I say?"

"Yup," I reply. "I didn't really mind, though. I don't know if I would have been able to sleep anyway." The hallway behind Laurence moves, but I know that's not true—exhaustion is messing with me, causing me to see furniture shift, think I see people who aren't there. Yeah, hallucinations are fun. This isn't the first time I've pushed off sleep longer than I should have. So, I know the signs.

"Yes," Laurence says, staring down at the floor.

This is awkward. Laurence just stands there, silent. "Okay, well, I need to get a bath. And try to get some sleep," I say, hoping he takes the hint. Right now, exhaustion descends on me, and Laurence's voice and the hallway wobble.

"Good night, Jayden," he says. Placing a hand on the doorknob, I push it open, "If you have trouble sleeping," Laurence whispers from several feet down the corridor, slouching, which is unusual for him. "Sorry," he says. He throws another apology over his shoulder while he shakes his head, speeds up, and turns around the corner.

I watch him until he's not there anymore. I stare at the handle and push the door open. I'm relieved to find Petronilla's room is mostly undisturbed. I walk into the bathroom and stick my hand in the water in the bathtub, and it's lukewarm. "Oh well," I say. Undressing, I sink into it, and even though the water's cool, I fall asleep.

***

Wide awake, I've already tossed and turned for at least half-hour. My bath put me to sleep, but when I got up and changed into my pajamas, bam! my brain would not shut up.

Did Olin have anything to do with this? Has Petronilla heard what's happened here? Oh my god, is Eustace okay? I don't remember seeing him. What about Emma and Hugo? Laurence and I are to leave at dawn. Am I going to sleep in now? There's so much to do here. I should stay and help. Or maybe I should get up now and help because I'm not sleeping anyway. No, I need to go and do what Wyndham's asked me to do.

STOP IT!

I throw the sheets off. Sitting on the edge of my bed, I slump forward. My boots are beside my bed, and it's enough of an invitation for me, so I yank them on and leave my room. I start down the hallway, and as I pass rooms, there are people I know, and some I don't that are asleep in beds and others wrapped in blankets on the floor. Guilt consumes me.

I should have offered up my room. Or at least let other people sleep there. Especially given that well, I'm not sleeping.

I pass one of the large sitting rooms, and Osgoode playing the violin there after dinner or Wyndham reading a story to Emma and Hugo haunt me. The rest of us always listened to the music or Wyndham's embellished voice when he read the stories. The room is filled with men, women, and the odd child where nurses and doctors circle. The medical team moves from patient to patient, checking bandages, offering water, or they'll place their hands on foreheads to check for fever. Still, others offer medicine to the injured who are awake.

I linger too long there, and a nurse looks up at me and gives me a small smile before she turns and places a glass of water to the lips of a man. Even from as far away as I am, I can see perspiration clinging to his forehead, and I wonder if he's fighting an infection from a wound.

I step lightly down the hallway, trying not to disturb our guests, and make my way to the kitchen. On the other side of the room is a door that's away from the cupboards, stove, and icebox. Placing my hand on the knob, I turn it, and the hinges creak.

Taking a breath in, I look around and wait a moment. No one's noticed. When it's safe, I climb the narrow spiraling staircase that's only big enough for one person. Petronilla and I would climb these stairs together when everyone else had gone to bed, so if one of us slipped, the other one would be able to help. We weren't to go here because both Wyndham and Constance forbade it.

Forbade? Shaking my head, I wonder how I haven't messed up more using old-time language at home.

Don't belong here. Don't belong there. Don't belong anywhere.

At the top of the stairs is a wooden door. I turn the handle and push on it, but nothing happens. I rattle the handle some more. Still, it doesn't open. I'm trying to be quiet here, but I'm losing patience as my face warms with frustration.

This—this childhood place that's always made me calm—and now the door's jammed? Of all days, it has to be today?

I swing my butt into the wooden door and give it a good shove, and the door bursts open. I stumble forward, and then I crash to the floor of the roof of Isons-Lydric Castle. I stare down at black leather men's boots. Looking up, Laurence says, "I was wondering if you were going to come?" he says, extending a hand.

"Thanks," I mutter. Taking his hand, I pull myself up to a standing position. I'm surprised to see him here as Petronilla and I were the only two that ever came up to the roof.

"As a child, I would come here," he says, staring out at the ruins of Rumbling Town.

I don't know why it never occurred to me that Laurence may have come here when he was younger, too. Laurence's head pivots from right to left, taking in the scene below and above us. There's very little light in the town now. So many buildings lean to one side, while others only have a few walls that remain. It seems a light blow of wind could topple the remains of what were once homes and businesses.

"Constance caught us one night when we were up here. She and Wyndham sat us down and told Petronilla and me we weren't allowed to come up here again. They said it was too dangerous." Red circles outline Laurence's eyes.

"You and my niece did it, nonetheless," Laurence says, with a crooked smile.

"Yup."

Before tonight, I loved this view. The billows of smoke that rose from the chimneys, the thousands of lights that blinked in the darkness, and it was almost as if I could see and hear the farmers and shopkeepers gathered around their dining room tables with their families having dinner. Sometimes, I even imagined I saw a small girl that hugged a stuffed dragon with a blanket pulled up to her chin, warm in her bed.

Staring out at the landscape before me now, those thoughts are replaced with only fatigue and sadness. Tapping my forehead, I say, "Wait, how did you know we came up here?"

Laurence's eyes shine. "We all came here at one time, even my responsible sister." Tilting his head, he says, "I showed Petronilla this place. I may have stumbled on you both a few times over the years."

Wiping my nose, I take a breath in. Despite the apocalyptic scene in front of me, the cold swells in my lungs, and I bite my lip. The destruction gives me a pang. At the same time, the budding light of some buildings gives me hope. I want to remember this. "I found it peaceful up here—to look out over the Town. Now, though—"

"'Tis difficult," Laurence says, his voice cracking. "I feel the same."

Walking over to the edge of the building, I sit down and swing my legs over the top. Laurence sits down beside me. Looking up, the stars flicker, like a bulb draining of energy. Pointing up, I say, "This view never changes."

"Yes, 'tis filled with the reminder of things that have lived and now are gone. Always, though, there is the promise of what might be."

Smiling, I say, "Well, that's poetic. Where did you get that from?"

"It came to me now."

"Good line," I say. "You should try to use it on a—err—well, you know, someone you like."

"Perhaps," Laurence says as he pulls his knees up to his chest and wraps his arms around his legs. "I am sorry," Laurence says, "for what I did earlier . . . forcing you to come with me."

"It's okay," I say, resting my hands on the edge of the roof. "First time you've ever done that," I say, shrugging. Looking around, I blink at the dirt road that leads to the Castle below us when I remember something I need to share. "Oh," I say, "I almost forgot. Hera and I met a woman tonight when we were handing out bread. She apparently hid when the Xyidaks were in her home."

"She hid?" Laurence says, his forehead crumpling.

"Yes. The amazing part was the woman had a baby with her. Apparently, if the mother says, shhh . . . ," I hold my finger up to my lips to demonstrate, ". . . the little girl gets very quiet—doesn't gurgle, or cry, or anything."

"How do you know this?"

"She showed us," I say, smiling while I stare up at the stars. "I know you thought Olin had something to do with the attacks because you'd told him—" I stop to hunt for the right word as I see Laurence's cheeks glow pink, "—of your concerns about Wyndham." I decide that's good enough. "The woman said the Xyidaks were told to destroy Rumbling Town. It wasn't about Wyndham. They had orders to do it."

"Why would the Xyidaks pretend to want Wyndham?"

"I don't know," I say, my jaw tightening. I stare over the edge of the building, past my dangling feet, to the ground below us. "The woman said there are people in Rumbling Town that want Wyndham and Enisseny to leave. Maybe that's why the Xyidaks did it? To isolate them?" Rubbing the bridge of my nose, I say, "Sorry, I'm speculating again." Shaking my head, I add, "I don't know."

"We all speculate," Laurence says, "even Wyndham. As he demonstrated tonight," he says with a slight curl of his lips.

"I know," I say, kicking my legs out that hang over the side of the Castle.

"I will be sure to relay the information to Wyndham before we leave in the morning."

"Good," I say.

"We should go back inside," Laurence says, standing up.

"Sure," I say. Taking a breath in, I scan the remains of Rumbling Town. "I'll go inside in a little bit," I add as I look up at the stars.

"Would you mind if I stayed?" Laurence asks. "If you prefer to be alone—"

"It's fine," I say, laughing.

Sitting back down, he whispers, "And I promise to be quiet."

"Good," I whisper as I stare up at the stars.

FIFTEEN

"I spoke with Wyndham," Laurence says. Our horses' tails swish as we enter a canyon that's a couple of hours outside of Rumbling Town. We'd primarily ridden in silence so far because I didn't sleep well on the roof of Isons-Lydric Castle last night, so riding and having a conversation is hard. I woke up at sun rise and woke Laurence, and then we both made it back to our rooms to change and grab our things before Wyndham came looking for us. "He plans to speak with the woman with the child. Wyndham will ask Hera to show him where the woman lives."

"That's good," I say.

The reins slide through my gloved hands as I tuck the cloak I wear under my arms to protect myself against the chill of the early morning. We plan to pick up the pace once we've passed Wringing Sound Station. Wyndham wanted us to leave early so no one could ask any questions. If anyone asks him, he'll tell them we're going to the King's Acres to deliver a message to the King. It's eighty percent true, twenty percent omission of fact. But most people don't ask Wyndham questions.

"I never asked," Laurence says, "have you had an

opportunity to see your mother?"

"What?" My mind fumbles. I'm not sure what he's talking about. The lack of sleep is starting to catch up with me, and then I remember, right, Mom. *How could I forget?* "Yeah," I say.

"How is she?"

"She's alright," I say. Shaking my head, I hesitate. I don't really want to tell him about my conversation with Mom, but I can't stop myself. "My Mom's known about Canonsland for years. She never said anything to me."

We're passing through a canyon with shimmering grey rocks on both sides of our horses, and Laurence's eyes are locked on the opening that shows rolling green meadows and red evergreen-like trees. This area was carved out by an animal, Qudsmaths, Wyndham had said. They were ten-legged, flying, and burrowing reptiles and were a distant relative to Enisseny more than a thousand years ago. The creatures were also very destructive. Well, according to legend

. . .

"Why did she say nothing?"

Raising my head, I say, "She said that the first time I came here, I came back different—more confident, not afraid of heights, or not as afraid of heights."

"I would like to think I had some small part to play in that," Laurence says, staring ahead and grinning.

"Yeah, I'll never admit that." Laurence laughs.

Between Laurence and me, there can be long, drawn-out periods of silence. It's never felt wrong, though, that we've got nothing to say to one another, or that we're avoiding a topic. Instead, it's a comfortable silence where the quietness needs no music to be played or tongues to be flapped. Taking a breath in, I suppress a laugh by rubbing my knuckles across my nose. With David, I feel the same way.

"My mom talked about her mother." I pause, and so I'm clear, I add, "She was my grandmother. I called her Grandma Nettie. Anyway, Mom said Grandma could never send her to museums or on school trips when she was a kid because they never had any extra money. And my mom wanted to be able to do those things for me," my face warms, and I don't think it's just because of the sun's rays, "and well, my parents can't do it. Everything costs something, and they don't," I fiddle with the reins through my fingers, stare at the saddle horn, and say, "really have anything extra."

God, why am I so embarrassed?

Right, my mother never knew her father. One of Dad's friends brought it up once when I was around eight and said stuff about my mom and Grandma Nettie. Grandma Nettie had died several years earlier, and Dad still lost it. It was the last time Dad ever spoke to Jacob Script.

And of course, there's the whole, *my parents can't afford stuff,* thing . . .

Looking around, I sit up taller in my saddle. We're close to the opening of the canyon, so I scan the area. Dad's love of Westerns has burned into my brain that a canyon is a perfect place to be attacked. Sure, Laurence is pretty good with a sword, and I'm okay. But between the two of us, we wouldn't be able to fight off thirty Xyidaks (or more) if they were hanging around waiting to ambush us.

"Does your mother know what's coming?" Blinking at him, I don't know what he's talking about, so I stare at the ground, trying to figure out what he means. "That Canonsland is in danger, and there is a chance of war?" We're not out of the canyon yet, so there are shadows under Laurence's eyes and across the right side of his face that fade as we exit the gorge.

"Not really," I say. "But my mother said she doesn't need to know the specifics." Laurence's eyes flicker at me. Smiling, and with a lift of my hand, I clarify, "No, she doesn't want to know—" Looking around, I shrug and add, "She understands things happen when I'm here. And she's been told I'm in training to be a knight. So, she knows . . ." I decide that's all I need to tell him.

"Yes. But there is a difference between training and war."

"I know," I say, shifting slightly. I'm never sure how much

to tell people in Canonsland about my life back at home. When I was five years old, I had a friend who lived across the road from me, and Mom said we were inseparable. I didn't remember her well. It was more like flashes of images of playing dolls, running outside, and playing hide-and-seek. Then her family moved away and came back to visit a couple of years later. Our parents reconnected, no problem. Us? Everything was forced.

Trying to explain Alberta, Canada to someone from Canonsland is worse because I need to explain the geography, how things work, the time difference . . . It's nearly impossible. When I've tried, it's taken me hours. So, now, unless I'm talking to Dr. Eastwood, I don't talk about home.

"Your mother needs to know."

Mander's bite. I'm going to have to tell him.

"I want to join the CAF." I feel my shoulders slump as I run a hand across my face and sigh. "Sorry, CAF stands for Canadian Armed Forces. It's our military." Laurence's head hangs. He blinks at his horse's shoulder, mouth gaping, as bewilderment tugs at his lips. "It's like an Ikansterup soldier or being a knight. Except if I make it in, I'll represent the Canadian military." Rubbing a hand under my eye, I add, "And our weapons are different."

There's a thumping coming from somewhere. Looking around, I hold a hand up, and Laurence stops mid-sentence. We stare at each other, and then we both swivel in our saddles. Leaning forward, I know the vibration is getting louder, and it sounds as if it's moving toward us. We sit there and wait.

Waving high, a flag flutters from the crest of the hill, and it looks like fifty Trygolish on horseback galloping towards us. "Back to the canyon!" Laurence hollers. I turn my horse, spinning around, kicking my stallion into a gallop, and following Laurence's lead.

Once back in the canyon, Laurence and I slink back into a corner. I'm not sure if we were seen. The horses' hooves pound the ground as the Trygolish pass by in their regal colors. Lanky, grey-skinned men and women gallop through the corridor.

Laurence yanks his sword from its holder, and the sun catches what little light there is and reflects it. I grab Laurence's arm and hiss, "What are you doing?"

Laurence's jaw pulses, and he whispers, "I am defending my home!"

"Really?" I say. "There are . . . ," peering out at the Trygolish, I know now I was wrong when I thought there were fifty, ". . . at least two hundred armed Trygolish!"

Slowly, he slides his sword back into its scabbard. "Still, we should at least return to Rumbling Town to warn them."

"They're already ahead of us," I say, sighing. "And Ikansterup soldiers are on their way—they're probably already at Rumbling Town by now," I add, nodding. "Besides, we're already running late. Wyndham only gave us a couple of days to see Olin."

"Jayden," Laurence says, rocking from side to side in one spot. He whispers, "When we first met and went to Ikansterup, you were able to disappear."

"Yeah," I say. "I don't have any magical powers," I say, wiggling my fingers in the air. "If I did, don't you think I would have used them by now?"

We're crouched down now, and the last of the Trygolish warriors disappear. A small smile forms along his lips, and he nods. "Yes. But did Wyndham ever explain as to how you were made invisible?"

"No, but I also never asked him."

"Is there a chance, as you come from another realm, that you may have some connection to Enisseny? Other than you can travel back and forth between the two worlds?"

"I don't know."

"Would you try this once to see if you can tell Enisseny the Trygolish are coming? And that there are many of them." Laurence pauses and says, "I worry what their intentions might be."

Laurence's eyes flick back and forth, and his lips are tight.

Holding the leather reins of my horse, I close my eyes. Yeah, I'm doubtful any of this will work. I'm old enough to know that there's nothing special about me. Still, I know I need to try for Laurence's family, Wyndham, and everyone else in Rumbling Town.

"Jayden, this is no time—" I follow Laurence's voice and shove my hand over his mouth, squashing his nose with my eyes still closed. When he stops talking, I try to settle my mind and focus only on Enisseny.

Enisseny. Enisseny. Trygolish soldiers, I'm not sure what to say next, assuming he can hear me at all. I try to sort it out in my mind. There were Trygolish soldiers, but their weapons weren't drawn. And they didn't seem to be carrying cannon drudges or have with them mammoth eidas with their saber tooth teeth, agility, and strength that can kill fifty people in seconds. They typically use eidas when warring with the Xyidaks. Both sides have them, so it usually results in no movement along the Xyidak and Trygolish border. The eidas are bad-tempered creatures, though, so they don't travel well. The Xyidaks had a couple when they attacked Rumbling Town. From what I heard, it wasn't too long before Wyndham, Enisseny, and the few Ikansterup soldiers arrived when the attack started. Enisseny took care of the eidas quickly.

Enisseny, several hundred Trygolish soldiers are heading toward Rumbling Town. Their purpose is not clear.

Enisseny's piercing cry bursts in my ear, and pain explodes from my temples and radiates through my jaw. I place both hands on my head, cradling it.

"Jayden! Jayden!" Laurence whispers.

I drop the reins, slumping into the dirt. Pulling my legs up to my stomach, I keep my hands on my head and begin to rock back and forth.

As quickly as the stabbing, throbbing pain in my head came, it disappears as if a snowstorm has descended and buried it. Numbness consumes me from the top of my head to the tingling in my toes. All I'm left with is exhaustion and no way to know whether Enisseny received the message.

***

I wake up groggy and sore with a blanket on top of me. Laurence sits beside me, his brown eyes watching me.

"Jayden, would you like some water?" He reaches over to his canteen and unscrews the lid before I can answer.

Struggling, I sit up, take it from him, and swallow the cool refreshing liquid. Water dribbles down my shirt, and I take my arm and wipe my mouth with my sleeve. Placing my fingers to my lips, it's dull to my touch.

I stumble to get to my feet and mumble, "We need to go." Blinking, I notice Laurence has let go of the horse's reins, and they stand in a nearby corner. Peering up, I can see white clouds above us, and the grey stone is still on both sides of us. Remembering where I am and what we saw, I say, "The Trygolish?"

"They passed," Laurence says, walking toward the horses and grabbing the reins. "They either did not see us, or they did not care."

Extending my hand, I say, "I'll take my horse."

The reins, one in each of his hands, sag at his sides. "I do not think—"

"You don't think what?" I growl.

He glances over to the horses. What's he doing? Looking for help from them? "We must leave," Laurence says, his eyes rest on the powdery yellow dirt under our feet, "but I do not think you are well enough to ride alone."

Leaning forward, hands on my knees, I squint up at him. Laurence and I have had this conversation before. He knows I don't like riding with other people. Give me my horse because I want to control how we travel (trot, canter, or gallop) and what direction I'm going.

Trapped, echoes in my ears.

I look away from Laurence, stare at a rock, and then peer up at him again. "I think we should ride together. You are—" hesitating, his lips purse together, and his eyes shift, searching for something.

"Weak?" I offer.

"Not well," he says.

"I can ride." Stumbling toward my horse, I reach for the reins and snatch them out of Laurence's hand. I bounce along beside my horse, trying to hook my foot into the stirrup, and I nearly fall over several times. "Stay," I mutter, hopping along beside it again as if it were a twenty-two hundred-pound dog. For some reason, he listens and stops. Unwilling to let the opportunity of my cooperative horse moment slip by, I bounce once, swing my foot over the saddle, and it lands on the other side. Grinning, I wiggle my foot into the other stirrup. Spreading my arms open wide, I look up to Laurence as I slump forward in the saddle with my head resting on the horse's neck. "See, no problem!"

Someone places a hand on my stomach and shifts behind me as I drift off to sleep again. My head knocks against a door.

Wait? Door? No, it's someone's chest. Then arms wrap around mine. I look up at Laurence. Laurence peers over at me, his lips tightening into a smile. He clicks his tongue once, and we start to move.

"Don't you tell anyone that I rode with you," I say, sticking a finger in his face.

Staring forward, he nods and says, "It will be our secret. I promise." He winks once at me, and I fall back asleep.

SIXTEEN

It's dark when I wake again, but there's the warmth of a fire and the crackling from wood burning, and the scent of meat, potatoes, and carrots. Laurence is there, staring into the flickering light of the fire. I recognize his outline from the crookedness of his nose, his long jawline, and his mid-length brown curls. He's seated on the ground, his legs pulled up to his chest with his arms wrapped around them.

And I'm busted. Smiling at me, Laurence says, "You are awake. How do you feel?"

"I'm alright," I lie. The throbbing in my head has stopped. But now, there's a sluggishness that's taken over. Of course, I know that might be because I've most likely slept for ten-plus hours. I flop my leg to muster the energy to sit up.

"I made some dinner," Laurence says, offering me a plate of food. Sitting up, I take it from him and glance over at his bedroll beside mine.

I take the fork and scoop the vegetables up, shoving some into my mouth. Mumbling, I say, "I don't know if I reached—" pausing, I add, "Enisseny." With each mouthful of potatoes, carrots, berries, nuts, and meat concoction Laurence created, I scrap the fork across my plate faster. It's almost as if I haven't eaten in a week.

Laurence lifts his eyebrows at me when I start to lick my plate. I laugh and say, "Sorry," as my cheeks warm. "I'm starving."

"Perhaps I should have become a cook instead of a knight?" Laurence says, grinning.

"I don't think so," tilting my head, I add, "it was alright, but it wasn't great."

"Very good," Laurence says. "So, there is no alternate path for me."

It's a trap, and I know it. Laurence is fishing for a compliment. I don't bite, though. "I don't think I connected with Enisseny."

Laurence gazes into the flickering flames. His eyes flutter, "You do not think so?"

When he turns, he stares at me. There's no shifting or turning on his part. And there's no smile there. I stare down at my empty plate and place it on the ground. "There was no response. He didn't send a message."

"There was nothing?"

"Well, I mean," I cross my legs and stare up at the shadow of a tree. The limbs stick out in all directions, and the leaves rustle with the wind. Shaking my head, I intertwine my fingers together and place them in my lap and say, "I think I might have heard his war cry."

"Ah, well, then we have an explanation as to why you suffered such discomfort right after."

"I don't know—"

Laurence touches my arm, stopping me mid-sentence, and says, "'Tis alright. You tried. That was all I asked."

There's something different about him. Some melancholic version of Laurence has emerged. I want to tell him he's already a great knight. Everyone thinks so because I've heard them talking: Wyndham, Abelard, Kemena, and even King Nicholas. All the younger knights want to be as fast with a sword as Laurence is, strong, and clever.

The problem is, Laurence has done this to me before

where he's pretended to suffer from some insecurity. I've fallen for it and praised him. Only then would he smirk and say, *yes, I know.*

"Where are we?" I ask.

"We are perhaps halfway to Ludswup."

I cover my face with my hands. "Sorry. We should have been able to make it in a day."

"No," Laurence says. "You were not well. It happens. And I have my suspicions that may be of my doing."

I close one eye, squint at him through the other, and say, "Are you alright?"

"Yes," he says, staring into the fire.

Gulping, I take a breath in. "I can't imagine what it's like for you. Your home . . ." Laurence turns to me, and with him watching me the way he is, it makes me unsettled. I'm trying to say something here but I just don't know what it is. I know Rumbling Town wasn't my home, and I was always just a visitor there. For Laurence, though, it's where he grew up.

"Yes," he blinks at me. His mouth opens, closes, and then he turns back to the orange-red glow of the fire.

"I'm sorry what happened to Rumbling Town." Laurence doesn't say anything. He doesn't even face me. "Are you sure you're alright?"

"Yes," he says, stretching his legs out and sighing.

"Something's wrong. Just tell me." I wait. Laurence huffs and picks some soil up, sifts it through his fingers, and it disappears to the ground.

"I don't remember my parents. Wyndham is the only father I have known."

The wind picks up. Or maybe it doesn't really . . . I take a big breath in to keep my own emotions in check. I've never seen him so vulnerable.

Waving a hand, I say, "Wyndham's fine. He's fine. He's probably going to outlive both of us."

"He rubs his hands together with such frequency I wonder if he is plotting something," Laurence says, smiling. "Sometimes, he limps. And I have found him asleep in the rocking chair in Hugo and Emma's room when he was to read them a bedtime story. He was not even past the first page."

"Well, at least your greatest fear is something worthwhile. Mine's just dumb."

"That was what I was going to ask you," Laurence says. "But I should not ask."

I look up at the stars above us and see the outline of only one moon. Tonight is an eclipse, so only one moon is visible. "I guess it's only fair, after all. Please, don't tell anyone, though. It makes me sound selfish."

Frowning at me, Laurence leans forward. "I am certain that is not the case."

Gazing up at the stars, I say, "I thought it would be my mom. Like you. I thought my worst fear would be losing her."

"Yes. There is nothing selfish in that. You are so young to face such a thing."

"Yeah, that wasn't it." I shake my head, shrug, and say, "I'm afraid of being trapped."

Silence is between us now. And for the first time, it's uncomfortable.

***

"Jayden," Laurence says, "what you said last night, the one fear you have above all else—" We're standing next to each other, hooking up our bedrolls onto the backs of our horses.

I'd hoped he'd forgotten about our conversation or at least would have the decency not to bring it up again. Sure, the silence between us has been stifling. But not as unsettling as actually talking about how I feel. I struggle to hook up my sack with some food, water, and clothes in it to the back of my saddle. If we were going to talk about it, why couldn't we finish the conversation last night? Instead, we just sat there, me looking at the stars, him saying nothing, and then to break the stalemate, I pretended to be still tired and went to sleep. The truth is, I was up for hours thinking about what I'd told Olin.

"You said last night you were afraid to be trapped. Were you speaking of physically being buried? Or was it something else?"

One of my hands is on the horn of the saddle. Facing Laurence, I say, "Something else." My throat tightens as Laurence stares at me. Rubbing my thumb under my eye, I say, "I'm afraid of being trapped at home where I might not have a chance to be more than I am right now."

"You are already more than you were," Laurence says.

I shake my head. "No, I'm not. Maybe here, I might be . . . ," I check the stirrups to make sure they're fastened tight. "Even that's debatable depending on who you talk to. But at home, I need to make choices now about what I want to be," sighing, I add, "when I grow up." I raise my fingers and make air quotes. I flick my eyes at Laurence, "There are different levels of education that you can take where I come from, and each one either opens doors or closes them. So, I need to decide which way to go."

"In Calgary," Laurence says.

Stiffening, I nod. "Yes," I mumble. I don't think I've ever heard Laurence say the name of my city before, and my two worlds colliding again makes me shift. What I've loved about Canonsland is that I can be different here. At home, I'm Jayden Heneck. Here, I'm simply Jayden.

"I have heard you say the name of Calgary before. You do not wish to stay there?"

The thought of leaving my parents makes my stomach flip. And then it flips again. Chewing on my lower lip, I say, "I love Mom and Dad. I just don't know—" I struggle to explain. It's like trying to catch a snowflake that you plan to keep in a glass. "I don't know that I can be what I want to be there."

"Your parents do not wish for you to leave?"

"No." Leaning against my horse, my temper bubbles like the scorching water in the lake found at the base of the mountain of St. Agatha. *Can we end this conversation?*

"Jayden," Laurence says, placing one of his calloused

hands on my shoulder.

I run my hand across my face. "My guidance counselor thinks—" I struggle to find the right word, no, not, *dumb*, instead, I say, "—he doesn't think I should go to University. He doesn't think I work hard enough." There. I prefer Laurence believe I'm lazy versus stupid. I cross my arms behind my back and add, "I want to be a CAF Pilot." I scratch my face and neck as if I have a rash and add, "But math and science are a struggle, and I need to have a good understanding of those subjects to have a chance." I bow my head. Sighing, I say, "I mean, I could still go to University and go into a Business Program or Arts Program and become an accountant, or something else, I guess. Or don't waste the money at all. Stay in Calgary, get a job, get married, have a couple of kids, or a dozen . . . ," I say, groaning.

Laurence's head is bent but hidden under his lowered chin is a smile. So, crossing my arms, I wait for the teasing to commence.

"A dozen babies would be too much, I suspect, for even Constance and Osgoode." I laugh and run a hand across my cheek. "Eustace struggled in school with mathematics, astronomy, and such. I have never been good at opening a book and settling down to read it. Constance will read for hours. There are many things you can do—" we lead our horses to an open area. Seated on top of our horses, Laurence pulls on his riding gloves, nods as if he's either agreeing with himself or trying to convince me, and says, "—that does not include bearing a dozen babies," he pauses, "unless, you wish to. There is nothing wrong—"

"Stop," I say. While I've enjoyed watching Laurence stumble his way along in this conversation, I want it to end. It's almost as if the more we talk about it, the more likely it will happen to me. "You're right. There's nothing wrong with it if that's what someone wants. My friend, Ava, can't wait to get married and have a family. She's one of my best friends," I say. "But it's just not the path for me."

Our horses step forward as Laurence says, "When I was

your age, I felt as you do. I was worried about leaving Wyndham and my brothers and sister. They were the only world I had ever known." Glimpsing over at me, he tilts his head in my direction, "And worried I would fail as a knight. It was all I had ever wanted. If I failed, what would I do then?" I don't interrupt. This is the most honesty I've ever gotten from Laurence. "Eustace came to diplomacy late in life. But he has found his way. You will, too, Jayden. I am certain of it."

I exhale. I've been going around in circles for months because I didn't have anyone to talk to. This conversation hasn't solved all my problems. But it's nice to know other people have struggled too.

Laurence's eyes flick over to me. A small smile crosses his face and widens.

"Oh, you!" I flip my reins once and squeeze my legs into my horse's sides. My stallion's pace quickens as he moves from a walk to a gallop, and I lessen the slack of the reins, so we stand a chance of beating Laurence.

Laurence is right beside us, our horses' necks are side by side, and there's the thunder of hooves that pound the road. Laurence's words are fast and loud now, and he says as he sticks a finger out to a cluster of trees ahead of us, "To the trees on the ridge!" as his horse's head lengthens.

"Go, go!" I shout. My horse grunts and snorts as I urge him forward, and we try to close the widening gap between Laurence's horse and us.

SEVENTEEN

Same Inn, same Ludswup.

Except right now, high winds and rain are coming down. Laurence and I pull the hoods up over our heads on our long leather riding jackets as we race from the stables to the Inn doors side by side. The streets are covered in brown, slippery sludge that pools, and as I splash through a puddle, my feet slip out from under me. But I catch myself and avoid falling forward in the middle of the road.

Well, mostly. Laurence's outstretched hand holds mine. We stand there for a second, and he squeezes it once and says, "To the Inn!" and his gloved hand is gone as he sprints toward the main entrance. I watch him run and then look to the sky as water pours down my face.

Lightning strikes. Black waves of wind illuminate tree limbs that bend, fallen leaves spin around, and walls of homes and buildings shake from the gusts, and shutters rattle.

I wipe my face and stare at the blinking lights in the Inn. My shirt and pants are soaked through. Laurence and I had tried to outrun the storm. It's safe to say we failed.

I've cursed weather like this recently: When I went hiking with David last fall in Bowmont Park and the sky unexpectedly turned grey-black before swaths of white rain drenched us. We made it back to the car before the lightning started. Yeah, that was close, and we made a pact to check the weather radar next time.

Today, though, this storm might be a blessing. It gives us a reason to cover our faces with our hoods. And with the soggy, blustering weather, few Ludswup residents are hovering around who might recognize us from a week ago.

"Isabel!" Laurence holds the door open and says, "Is this where you plan to shower?"

Smiling, I run toward him. And say, "Thanks, Michael."

Yeah, we're really hoping no one remembers us.

Dampness and grey stone greet us, as does a crackling fireplace. A man roughly the same age as Laurence is at the counter with a silver bell in front of him. "Welcome," he says, his mouth opening into a smile. The Innkeeper's eyes flash to me. He nods and rests his hands on the old black, flaking wooden countertop. "You have picked an odd night to arrive," he says, with more warmth than the building we're standing in.

"We were delayed in our travels," Laurence says, dropping his bag to the wooden floor. I straighten up, waiting to see what Laurence will say next. I hesitate to interrupt and allow him to take the lead. The last thing we need is for someone to figure us out because we're giving conflicting stories. "One of our horses lost a shoe. We needed to stop along the way to have it repaired."

Also, Laurence is a phenomenal liar when he needs to be. His face, his form, his eyes are solid. Unlike me, he doesn't tug at his clothes or fiddle with his fingers. I place my bag against the side of the wall and rest my hands at my sides before I shove them into my pockets and try to relax my shoulders.

Tilting my head, I stare at a few books on the shelves behind the attendant. I don't remember the bookcase with books on it last time we stayed here. He opens the registration book and swipes his wispy hair in his eyes. It's an odd style not typically seen in Canonsland. "One room or two?" the man asks.

"One room," Laurence says, looking over at me.

Walking around the small reception area, I cross my arms behind my back and stare at musty wooden framed photos of Lord and Lady Rodnar, who were the last landholders of Ludswup. For better or worse, they'd never had children, and so they left the town and land to the people to manage themselves. Their intentions were good.

But when theft of property and murders occurred, the King stepped in and made a few rules. Overall, though, there are minimal laws in Ludswup. It's part of the reason why the Ludswup residents love the King and hate the knights. The knights sometimes overstep their bounds and issue fines that don't apply here.

We sign our names, *Michael Watkins* and *Isabel Tyrell*, and pay for our room. "Let me help you with your bags," the blue-eyed, wispy-haired man says, bending forward to take my bag from my hand.

"I'm good," I say. The Innkeeper's lips pucker, his blue eyes shine, and dimples in his cheeks and chin appear.

"I would be honored to help you, my lady," he says, bowing his head and bending forward.

"Surely, not," I say.

He laughs. "You do not think I would be honored?"

"I think I'm not a lady," I say, clutching my bag tighter.

His hand extended, "I would be honored to take both your bags." Tired of arguing with him, I let go. He reaches for Laurence's. While the Innkeeper is bent over, Laurence's eyes dart at me, and his forehead crinkles. I shake my head at him. Grinning, the man in the jacket and tie with the ill-fitting baggy pants straightens and glances between Laurence and me and says, "And then I could show you around."

"No need," Laurence says, "we are only here for one night."

"Still, I suspect you will need food before you depart tomorrow? I can show you where you might find breakfast." Climbing the stairs, he bumps our luggage against the wall while Laurence and I trail after him.

"What happened—" Laurence places a hand on my shoulder, and I stop talking. Right. I can't ask about the last guy who was at the front desk.

"What happened?" at our door now, the wispy-haired man repeats my half question while he wrestles with the keys. He shoves one key in, and it doesn't open. The keys rattle in his hand as he tries another. "Sorry, I'm new here." His cheeks turn pink, and then the door clicks open.

"Friends of ours had been here some time ago," I say, looking over at Laurence, "and they had recommended this place. They mentioned the owner was an older man."

"Ah yes," pushing the door open, "there we go!" he says, beaming. "He has sold it to me. I am still finding my way around, figuring out all of the Inn's secrets." Dropping our bags on the floor, he shuts the door behind him. His eyes skip between Laurence and me. His smile vanishes. "Why have you returned to Ludswup?" he snaps.

***

Laurence places his hands on his hips, turns to me, his eyebrows bunching. Facing the Innkeeper again, he says, "I do not know what you mean." Leaning against the door now, the Innkeeper's arms are folded across his chest. "We never have—"

"Stop," he says, flashing a hand at Laurence.

"I remember you." His eyes flick back and forth between Laurence and me. Nodding, he says, "I remember you both well—'tis not Jayden and Laurence?"

Laurence's face flattens. Clearly, neither the weather nor the jackets have given us an advantage. "Olin?" I ask.

"Yes," the Innkeeper says.

"You look different," I say. Laurence stands there as a blue vein on the right side of his temple pops. There's a slight wiggle of his ear.

"Yes, when I'm here, my eye color and hair change. Trepid Divide, it changes how I appear. You would be surprised how subtle differences would make someone who you know well become almost unrecognizable. If you find yourself in a town unwelcomed again, might I suggest you consider changing something simple if you truly wish to remain undetected?" I assume he's not looking for an answer to that question.

"Now, I have answered your questions. Why have you returned?" Olin demands.

"We have questions," I say. Laurence's face reddens. He clasps and unclasps his hands into fists at his sides. "How did you know we were here?"

Olin walks around the room, crosses his hands behind his back, and stares at a framed watercolor portrait of a bridge with a river below it. "The man you held a knife to his throat, he saw you and Laurence approach the town, and he warned me. I asked him to make sure it was you, and he received that confirmation when he saw you both bring your horses to the stables. He was hidden in a corner of the barn." Facing us, Olin stares down at us and says, "You have still not answered my question." His jaw pulses. His eyes are locked on me.

Laurence runs his hand over his mouth and faces Olin. "Did you share the information we told you with anyone?" Laurence says.

"That is the reason you have returned?" Shaking his head, "You return for foolish reasons!" he says, laughing while rubbing his eye. "There are those who would kill you." He nods once at me and says, "Both of you."

"Rumbling Town," I say, touching Laurence's arm. He was mid-step, moving toward Olin. I don't know what Laurence intended to do, but his hands are shaking. "It has been attacked by Xyidaks. Witnesses say they were looking for Wyndham."

Olin nods, "Yes, I have heard." Shrugging his shoulders, he says, "But everyone knows that Wyndham and the Winter Dragon are connected. The Xyidaks could have planned to capture Wyndham to convince Enisseny to help them win their border issues with the Trygolish. Or for some other purpose . . ."

"You did not answer the question," Laurence hisses.

"No! I did not share your secrets. I am bound to keep them," Olin says.

"Bound? Bound, by who?" Laurence demands.

"Bound by the spirit of my mother."

I glance over at Laurence. "The spirit of your mother?" I say.

"Yes," Olin says, "she died giving me life."

"And your father?" Laurence says.

Olin's eyes flutter. His skin glows with the lanterns in each corner. "I never knew him," raising his chin, he says. "So that was why you came? To find out if I was responsible for the attack on Rumbling Town?"

"No," I say. This conversation isn't going well. "There was a woman I saw in my world. She had long dark hair and a red birthmark, I think, by her mouth. When I saw her, she was wearing a green dress." Hesitating, I wonder how much I should tell him. "When we were here last time, we were going from town to town, trying to find out who the woman was and if anyone knew her. We forgot to ask you at Trepid Divide."

"You came back to ask me about this woman?" Olin says, frowning and crossing his arms.

"Yes." I know I can't tell him about the possibility the King could be his father. And I'm not good at lying. But I can do half-truths. "Someone from Stock Castle remembers meeting your mother once in your land. He came a long time ago, and he thought your mother and the woman in our sketch were friends." From the inside pocket of my coat, I carefully unfold the sketch and show it to Olin. "This is what the woman we're looking for looks like. The person from Stock Castle thought her name might be Nesta," I add.

"Has she done something?"

"No," Laurence says. I tug at my jacket and take several steps backward, and stare at the wooden floor. "We only wish to ask her some questions," he adds.

Olin walks over to me and leans forward. His warm citrus

breath makes my cheeks warm. "Jayden?" he says.

Breathing out, I look up and say, "She stabbed Sir Edric, and he's been missing for some time now." Laurence huffs. I see the color drain from Olin's face. "And she threatened my mother and me with a knife and caused my mom to fall into a river."

"What?" Olin's hands flick at his sides, his mouth gapes. "How is that possible? You are from another world."

"Edric was with Enisseny, and they came to my realm. Then Edric was stabbed, and they both disappeared into the river. The woman was left behind, and she pointed a dagger at my mom and me and threatened us with it. But Enisseny and Edric returned, and the dragon hit me with his wing and knocked my mom into the river. My mom hit her head on some rocks. She nearly drowned." Anger rushes through me. Somehow, though, my words are steady.

Remembering the scene, I stagger backward and turn away. I walk over to the wooden mantle and rest my hand on it. There's no fire lit yet. We'll need to do that later. The room is damp, cold, and what little light the lanterns were giving off is fading. Sliding my fingers along my cheeks when I get to my lips, I squeeze them together, trying to remember. Mumbling, I say, "Enisseny knocked my Mom into the water, and it was an accident. But the whole thing was Nesta's fault."

Olin's left eye twitches. He sighs and says, "She is my guardian—and is a troublesome guardian on the best of days."

"Any chance she's your mother?" I ask.

"No," Olin says, "my mother died in childbirth."

"Do you know that for certain?" Laurence asks.

"Yes," he says, "if she were not my mother, I would not be able to be the broker of Trepid Divide."

"But Nesta—"

"Do you listen? I said Nesta is not my mother." Laughing, he says, "I know."

"But how do you know?" Laurence sputters. "You would

not remember your own birth."

Standing taller, Olin says nothing. His eyes rest on Laurence.

Standing between both men, I don't say anything. My face contorts as I think of—

"What?" Olin's chin sticks out as he glances down at me.

"Nothing," I say. Having a child anywhere, I guess, is risky.

"'Tis not possible," Laurence says, "you could not be there!"

"'Tis not possible, that the simple act of lying would cause someone to come down with a fever. Yet, it happened, did it not?"

"Yes, but—"

"Why would I not tell the truth about my mother?" Olin says. I rub my neck as I wait out the battle of wills.

"You could not have been there!"

Frowning, Olin laughs, rubbing his forehead. "We are all there. Whether we remember the beginning or not is another thing," Olin says hoarsely.

"Do you happen to have a photo of your mother?" In Canonsland, they've been able to take photos for some time now. But in case Olin doesn't, I say, "Or maybe a drawing?"

"Why?" Olin asks.

"Someone might remember her," I lie.

"It has been more than twenty years. Memories fade," Olin says with a shrug.

Tilting my head, my mouth opens and then closes. Grandma Nettie has become a little more unclear over the years, but I can still smell the mixture of cigarettes and her floral perfume on her clothes when I think of her. Closing my eyes, I see her curly grey hair, the light in her eyes when she laughed, the brown spots on her skin from being out in the sun too long. And in memory, she's as big as she was when she was alive. "If they knew her well, they might still remember, even with the time that's passed."

"No one knew her well," Olin says, "she drifted in and out

of this world and the other. You will need to trust me." He peers down at me, and there's something there, a question or a hope.

I don't know why, but I believe him. "So, Nesta's your Guardian?"

"Yes," he says. "If you know for sure who your mother is, you must know who your father is?"

"No," Olin says. "He was an ordinary man of no particular abilities, or so Nesta told me." His eyes stare down at the wooden floor.

Uh, sure, there's a good chance he's only the King. I don't say that, though. Nodding, I say, "Do you know where Nesta is?"

Olin takes a step back and says, "No." He lets out a long sigh. "Even when I was a child, she was barely there. My mother left her as my Guardian as she was a good friend and thought she might make a good mother. But Mrs. Bellows and Mr. Bellows—"

"The two cooks?"

"Yes," Olin says, lengthening his neck. "You remembered?" I nod. "Well, Mr. and Mrs. Bellows raised me. I did not take over my responsibilities until I was old enough. That only happened in the last four years."

"When was the last time you saw Nesta?"

"Perhaps a month ago?"

"I think it's too long," I say, turning to Laurence. Staring at the ground, he nods.

"I am sorry for what happened to your home, Laurence," Olin says, his hands clasped behind his back. "If I had known and if there were something I could do, I would have done it."

"There is something you can do," Laurence says. My heart skips a beat.

"You wish for me to play some part in finding my Guardian? So she can be arrested?"

Rubbing the back of my neck, I watch Laurence and Olin negotiate. "Would you?" Laurence says.

"Nesta rarely returns now," he says, biting his lower lip. "I would be remiss if I did not admit I do have some affection for her. I still call her mother."

"Is there a chance there might be someone else who heard what Jayden and I said? I mean to say, our secrets?" Laurence says.

"Are you worried about someone finding out your secret, Jayden?" Olin says, glancing over at me.

"No. I already told Laurence."

"Do you know Laurence's secret, Jayden?" Olin asks. I nod. "So, Laurence, what is this ridiculous concern you have in others knowing you care for Wyndham? He has been a father to you."

Turning away, Laurence mumbles, "I," he spins around, flicks his hand at Olin, "I worry I have placed him in danger!" he snaps. "I know him well, and others may suspect he is not as strong as perhaps he once was if they know my worries about him. I fear he will become a target in battles and such."

Groaning, Olin's eyebrows crumple together. He shakes his head, smirks, and says, "Wyndham is old. Everyone knows he is well over two-hundred-years. So, they would suspect some frailty there." Tilting his head, Olin adds, "As well, everyone knows you care for Wyndham. They know how you speak of him, how you behave around him, and all the praises you cast on him. Your father, Wyndham, is immortalized already while he lives." Olin sighs and says, "And still others speak of your devotion to your siblings, both by blood and by marriage . . ." Laurence's head's raised, and he blinks at Olin. "Even from where I am, I have heard of your family. You are lucky." Olin's head is bowed. He's quiet. "I have never known that," he whispers. "But before Wyndham was your father, he was a knight. As well, he is connected to the dragon." His lips twitch. "There will always be those that will threaten him and Rumbling Town because the knight and dragon reside there." The thumping of the rain off the windowpanes echoes in the silence. "In answer to your question, no, there was no one with me that would have heard your greatest fear. No one is allowed in until you either succumb to your lie, or you admit the truth."

"Will you speak with the King?" I ask. Oh no. I can't believe I just said that. I'm going to have to explain. I look past Olin and see a mouse crawl back into a hole that's beside the bed where Laurence's bag is. "He thinks he might have met Nesta."

Wow. I really need to work on my ability to lie.

"I am not allowed on the King's Acres. That was the reason I left you and Laurence on the outskirts of the City."

"Who told you that?" I ask.

"Nest—" his eyes shift back and forth as he runs a hand over his mouth.

"Well, in case this one time Nesta was telling the truth, and so you don't melt into a puddle or something if you step onto the King's Acres—" Olin laughs. Laurence smiles, and I add, "—we can arrange a meeting so that you can tell King Nicholas about Nesta. Right now," scratching my forehead, "you're the only lead we have."

Nodding, he says, "As you have told me, my mother may be responsible for the injuries to a knight and played some part in your mother's accident, I wish to help." He bows his head and whispers, "I hope Nesta had no part to play in the destruction of Rumbling Town."

Looking up, he walks to the door, rests his hand on the knob, turns around, and says, "I'll speak to Mr. and Mrs. Bellows and see if they know anything more about Nesta. Perhaps they know of a way to reach her. Stay in your room for the evening. I will bring you some food early in the morning." Pausing, his jawline lengthens, "You must leave before the town awakens. Neither of you won friends here by threatening Dr. Catcher."

"Sorry," looking at a clock, I say. My eyes meet Olin's again, and I add, "Laurence didn't have anything to do with that. It was all me. I know you can't tell the son. But please, tell Dr. Catcher, is it? I'm very sorry." Unclasping my hands, I wrap my knuckles on the mahogany wooden desk a couple of times as moisture gathers in my eyes.

"I will," Olin says.

I nod once, say, "Thanks," and place a finger to the corner of my eye.

Olin stares at me and then opens the door and closes it behind him.

EIGHTEEN

Warm above us, the sun shines bright. Our horses' hooves clop against the grey stone in the courtyard of the King's primary residence of Stock Castle, where we cross on our way to the stables. Laurence and I have ridden in silence for the last hour or so.

Before we left Ludswup, I fought with Laurence over why he didn't leave me any jam for my toast, and he snapped that I'd kept him up with my snoring. Our day didn't start great, though, with Olin opening the door to our room, dropping the food on the table, and telling us to be out before dawn. We barely had a chance to open our eyes before we were in the stalls, walking our horses to the outskirts of town, and then riding hard to Stock Castle.

"Laurence!" Vik says, running over to him. "Jayden," he says with a flick of his head that barely counts as a nod. "Some soldiers and knights have gone to Rumbling Town. And Wyndham has arrived," he says. "Do you have news?"

You may have news, Laurence, only you. Not me.

Laurence jumps down, sighs, and says, "Yes." I swing my leg over the saddle and drop to the ground as I hear Laurence say, "Where is Wyndham?" There are mumbled words as I lead my horse to the stables. The last thing I overhear

Laurence say to Vik is, "I am sorry. I cannot tell you."

As a knight-in-training, the other knights acknowledge my existence, sort of. But I'm not someone who has anything valuable to say.

"Jayd'n," a husky, female voice says from behind me as I take the saddle off my horse.

Turning around, I smile, "Hera!" I say. I don't know why but I'm happy to see her. "What are you doing here?"

She strides over to me and pulls the bridle off my horse. "Gamel and I have come with our soldiers." She looks around.

"They go over there," I say, pointing to a wall on the far side of the room.

Before she leaves, she says, "Have you spoken to Wyndham?"

"No, Laurence and I—" I nearly say Ludswup. But, instead, I say, "We just got here."

Hera nods. "Am I allowed to use this?" Hera pauses, looks around, and says, "On any horse?" she asks, holding a brush up.

"Yeah," I say, picking up another brush. Together, we walk back to the horse that Gamel gave me at Ikansterup and clean out the sweat and dirt that's soaked into his coat.

She looks over my horse's shoulder. "You did not stay and speak with Vik?" Hera asks. Her hand stops moving with the long brush strokes, but she pats the horse along its shoulder.

"No," I answer, placing the brush down on the ground. I tap my horse's foot, and he lifts his leg, and I check his shoe.

"Vik does not speak with you?"

"He doesn't care to," I say with a sigh. "I'm not taken seriously. Lots of people train to be knights. Very few make it."

"Ah. Well, if it does not work out, you could come to Ikansterup and be a soldier. I will happily train you."

I cradle the stallion's leg in my hand, and bending forward, I say, "Careful, I might just take you up on your offer."

"You would make a good soldier," she says.

Is she serious?

"Thanks," I say. "But you're just kind. You don't know me," I say, dropping the horse's leg. I stroke the stallion's sleek coat and whisper, "Good boy," and he blows warm air into my face.

"Jayden, I appreciate you taking care of the horse," the senior Stable Master says as he walks toward us along the corridor with stalls on both sides. "But if the King discovers some are willing to tend to their own horses, where does that leave me?"

"Sorry," I say, smiling. We've done this dance so many times I've lost track. I hand him the brush that I'd placed on the floor, and Hera gives him hers and apologizes too. I thank him for caring for Lyra while I was gone and for this horse as well.

"'Tis a long road to becoming a knight . . ."

"Yup," I say.

I close my eyes and take a deep breath in, and the scent of berries, grass, and salt are in the air. When I open my eyes, Hera's staring at me. "Do you ever feel like you don't belong anywhere?" She laughs while raising her eyebrows. Rubbing my eyelids, I shake my head. "Sorry," I say. "I sometimes forget." Then, taking a step back, I add, "I can be so dense sometimes."

She stares up at the plumes of clouds that drift in the sky. "You are not dense," she says, shrugging. "You make mistakes and forget things. I still do—feel as if I don't belong," she says. "But it must be hard for you. You do not come from Canonsland, and the more time you spend here, the less familiar, you must become with your own world."

Blinking at her, I don't know what to say. No one's ever understood that. Not Constance or Laurence. Not even Dr. Eastwood because by the time I started coming here, he'd already spent most of his time in Canonsland. Although, I guess he might have felt like that at the beginning. And well, Wyndham's always known where he belongs . . .

We pass apple and pear trees and rose bushes in the

garden planted when the King's daughter was born. Shrubs have been trimmed into men, women, and children, multiple blue ravens, dragons, and tilting my head, I peer at one thing that I can't make out. "I believe 'tis one of our Jack Rabbits," Hera says.

Smiling, I remember the first time I saw them in the cave in the mountain. "Right," I say. Then, squinting, I finally make out the ears and whiskers.

We walk up the steps in silence, and the quietness is starting to rattle me. "So, you said you and Gamel have come with the other Ikansterup soldiers? Why?" I say.

"The King sent a messenger and asked if we could supply some troops. Kemena and Abelard, he said, have remained at the Xyidak and Trygolish border, and they heard what happened in Rumbl'n Town. They sent a messenger who said no one saw any Xyidak soldiers leave the border before the attack. So, the King plans to march troops to the Xyidak and Trygolish border to confront the Xyidaks. When we go, I will lead Toly's Troops, 'tis my soldiers, and we will return the prisoners to their city and escort some diplomats. The diplomats are to ask the Xyidak leaders the reason for the attack. Gamel has already left with some soldiers. I am to wait here until Gamel sends word I am to come."

We've passed through the first level of steps that are outside the King's Palace. Knights passing us offer a nod of recognition to Hera. I rub the side of my head and look around to see a couple of diplomats seated at a small round marble table under the red ivy tree. They have a couple of small goblets at their table, and their plates are empty. A thin-haired male server appears, bends forward, says something to the two men, and then gathers up the dishes with another woman dressed in the same black and white pants, shirt, and jacket. She eagerly trails the lead waiter.

We walk up more steps and into the main lobby of the King's primary residence. Knights stand at attention leading up the stairs and are positioned at the entrance to each room. The main hall has white marble that, when it rains, is slippery.

We're in the south, though, so that seldom happens. There's lots of gold here—gold edges of mirrors, statues made of it, and crystal chandeliers hanging above us. Even the chairs in the corner shine a bright yellow with the sun's rays.

"Jayden!" Laurence says as he walks out through one of the side rooms. He strides toward us, and I notice he's already changed. His boots and belt buckle both shine, and he's dressed in black trousers, his tunic, his vest, and a jacket that marks him as a knight.

I relax my hands at my sides, chew my lip, and shift, looking around at the opulence that surrounds me. *Yeah. I really don't belong here.*

Laurence frowns between Hera and me. His curls bounce when he swings his head back and forth. Taking a breath in, I place my hand on my belt and say, "It's Hera. She was at Rumbling Town."

"Yes, yes, of course," he taps his forehead, saying, "'Tis good to see you again. If my memory has not failed me again, you are Gamel's second in command?" he says, extending his hand to her.

"Yes," Hera says, blushing as she places her hand in his and gives it a shake.

"Gamel speaks highly of you. He says you are good to your team and are well respected amongst your soldiers."

"Thank you. I alone cannot take the credit. I was taught at a young age to always strive for excellence." She steps back, her eyes shining. "'Tis something my parents taught me before they passed."

"Yes, yes," Laurence says, looking down at the floor. "They would be very proud," Laurence says, nodding while he stares at the ground.

Something sweeps across me—it's cold and dark, and when it leaves, it casts a shadow that lingers long after the ghosts have gone.

I *was jealous* of Hera. She's climbed to a high rank in the military, and she's not that much older than me. But she's young, too young to have no one. We stand in silence for several seconds until I can't take it anymore. "Hera, thanks for helping me with my horse," I say.

"'Tis my pleasure," she says, nodding. "I should return to my troops. I have left them without a leader for too long. They sometimes get into trouble when no one is watching," she says, winking and grinning.

"Yes, yes, we should go as well, Jayden." I gape at Laurence. *Right.* Olin's probably waiting on the outskirts of town. "We need to speak with Wyndham."

"I'll see you later," I call to Hera. Her back's turned, and she's almost at the doorway to the next room.

"Yes, you will," spinning around, she says as she disappears through the corridor.

***

Laurence and I cut through a few more rooms and head towards the west wing.

Before we're there, though, we slip into a small room that can barely fit five full-grown men. We're greeted by Crayton, a young man who's a cook-in-training. He says, "Wyndham has asked that you remove your jacket, Laurence. I will ensure the jacket is returned to your room." Crayton hands us long black robes and says, "And that you should wear these as well."

I take the robe and pull it over my head. Remembering my conversation with Olin about changing my appearance, I slide the elastic from my hair, and it falls down to my shoulders and to my arms. "Thank you," I say before we exit through the door as I flip the hood up on my robe.

I see two men standing along the wall, wearing similar robes, speaking to one another while they stroke their horses. Touching Laurence's arm, I lift my head in the direction of the two other priests. Walking up to them, I keep my head bowed forward until we see the eyes of the two men— Wyndham and the King.

We mount our horses in silence, keep our heads down, and pass through the gates of the castle and the outer walls.

"Please, Nico, ride ahead. I must speak with our friend

here. And my son," Wyndham says, lifting his head to Laurence, "please stay close to Nico."

Why, oh why, do I think I'm in trouble?

Wyndham touches the side of his hood and looks around over hills and along the length of the treeline. He takes only a second to peer behind him. Laurence and "Nico" ride together discussing I don't know what.

I blink at Wyndham, who squints at me. "I wish to be clear with you," Wyndham says, "do not *ever* do that trick again with Enisseny."

"Trick?" I say.

Glaring at me, Wyndham says, "You connected to Enisseny's mind, did you not?"

Mander's bite. I sit there on top of my horse, holding the reins, trying to figure out what to say next. I could tell him it was Laurence's idea, and it was his fault. But I'm still responsible for my actions. I don't know why it was wrong, and then it occurs to me, "Did I hurt Enisseny?" I ask.

Wyndham looks around, shaking his head from side to side. "A mild discomfort, that is all," he says, sighing. "But please, describe your experience when you were so bold as to connect your mind to Enisseny's?"

Slouching forward, I stare down at the dirt road we're traveling on.

"Jayden?"

I raise my head to Wyndham. I could lie, and I know it. But I also know I shouldn't. "It was terrible," I say. "It was as if I was in a hurricane of voices, ideas, losses, and endings. I couldn't stand or sit up after I did it. And I slept for the rest of the day." Oh boy . . . I'm getting nauseous just talking about it.

"Good," Wyndham says. "So, you will promise to never do such a thing again?" he asks, his eyes flashing with anger.

I tighten my stomach, sit up taller in my saddle, and force myself not to flinch under the old knight's gaze. "I promise," I say.

Wyndham stares at me too long. Then he turns away. "'Tis

not because I do not trust you to see what Enisseny thinks," Wyndham says. "If you were to do it again, you might not survive," he says. "And then, what would I tell your mother? Yes, yes, Jayden was on her way to becoming a knight, I am sure of it." He gives me a sideways look. "But her mind burst under the weight of witnessing everything that Enisseny has seen in his thousand plus years . . . I am truly sorry."

I want to laugh. But I don't dare because Wyndham still looks furious. Then a thin line crosses over his lips, and I know we're okay.

Something's been bothering me since Wyndham and Enisseny were wounded. Something he said in the first few days after Dr. Eastwood stitched him up. "Wyndham?" I say.

"Yes, Jayden."

"When I first saw you, after Dr. Eastwood helped you . . . you said something to me . . ."

"You will need to remind me. Those early hours after my surgery, I remember little. It was as if those who visited me were nothing more than phantoms."

"Oh."

"Tell me. Perhaps I can offer some explanation."

I stare ahead at the backs of King Nicholas and Laurence. "You said that I was *changed* after what happened to my Mom." I want to say: *Do you mean in a good or bad way?* But I don't want Wyndham to give me an answer to make me feel better. "What did you mean?" I say.

"Yes, I do remember saying those words." A bird sweeps close to us as if he's listening, and Wyndham smiles at it. "I meant that you were changed. Some things happen in life that will make us braver or more terrified, or force us to reassess relationships with other people, or things we do in our lives. They are moments that transform us," he says, glancing over at me. "And the experience can change us in ways we did not expect."

Looking away, I stare over at the river, the same river that runs beside Dr. Eastwood and Dr. Wretchell's home. Now, I'm back with the old man at Ludswup, the one I held my dagger to his throat, and I wonder: *Was there another way to help Laurence?*

"It has not changed you for the worse," Wyndham says.

How does he do that? It's almost like he's reading my thoughts. "I don't know about that," I say, staring at the swishing tails of Laurence and King Nicholas' horses.

"I do," he says. I peek over at Wyndham, and he looks from side to side. His smile is small. Wyndham says, "Jayden, you are young. You will be at times hot-tempered and, from there, make mistakes." Wyndham gives me a yellow toothy grin, "So long as you are like that for only a few years, you will do better than Laurence."

Leaning forward in my saddle, I look out at the horizon. "The man in Ludswup—"

"Are you remorseful?" Wyndham asks, glimpsing over at me.

"Yes." I hold the reins with one hand now. I place my hand on my thigh and watch the green grass move under our horses' legs.

"And?"

Nodding my head, I say, "I had other options. I didn't need to take a hostage. I could have waited. Yeah, they were punching Laurence, but he was still making jokes," I purse my lips, smiling, "so he was probably doing okay. Or maybe I could have lied and said other knights were waiting, and if they didn't let us go in the next five minutes, they were going to tear Ludswup apart looking for us."

"See. I have no doubt you will be a fine knight."

I want to ask him: *How do you know that? Why do you think that? And have you talked to Kemena lately? Because I'm sure, she feels differently.*

I can't say anything else, though, because Olin's standing in front of us, waiting.

NINETEEN

Olin stands beside a wild rose bush, his face pale, his hands rest at his sides, and he steps forward, starts to bow, and says, "My—"

Under the cloak, I see a hand rise. Olin straightens himself.

"Hello, Olin," the King says, extending his hand to him, and they shake hands instead. The King turns his head and peers at the bush behind Olin, right, then left, and out over the horizon, the black fabric swaying with each tilt-turn of his head. Shifting, I notice Laurence scanning the area too. "I was told you might have some information about a mutual acquaintance?" the King says.

Olin coughs into his hand and clears his throat. "Yes." His eyes are misty, his jaw pulses, and the dimples in his cheeks and chin appear. "Do you know where I am from?" he asks the King.

"Yes. When I was young, I visited the Trepid Divide." The King pauses, and says, "In truth, I was a boy at the time, and I had played the game, too, and nearly lost my life because of a lie."

"Many people do not know they are lying," Olin says, glimpsing at Laurence and me. Rubbing his forehead, he says,

171

"Nesta is my Guardian, but she was an absent Guardian. I was raised primarily by the cooks." Shaking his head, he says, "I do not know if this is helpful or not—I have no specific details to share, except to say that Mr. and Mrs. Bellows noticed a carefree step in the way Nesta moved the last time she returned to check on me some ten days ago." Olin pauses and says, "They said she nearly skipped when she greeted them and gave them each a kiss on their cheeks. She asked questions about my welfare and enquired about their children. Mrs. Bellows said it seemed as if she had fallen in love, or at least found someone she was fond of." Olin smiles, stares down at the ground, and crosses his hands behind his back. "Her behavior was quite unlike her." He raises his eyes to the King.

"You said it had been a month," Laurence says. I bite my lower lip and shake my head.

"I did not see her. I was asleep when Nesta came, and she did not wish to disturb me." He looks back and forth between the King, Wyndham, Laurence, and me.

"What are your thoughts?" the King says, pushing his hood back to look at Wyndham.

"There is a missing knight and a woman who appears happy. I would guess Edric and Nesta had a relationship," Wyndham says. "Perhaps there was love there?"

"Or perhaps she was looking for information?" Olin says. His eyes rest on large red trees with trunks the size of transport trucks. Then he looks up at the clouds where a white eagle soars above the treetops.

I shake my head at the thought Nesta only used Edric. "Maybe she did love him?" I say.

Keeping one eye open, closing the other, Olin's face contorts. "No, Nesta is not one for love."

"How do you know? You said yourself you didn't spend much time with her when you were growing up."

Slouching, Olin says, "She loved my mother, for certain. That is why she agreed to care for me and checks on my well-being. But everything she does comes with a price, even when it comes to me." I tilt my head and stare at Olin. "She would bring me gifts on my birthday and make me call her mother even when I was young and rebellious and wished not to. There was also one time she took me to a village where I played with a boy, and I watched her steal a golden necklace from the boy's parents," Olin's voice is hoarse.

Wait. Wyndham said that Nesta and Edric had a relationship? "What makes you think that Nesta and Edric had a relationship?" I say to Wyndham.

"Vik, Roul, and Yaromil remember Edric spoke of a woman with long dark hair." Wyndham catches my eye as I shake my head, shrug, and flip my palms up in the air. *When did this happen?* "They only recently recalled the conversations they had with him. They said they never saw the woman," he adds dryly, his eyes crinkling.

Laurence lets out a long sigh and places his hands on his hips. "He never spoke of her to me."

"No, Edric has never been fond of you." For the first time, I notice Laurence is uncomfortable, and a flash of hurt crosses his face. Wyndham sighs, and says, "Edric wished to be respected the way you are by the soldiers and knights, so perhaps he shared more with them to be friends in the hopes the respect he desired would come to pass through friendship. Laurence looks away. "Laurence," Wyndham says, "you are younger than Edric and are a better knight." Wyndham turns to Olin and says, "Thank you for the information. We appreciate the details about Nesta, and the warning of war you shared with Laurence and Jayden when they visited Trepid Divide."

"I hope this has been helpful," Olin says. "Now, I must return."

The King moves toward him, "You should come to Stock Castle." he says. "Unless—have you visited?"

"I have not, my K—" his chest expands, and Olin says, "—my Lord. I do not think I should. I was told by someone," he rolls his eyes, "I cannot trust . . . that I should never visit. But given the circumstances," Olin's eyes survey the ground, his hands are clasped behind his back, and he says, "I do not think I would be trusted."

"Jayden? What say you? Can Olin be trusted?" Wyndham says.

Laurence's face straightens, his jaw and mouth are tight. I see him, but I don't care. "Yes," I say. Olin's cheeks redden. His eyes shine like water in darkness with only light from the moonlight.

"No," Olin's voice cracks, "I should not."

"Please," the King says, "come and let me offer you some food before you return home."

Olin's face lengthens. Relaxing his hands at his sides, he nods and says, "Thank you, my Lord."

***

We follow Wyndham and King Nicholas through rounded tunnels below Stock Castle. As we turn down a long corridor, Eustace stands by a door.

"Ah, you have returned?" Eustace says. His face is lined with thin wrinkles, and his eyes have blue and dark circles under them. "Your travels were safe?" he says evenly.

King Nicholas removes his robe, handing the black garment to him, and says, "Yes. Olin has provided much-needed information." The King places a hand on Olin's shoulder, and he slumps, and his head sags forward. Any sureness in Olin's step has evaporated under the King's hand.

"'Tis good to see you have returned," the King says, removing his hand from Olin's shoulder and facing Eustace. "Your sister and brother and all those you hold near and dear?"

Eustace flaps the robe and folds it into squares. I want to walk over and help, but I stay where I am. I'm never sure when I should help and when someone just wants to be left alone.

"They are fine, my King," Eustace's words catch on the way out as if he's inhaled too much pepper.

"I am happy to hear. Wyndham mentioned Osgoode was hurt."

"Yes. But Osgoode will make a full recovery, Doctor Daynta has said." Eustace says, folding the King's robe.

"Very good." The King turns to Wyndham, "I will find Olin some food. You will tell Jayden and Laurence the plan in the Room of Things," the King says.

"Yes, my King," Wyndham says.

Laurence and I frown at each other. Weird. I've never heard of that room, and from the look on Laurence's face, he hasn't either.

"When you are done, find me," the King says. "I will be in my office. And we will review the details together. We want to ensure we have not missed anything. Nesta has been several steps ahead of us up to now." He watches Wyndham closely. There's a hint of other things he means, but I'm not sure what they are. My mother? Rumbling Town? Or is there something else?

"Yes, my King," bowing, Wyndham says. Laurence and I follow Wyndham's lead.

We watch as the King and Olin walk up the stairs together, and when they're out of sight, Eustace lifts his head while saying, "Remove your robes. I need to return these before anyone knows they are missing." We all pull the robes off and hand them back to Eustace. Wyndham and I take a few minutes to fold ours. Laurence rolls his robe into a ball and hands it to his brother.

Eustace stares at him, his eyebrows arching.

Laurence stands in front of Eustace, frowning, and says, "What?" Eustace shifts and looks over at Wyndham. "Ah, oh!" Laurence stammers. I watch him shake it out and make his first attempt to fold it. I wrestle with my own robe, trying not to let it drop on the ground, and do my best to turn the garment into a tidy packaged square.

"Sorry," I say, handing the robe to Eustace. "It's the best I could do."

"'Tis a valiant effort, Jayden," he says, smiling.

"I did try," Laurence says from behind me.

Sighing, Eustace looks at the crumpled black mess

(turning around, ahem, I notice Laurence's "folding skills" are worse than mine) and says, "Yes, yes, you did. Thank you, brother." Laurence places a hand on Eustace's shoulder, and they stand like that for a few seconds.

I stare at the ground, shifting. I look at the brick of the tunnels and peek over at Wyndham. Wyndham's eyes shine when they meet mine, and he places his hands on his hips and says, "Let us go!" Turning away, he hustles down a hallway, and now he's out of sight.

Laurence and I chase after him through the tunnels.

For an old knight, he sure can boot it when he wants to.

***

The Room of Things is just that—wooden trunks stacked in corners rusted and closed while other suitcases have fabric hanging over the edges: clothes, blankets, and curtains with books, statutes, and other things between the material. There are also worn rugs laid out on the floor, and others rolled up leaning in corners, yellow scrolls and maps, jewelry, shields, swords, and odd trinkets that I don't really know what they are.

Mildew is in the air, and I wipe my hand across my nose as I stare at marble statues of half-naked men and women similar to pictures I've seen taken at ancient sites in Italy and Greece. There are many gold statues, some in human shape, and others a combination of animal and human form. I recognize some like the God of Snow, the Goddess of the Past, and the Lion of All Creatures.

In the center of everything is a gold dragon with blue diamonds as eyes. His head's more prominent than the rest of his body and his wings are extended as if ready to take flight.

Wyndham pushes some clothes off a red fabric chair and collapses into it. "We will be going north," Wyndham says as he leans back into the chair, his hands on the armrest as he taps his fingers on the wooden arm of the chair.

"Why?" I ask.

Raising his chin, he says, "You remember the Trygolish?"

"Yes," I say, groaning. I place my hand to the side of my

head and rub it, the memory of the headache now tied with the Trygolish name.

"We saw them—the Trygolish!" Laurence looks at Wyndham and places the sword back down that he'd picked up.

"Yes, I know," Wyndham says, staring at me.

"It worked!" Laurence cries, smiling. I cross my arms in front of me, let out a long sigh, and stare at the floor.

Mander's bite, now Wyndham will know.

Slowly, I look up at Wyndham, and his fingers are intertwined. His blue eyes shift back and forth between Laurence and me. The lines in his face deepen as he frowns and squints. I do a sideways glance, and Laurence's smile is gone.

"Do you know what Jayden did?" Wyndham asks.

Yup. I'm just going to stand here and say nothing.

"Yes, she tried to connect with Enisseny's mind," Laurence says.

"And what part did you play in it?"

"It was my idea," I say, interrupting.

"No, 'tis my idea," Laurence says, his chest widening.

This one time, could Laurence keep quiet? Just once? Rubbing my forehead, I sigh and add, "I chose to do it, Wyndham. It's my fault." My cheeks flame.

"Yes, you are right," Wyndham says. "But I believe it necessary you share with Laurence our conversation from earlier this day."

With my head down, I mumble, "Wyndham said that if I did it again, I wouldn't be allowed to come back to Canonsland—if I connected with Enisseny's mind."

Laurence's face flushes red. His mouth widens, and his brown eyes sharpen at Wyndham in a scowl. "Why?" he barks.

Wyndham says nothing. He just sits there. I guess I'm up again? He could tell Laurence some of this. Laurence wipes a brown lock from his forehead, pushing it out of his eyes. He frowns as he looks back and forth between Wyndham and me.

"Wyndham said I could die."

Laurence blinks at me a few times and then faces Wyndham.

"I am not lying," Wyndham says. "It has happened before." He pauses, runs a hand across his beard, and says, "So, we are all in agreement?"

"Yes," Laurence and I mutter in unison.

"Good. Now that matter is settled . . . ," Wyndham says, leaning forward in the chair. "We will go north to Winter Dragon's Lake that was Enisseny's home," Wyndham says, standing. He stares at a mirror that hangs on the wall, and when he sees his reflection, he shakes his head and pushes his loose hair back. Turning away, he faces us and says, "The Trygolish heard the news of the attack on Rumbling Town—they had left their borders a month ago for a pilgrimage to St. Agatha's when on their return, they encountered the Xyidaks who had escaped from the battle. The Xyidaks attacked the Trygolish first, or so the Trygolish said. The Xyidaks were terribly outnumbered, though, so the Trygolish prevailed, and they took prisoners and questioned them much more *persuasively* than we had in Rumbling Town as to the reason for the attack," Wyndham says, frowning. "They confessed there was none except to pose as a distraction for the dragon and myself. They also claimed a seer ordered them to do it, and she had said they (the Xyidaks) would be victorious in their land dispute with the Trygolish if they attacked Rumbling Town. On further interrogation, the prisoners told the Trygolish that Nesta was the seer and was at Winter Dragon's Lake. The Trygolish did bring a couple of Xyidak prisoners with them to Rumbling Town, and when we questioned the prisoners directly, they said the same."

"They believed her?" Laurence says with his hands on his hips, shaking his head.

"They claimed Nesta was able to foretell certain events—a baby's breached birth, a man who would fall into a river and drown, and a fire that would start in a home but no one would die . . . so yes, they believed her," Wyndham says, shrugging.

I shake my head and roll my eyes. "How many of us are going to Winter Dragon's Lake?" I ask. It's so bizarre. I swing wildly between wanting to make Nesta pay for what happened to Rumbling Town and my mom, and also searching for some example that there's good in her. After all, Olin had no one, and she took care of him. Now, to learn she manipulated the Xyidaks into attacking Rumbling Town . . . maybe looking out for Olin is the only good thing she's ever done?

"There will be the three of us with swords. Eustace will come to see if he can reason with her. Even though Rumbling Town was destroyed, and his family was threatened, he still has a grasp on his emotions and wishes to bring her to be tried, unlike some of us . . . ," Wyndham says, leaning against a wall.

"Do you think that's safe?" I ask. "I mean, shouldn't there be more of us?"

"Yes," Laurence says, "for someone who has gone to great pains to avoid capture, this somehow seems too simple."

Wyndham smiles, and says, "Yes," and his face gives us a crooked smile. "And that is why Gamel has left with some of his troops. This evening, we received a message from the blue raven that Gamel and his soldiers have arrived at the base of the mountain. So, we will need to leave tonight." Wyndham places a hand on the door and says, "As well, do not share this conversation with anyone. If it is a trap, we will place ourselves at risk as well as Gamel's troops. If anyone asks where we are traveling to, tell them we are returning to Rumbling Town to assess the provisions and report back on the status of those injured and how many troops we have in the town."

"In particular, do not say anything to Olin," Laurence says as he walks by me.

I drop my head and run a hand over my face. Wyndham crosses his arms and leans against the door. "'Tis not only

Olin we need to fear," Wyndham says. Kemena and Abelard were at the border, and they did not see the Xyidaks leave. So, they may have been afoot before King Nicholas' troops arrived. There might be treachery within the King's court, or perhaps it was only with Edric. We cannot be sure, though, so we shall err on the side of caution." Wyndham pauses and places a hand on Laurence's shoulder. "But you need to search within yourself to find out why you fail to believe what Olin says is true. Jayden believes him, and I share her opinion of him, as does the King."

"Yes, Father," Laurence says, nodding stiffly.

"I thought the King was going to tell Olin he thinks he might be his father," I say.

Shaking his head, Wyndham says, "'Tis not the type of thing you can share after one conversation. As well, without Nesta, we may not be able to confirm it." Wyndham turns to face the door and turns back again. "That said, let us keep this conversation between us. In case we are wrong about Olin."

Opening the door, Wyndham says, "Be prepared to leave in two hours."

TWENTY

This is the first time this has ever happened.

I'm on Enisseny. I didn't fall or slide backward, and I did it in just one try. Have I gained Laurence's ghost-like ability to move from one room to another without making a sound?

I'm doubtful. I assume it's nothing more than sheer luck.

Enisseny runs, we bounce, and then his wings expand. The night air is cool, and I close my eyes. When I open them again, I look down at stone and wooden houses with thatched roofs below us. Wind runs a hand across my face. It doesn't sting or burn, though, because we're not flying fast. It's more like I'm standing on top of a mountain in British Columbia. Then we turn left and fly out over the Tadders Ocean, and I see the top of the green rock that sticks out on the shoreline.

Enisseny sweeps across mountains, hills, and valleys as we fly north. Halfway there, with the sun still setting, I see a large stone monument to Edmund Stoneledge, the last knight connected to Enisseny.

Some pictures and paintings commemorate Enisseny's last friendship that some told me lasted close to four hundred years. Sir Edmund had married four times, with each wife passing before him. That didn't stop him from marrying a fifth time. Unlike his life, his death was unremarkable because he didn't die in battle; instead, he died in his sleep next to his fifth wife. They'd been married more than thirty years, or so they say. She passed a few days after him.

There's nothing but stars and sometimes the shadow of a drifting cloud to see in the darkness now, and the outline of trees, black puddles of lakes, and the grey smoke from chimneys. It's all subdued, though, without color, and as we start to descend, a short, stocky, lone man comes into view, sitting on a horse at the edge of a hillside, with four horses next to him. Behind him is a snow-covered mountaintop. Enisseny slows down, and we sail to the ground, dismount, and then when we're all off, Enisseny rises back into the air.

"Where's he going?" I whisper to Wyndham as we approach Gamel.

"He's going to find somewhere else to rest for the evening. He is difficult to hide," he quips.

I salute Gamel when I see him, and he smiles, and we mount our horses in silence. We say nothing until we reach the camp of the Ikansterup soldiers.

***

We've had dinner with the soldiers, and after we were done, Wyndham spoke to Gamel privately, and then Gamel and his troops packed their belongings and left to climb the mountain. Wyndham, Eustace, and Laurence are still sleeping at the campsite.

I couldn't sleep. So, I do what I do at home and wander. Staring up at a tree with low-hanging limbs, I reach up and grab the branch and swing myself up into a sitting position. Then I wedge my foot into each tree limb, gently at first, and then lean into it with more of my weight until I know the branch won't break. I do this over and over again, climbing higher into the treetop.

"Jayden," a man's voice says from below. Looking down, it's Laurence. "Where are you going?" he asks.

I lean against the trunk. *How do I explain to Laurence that I just needed some time alone to think?*

"Jayden?" Laurence says, staring up at me with his hands on his hips. Through the shifting black limbs and leaves, there are the two moons above that shine bright. And from where I am, I can see white and fiery red stars tonight. But the red stars don't happen every evening, and this is one of those rare nights.

"I just needed some time to myself," I say, wedging my foot between the trunk and a limb and holding onto another branch above my head with my hand.

"What is it?" Laurence says. He watches me, and the weight of his eyes makes me shift. "Jayden, come down," he says, rubbing the back of his neck, "if you are upset about Rumbling Town . . ."

I look past him to our campsite, where Eustace and Wyndham are sleeping. *Right, Rumbling Town. How could I be so selfish?* There are other things to worry about, other people who have more significant problems. So, Nesta, she only wanted to get Wyndham and Enisseny's attention? I tighten my jaw. I want to believe there's some good in her but she's not making it easy. Sure, she sort of took care of Olin and checked in on him. Still, she left most of the responsibility with Mr. and Mrs. Bellows.

"I am coming up," Laurence says, jumping up to reach a low-hanging branch. He huffs, groans, and struggles to climb up to where I am.

The way his hands reach for a branch, the way he checks to make sure each one can hold his weight, the way he uncomfortably shifts and clings as close to the center of the tree—it's clear he's not alright with this. Smiling, I can't help myself. Finally, there's something Laurence can't do easily. Slowly, he creeps toward me. It's impressive, though, that no matter how uncomfortable he is, he's still climbing up.

"Is this as far as we will go?" he asks, his eyes flicking back and forth and then up and down.

I planned to go higher. But Laurence's back is against the heart of the tree as he stares down at the ground, breathing heavily and with flushed cheeks. "Are you uncomfortable?"

"Not in the least," Laurence says, crouching down. "I am confident this twig can hold my ninety-five kilos," he says, with a slight nod. He pushes himself back into the tree, lets go of the limb for not even a second before he grips the branch again.

Staring down at him, I say, "You're not afraid to climb mountains."

"No," he says. "Rock is predictable. I suppose trees are too. If there is too much weight, they will break." Smiling, I nod. "You are comfortable here?"

"Yeah," I say. Above us, white and red stars flash against the dark sky from opposite directions.

"'Tis Rumbling Town, you need time to consider?"

"No," I say. Shaking my head, I add, "Sorry."

"Do not be." Laurence lets go to wave, and as soon as he tries to flap his hand at me, he reaches back up and grabs the branch. I know I should suggest we go back down. But I don't want to. This was my spot. I needed time to think. And I wanted to do it here. "Something bothers you. Someplace where you might be trapped?" he says.

How did he figure that out? I scratch my collarbone and then my cheek. I can't look at him. So, I look to the sky, to the limbs, and then wedge myself further into the center of the tree, reach up and grab a leaf, and shred it with both my hands. "Yeah," I say.

"Home?" Laurence says. Leaning forward, lines map his forehead.

"No, of course not." I shift and rip the leaf faster. I add, "I love my parents."

"No one who knows you would doubt such a thing," Laurence says. "When I was younger, 'tis what I feared— becoming my brother, Alwyn."

"No, it's not that," I throw the remains of the leaf into the air and grab the branch above me. "Do you remember the night we saw that thing that Enisseny showed us with Wyndham?" *How do I describe something that Laurence has never seen?* "It kind of looked like a grey bird?"

"Yes," Laurence says, "the roaring bird."

"Yeah," I say. "I want to fly those things. I want to join the Canadian Armed Forces and fly those. I want to be a fighter pilot."

Laurence looks at the branches again, shifts his weight, and stands taller. Nodding, he says, "You should."

"I don't know if I can," I say, shifting.

"Why?" Laurence says. If I tell him I'm not smart enough, is this one of those things he'll hang over me? "Jayden?" he whispers.

I tighten my lips. I half-laugh, half want to cry. The irony isn't lost on me that I want to join the army, yet I'm about to shed some tears because I think I might not be able to make it. *I'm not smart enough.*

No, I can't say that. "I need *really good* grades in math and science. I don't know if I can get them up high enough." I add, "And while I'm in training, I'll need to keep them high."

Okay, that works. I'm not saying I'm dumb, just that my grades might not be good enough.

"If 'tis something you want, you must try."

"What happens if I can't do it?" I say. "I'll have put in all that time and effort, and then what do I do?"

"You will fail," Laurence says, chuckling.

I scrunch my face. *So says the glorious knight who can't climb a tree without shaking in his shiny leather boots.* I never asked for him to come up here. I never asked for this conversation . . .

"Everyone fails," Laurence says. Gone now is his smile.

"You never have."

His teeth shine in the darkness. His eyes glisten. "You are kind to believe such a thing. But I struggled to write as a child reversing letters and such . . . only after Dr. Eastwood came to Canonsland and diagnosed me as dyslexic that reading and writing became less of a hindrance. Still, to this day, I find it challenging."

I gulp and snap my mouth shut. Shaking my head, I say, "I didn't know that."

"By the time you came to Canonsland, I was already well

on my way in training to be a knight. And most of my reading and writing was done with Wyndham or on the King's Acres."

"Oh!" Laurence cries. His foot skids off the limb, and the branch sways up and down.

I grab Laurence's upper arm, and he places his hand on top of mine. I use my other hand to tighten my grip on the branch above my head, wedging one foot into the center of the tree while the other foot teeters on the branch. The limb sways, and I struggle to steady myself on the branch.

It's the first time I've noticed how muscular Laurence's biceps are. My cheeks warm. I know it's not so much from the effort as the—

No. Laurence is a mentor to me. That's it.

Laurence clings to the branch above his head, his brown eyes shining.

"Maybe we should go down," I say.

"No, I am fine." Nodding, he lets go of the branch with both hands, drops his shoulders, and smiles.

I try not to laugh. "You've helped," I say. "Thank you."

It's true . . . sort of. I inhale the damp cold air and look between the limbs of the trees as another white star flies across the sky.

I don't know how I'm going to get my marks up. Tutor? Can Mom and Dad afford one? I peer over at Laurence, his face pale. "Let's get down," I say. "I'm good."

"Finally," he says, grabbing the branch above him. Carefully and quickly, Laurence begins to navigate his way down, and within a few minutes, we're standing on the exposed roots that snake along the ground near the tree.

***

"Why do you trust him?" Laurence says.

We're crossing an open field that's probably about four hundred feet from the campsite. "Trust who?" I say, frowning.

"Olin," he says.

The air is cool against my face, and I stare up at the

mountaintop to our right. On that mountain is where Enisseny lived before he moved to Rumbling Town and where Winter Dragon's Lake is. It's less than a day to travel there. My mouth tightens. "He's never done anything to us. Sure, we got a fever, but he didn't let us die. And his people took care of us. Actions speak louder than words," I say. "Besides, if Olin wanted to kill us, we were easy targets. And he let us escape there." Biting my lip, I add, "Thanks to me, they probably would have killed us in Ludswup."

"You were angry," Laurence says. "Even the best of us make missteps."

"That's no excuse. I've always been in awe of people who can be good in the worst of circumstances and they don't lose their compassion for others. My Mom and Dad give to the food bank even though money's never been easy for them. And Osgoode," I stare at the red-pink sun that peeks out over the horizon, and add, "Osgoode lost all his family and friends in the Civil War but didn't blame the people in Canonsland or the other Ikans. He only blamed Droart and Fulke. That's where it ended."

"Yes," Laurence says, rubbing his eye. "Osgoode is truly exceptional, and your parents."

"Yeah." What else can I say? "I can't undo what I've already done. Unless? Is time travel a thing in Canonsland?"

"Time travel?"

"Yeah, you know, go back to a time before like one-hundred years ago, or four days ago, or a week ago and change something that you wish never happened? Or that you did?"

Laurence smiles and says, "No. I have not heard of such a thing."

"Well, then, I guess I'm out of luck."

"If you are unhappy with something you have done, learn from it. Be better."

"Lessons learned?" I say.

"Yes."

"That sounds like something Wyndham would say."

As we approach the campsite, I see Wyndham kneeling in front of the fire, and embers begin to crackle. Eustace's head is still under the blanket, and he's snoring.

"He did," Laurence says, peering over at me.

"Where have you been?" Wyndham says.

"Climbing trees," I say, grabbing a pot and placing it over the fire as the flames fan out across the wood.

"What were you discussing now?" Wyndham asks. "I heard my name."

Laurence reaches into a bag, grabs a can of food, and opens it with a can opener. I smile because it's obviously a gift from Dr. Eastwood. It's funny that the people of Canonsland can take photos, but can openers weren't thought of. "You," Laurence says, without looking at Wyndham. "Wyndham's Wise Words," he says, dumping the food into the pot over the fire and looking up at me.

"What were they?" Wyndham asks.

"Nothing memorable," Laurence says, frowning, as he stirs the food with a spoon.

Wyndham pushes the wood around some more and looks up at me, stands, and says, "Thank goodness." Before Wyndham turns his back, though, I'm sure I see a smile . . .

TWENTY-ONE

My boots sink into the snow as I shift a small bag that I carry with food and water over my shoulder. The wind is calm, but the temperature has fallen at least ten degrees. I glance up at Eustace, who has his arms wrapped around his sides.

"I fear I have chosen the wrong coat," he says with a tired smile. He trudges beside me, then stumbles (over what exactly, I don't know. The snow?) and falls into a peaked white snowdrift sculpted by the wind.

"Are you alright?" I say, kneeling beside him. I touch his elbow and search his eyes for some indication that there's something physically wrong with him. Eustace blinks at me, with snow stuck in his beard, his hair, and on his shoulders. His lips are dry, and his eyes look tired. But his color is still good.

"Yes, yes," Eustace says. I brush snow off his shoulders and offer him my hand. He takes it, and I pull him to his feet. Laurence is stomping full-speed ahead, oblivious to the fact that his brother isn't doing well. Wyndham, on the other hand, is sprinting through the deep snow toward us.

"Team player, not so much," I mumble. I wave at Wyndham, hoping he understands that it means Eustace is okay.

Wyndham slows his pace, but he's still coming toward us. "Eustace?" Wyndham wheezes when he stands in front of us.

"I am fine," Eustace says, with a weak smile. "Jayden is here. She always takes care of me."

I shift. I'm not a fan of being named a caregiver.

Why is it okay for Laurence to abandon the team without anyone thinking less of him? I suspect if I did something like that, I would get "a talking to" from Wyndham.

"We are almost there," Wyndham says, leaning forward, sucking in air. He glances up at us, shakes his head, and says, "I am delighted Enisseny moved to the King's Acres when we were first bound together, and later we moved to Rumbling Town." He turns his back on us and walks sluggishly toward Laurence. The wind rises out of nowhere, and the snow circles. With all the noise, it's hard to make out what Wyndham's saying. But I think I hear him mutter, "To live here, I would have been named the arthritic knight!" he says, chuckling.

I roll my eyes and shake my head. Peering over at Eustace, his head is tilted to the side, and he smiles as he watches Wyndham plod through the snow. When Eustace starts to move again, I look behind me to ensure no one's following us. "Onward," I say to no one as I step forward toward the snowy mountaintop in front of us.

Laurence stops when he's at the top. As we approach, I see the lake—the lake that the people of Canonsland knew that Enisseny could travel through—the lake with unbreakable ice. Or so the fables say. It was part of two stories I was told about Enisseny when I first visited Canonsland. Now I wonder, as I've never been here before, if the story about Winter Dragon's Lake is true and only Enisseny can pass through it?

The lake is like glass. There's no moving water in the center of it like in springtime at home, and I don't see anything shifting below the surface like fish, frogs, or bugs. We're lined up along the edge and stare down through the ice. Lifting my chin, I want to ask Wyndham where Gamel's soldiers are hiding. There's only one mountaintop with a cave in it, and we're standing in front of it. I know better than to ask questions like that, though.

"Would you like to warm yourselves by my fire?" a woman's sultry voice says from behind us.

Eustace steps in front of me. "Yes!" Eustace chirps while rubbing his hands together. "My daughter and I would appreciate it." He wraps one arm around my shoulder and pulls me close to him. "The knights," his eyes turn cold, he scowls, and says, "were to escort us to the Trygolish border and have made some wrong turns, it would seem."

"Well," the woman says, placing her hands on her hips, "you should ensure the King knows and have both removed from their positions. We would not want them to be assigned as protection and to lead other diplomats and their families in the wrong direction."

The dark hair, the red birthmark by her lip . . .

It's Nesta. Calm down, Jayden, calm down. Deep breaths.

"Yes, I shall ensure—"

"She knows . . . ," Wyndham growls. Eustace removes his hand from my shoulder, and he blinks at Wyndham and me through eyebrows with ice and snow stuck to them. Nesta lifts her chin, stares down at us, and pushes the hood of her white fur coat back.

"I am not a fool," Nesta says. She turns her back on us and marches to the opening of the cave. Laurence places a hand on the hilt of his sword. Wyndham shakes his head and lifts one finger to Laurence before he drops it back down. Nesta spins around with red cheeks, her eyes flash, but I'm sure she's missed the exchange between them. "Of course, I know who you are—all of you! Except for this one," she says, stomping toward me. When she's in front of me, she pokes me with her finger. "Who are you?" she says, her voice rising and falling, her upper lip twitching.

Shaking my head, I shrug and say, "No one that matters." The words catch in my throat.

"We seem to have hit a nerve there, my dear," Nesta says, leaning forward. Seriously, she's so close I could grab her by her hair and shove her face into the snow. It's so tempting.

Her eyes narrow at me as she breathes into my face. I hold my ground and try to keep my facial expressions neutral as anger bubbles up in me. *How does Wyndham always stay so calm?* Not let his rage show when his family's lives have been threatened, people have died, and homes in his town have been destroyed. I can't look at anyone else right now. Nesta will know something is up. So, we stand there with our eyes locked on each other, and neither of us will back down.

Nesta spins around, snaps her fingers, and says, "Come with me!" she says as she struts toward the entrance of the cave.

Eustace and I look at each other. Neither of us moves.

Yeah, she's a weird one.

Standing at the entrance, she flicks her hair over her shoulder, glances at us, and says, "Come with me," dragging out each word slowly as if we're having a hard time understanding, "if you want Sir Edric back!" she snaps before she disappears into the cave.

I look at Wyndham, and Wyndham faces Laurence. Laurence blinks at Eustace, and I just look at everyone else, waiting for someone to make the first move. When Wyndham takes a step forward, we follow him.

Before I'm too far away, I look down into the frozen water of the lake.

And there, in the ice, two brown eyes stare back at me. I almost laugh when the ice fogs up from Enisseny's breath and his white teeth gleam. Instead, I place my hand on my belt and turn away without looking back. I force the thought of Enisseny out of my mind.

Wyndham was wrong.

For a giant animal, Enisseny's good at hiding.

***

"Did you get lost?" Nesta says.

"Yes, I fell into a snowbank," I say, sighing as I stand

beside Eustace.

"Edric," she says, lightly kicking a man in his leg with her boot.

There's the outline of a man. Based on his size, it could be Edric. But his features are hidden as he faces the wall. Where he lies, there are long spear-like rocks that hang from the top of the cave and glow with red, blue, green colors from the light from the fire near Edric. Where we stand, though, it's only black rock above our heads.

"Edric?" she says, with another tap. "You have visitors."

Groaning, he rolls over. "Yes?" he says, blinking at Nesta. His arms are folded across his chest, and I notice he's wearing a clean white shirt. Looking around, I see a Knight's Traveling Bag beside him with other clothes stuffed into it.

"Sir Wyndham has come to get you?" she whispers, staring at Edric. Her eyes flick over to Wyndham. Shaking his head, Wyndham stares at the ground and says nothing. He hates when his title is used outside of formal occasions. "What is with you knights?" Nesta sneers, "You knights are always going missing," she says, as a smile forms along her lips.

I look over at Wyndham. His eyes are locked on Nesta, his jaw tightens. I suspect that to be a shot at Wyndham, who went missing the first time I visited.

And the mocking continues . . .

"I loved you," Edric says, grabbing Nesta's ankle.

"You were a means to an end," she says, kicking her foot loose. Edric struggles to sit up. His face is pale. He stares up at her, eyes pleading. "I needed you to lure the knight and dragon to the Xyidak border because I wished to take care of them. And in case I failed there, I had to have a second plan in place. But for the second plan to be successful, I needed to be certain of some information. You were kind enough to provide that confirmation."

"The Xyidaks and Trygolish," Edric says, nodding, his eyes staring at the wall. "You needed information about the negotiations."

"You are a fool," she says. "I needed to know if the King planned to send troops to the Xyidak-Trygolish border. Because I needed time to move the Xyidak warriors and prepare them . . ."

"Prepare them? For what?" Edric says, his eyes reddening.

"The attack on Rumbling Town," Wyndham says, shifting forward and placing a hand on the pommel of his sword. One eyebrow rises.

I didn't think it was possible, but Edric's face changes to skeletal white. "You did not!" he cries.

Nesta's eyes flash, and she looks around the room at all of us. And then her head snaps back to me. My hand rests on my belt with my sword hidden inside of it. I spread my feet and ready myself to move. "I do know you!" she cries, her long finger pointing at me. "You are the girl! The girl from the other realm!" she says, taking long strides toward me.

I blink, and Edric's hand reaches out and grabs Nesta's ankle, and she falls to the ground.

Laughing, she cries, "Attack!"

***

Mander's bite! At least twenty-five Xyidak soldiers pour out of a tunnel with armor and swords, the metal flashing while they scream and charge toward us.

Laurence and Wyndham have their swords out and have them raised. I yank mine from my belt as I push Eustace into a corner and stand in front of him.

Did Wyndham really think Nesta was going to negotiate with us?

"Enisseny!" Wyndham shouts, snapping me back to where I am.

There are eight towering, robust Xyidak soldiers on Wyndham. He steps onto a rock, and his sword rises and descends as he blocks the warriors' blades. Laurence rushes toward Nesta, but she slips between two large, long spears. "Where did she go?!" Laurence barks. His sword rings as he defends himself against the steel of two Xyidak soldiers.

"Get me a sword!" Edric says, forcing himself up as he lists from side to side like a boat on windy waves.

"I do not have one!" Laurence huffs, his sword ringing in the cave. His sword flashes and chimes against the heavily armored ginger-haired troops.

Oh, no. Here we go!

"Hahaha!" one six-foot Xyidak soldier with crooked teeth laughs as he raises his sword at me. I step forward, tighten my hand around the grip and wait for his next move. With a flick of his wrist, his sword snaps up—

—and I raise mine, blocking him. The Xyidak soldier stops laughing, and I can't help but smile. I've seen what happens to arrogant soldiers. So, I give myself only a second to be pleased.

Lifting my chin, I steady my nerves, straighten my back, and look to my right and left as two more orange-haired Xyidak soldiers move toward Eustace and me. I usually only play defense, but I'm about to be seriously outnumbered.

I flick my hand, and our swords spark, and the clanging echoes in the cave. My movements are fast and precise.

I come at the Xyidak soldier allowing my anger to move my hand but not consume me, and with a few more strikes, I hit his sword disarming him before the other two Xyidaks are on Eustace and me. Quickly, I kick the Xyidak's sword toward Eustace, he picks it up, and I urge Eustace out the only entrance to the cave, always keeping my eye on the one disarmed Xyidak and the two others that are approaching us.

"ENISSENY!" Wyndham screams again.

There's the sound of shattering glass, and even through the Xyidak soldier's helmets, I can see their eyes widen. The Xyidaks stop and take a few steps backward.

Standing at the entrance, Gamel roars, his sword high in the air, screaming at the Xyidak soldiers. I look around. Right now, it's only Gamel. I scrunch my face at Wyndham and shift a look at Laurence while glancing over at the Xyidak soldiers. They don't move. We're all just standing there, waiting.

There's the sound of a dull roar coming from somewhere.

I know that sound. It's the sound of hundreds of feet

running. *Oh, I hope they're on our side!* Rushing in, swords raised, the Ikansterup soldiers arrive, and for once, we're no longer outnumbered. The Xyidak soldiers fight, and so do we. The sound of swords clanging together, heavy breathing, and shouting is everywhere. Our blades are high—we fight, kill, and lose some Ikansterup soldiers, too.

Looking up, I see Nesta standing on the outcrop of rock. Her arms are wide, her eyes fluttering. There's a sing-song of words she's chanting, but I can't make them out with the sound of the steel against steel crashing together, the yelling, the running, leaping . . . all of it.

Gamel and I fight side-by-side, both battling Xyidaks. I swing my sword high and fast while I glimpse up at Nesta. There's a groan, and I turn in time to see Gamel pull his sword from a Xyidak soldier. Standing on a rock, with Eustace behind me, I'm sick of this sword fight. So, I quicken the strikes against my armored opponent like Kemena taught me and scream at the soldier in the helmet. He stumbles backward with his sword down (*use surprise if you can*, Kemena said), and I leap from the rock with my feet directed at the soldier's chest and knock the Xyidak soldier to the ground. His head cracks against a stone. Getting to my feet, I shout, "Gamel? Can you take care of Eustace? I see Nesta," I say, pointing with my sword.

"I h've gut him!" he says.

I step forward, and a rush of polar vortex cold descends over us. Any warmth is a forgotten dream, and silence covers everything. There are no screams, no shouts, no words or breathing, and no ringing from swords striking together.

There's only the sound of my breath leaving my mouth and my heartbeat pounding in my ears. Looking over at Eustace, he's far away from me, and his face is twisted. I want to say something to him that Gamel and I are here. I don't think he can hear me, though.

I stare up at Nesta. She stands above us, smiling. We are her puppets. And whatever hope I had that she was something more than what I met on the day by the Bow

River with Mom is gone.

Now, all I want is for this to end. One way or another . . .

***

I take a deep breath in and watch white spirit dragons fly above the suspended sword fights of Laurence, Gamel, Ikansterup and Xyidak soldiers. Eustace and Edric stand motionless, too. Wyndham is on the other side of the cave, and he takes the weapon from the female Xyidak soldier he was battling, places it on the ground, and steps away.

Nesta laughs. "It worked!" she says, clapping. "I am now a Sorcerer!" she says, peering down at Wyndham, who strides toward her.

"Kill them!" she snaps. "Kill them all!" she says again, leaning over the edge of the rock. "Except for that one!" she says, pointing at Edric. And the Xyidaks—the ones in helmets and armor and such," she says, nodding her head. "Most of them have orange hair," she adds.

Enisseny's high-pitched scream comes from the cave entrance, his eyes watering, and his eyes glow red. Wyndham shoves his sword back into his scabbard, keeps his eyes locked on Nesta, and hooks his fingers into rock, climbing up to her right where she can see him coming.

A single droplet of water falls from Enisseny's eye. I'm standing between his legs, hidden from Nesta's view. Enisseny looks up at the ghost dragons that have stopped moving when they see him.

Nesta's eyes are locked on Wyndham, and she backs up from the ledge as he gets closer. "You stupid beasts! I said kill them!" she says again. Then from the outcrop above me, I hear, "Wait. Where is she?" Nesta bellows.

I stop and look up at Nesta. Her eyes are searching. "Where is she?" she cries again. Wyndham heaves himself up over the stone ledge. Enisseny looks up at the ghosts, and then he blinks once and looks down at me before the dragon turns and stares up at Nesta and Wyndham.

There's a wave of water and light that rushes over me— some tingling sensation where the hairs on my arms prickle

197

from terror and excitement intertwined together. Whispered words are sung in my ear that I don't understand. A memory snaps inside my mind. The song is the same I heard when I was smaller, the first time I visited that I didn't remember until this moment . . .

I step out into the middle of the floor where Nesta *should* be able to see me . . .

"Where is she?" Nesta hisses.

It's been a long time since this has happened. But I'm now sure of one thing: I'm invisible, so, I run . . .

Rounding the corner, I pass the shining colorful spear-like rocks and round another corner. This new tunnel is carved out of the mountain because the older stone is dull and worn, and the more recent part shines in the light. Around the next bend, I see stairs—stairs that lead to where Nesta stands.

I jump up the stairs, take the steps two at a time, and try to keep my breathing even and quiet with my sword in one hand. The sound of one pair of footsteps and a second pair coming down the stairs makes me stop.

"I don't understand it," Nesta says. I hear her words before I see her. Hidden in a darkened corner beside the steps, I ready myself to intercept her.

"You will stop, or I will force you to stop!" Wyndham shouts.

Laughing, she peers back at him, smiling. She moves one foot forward, and I stick the end of my sword to her throat. "Don't give me another reason to kill you," I say. Her face crumples in confusion as her eyes widen like mine might do while watching a horror movie.

"How did you—" she says.

"What?" I say.

"How did you evade my view? From there," she says, flapping a hand backward, "I could see everything."

Smiling, I say, "Not everything."

"Ah, Jayden," Wyndham says, "thank you." Shoving his sword back in his scabbard, he pulls rope from his belt. "By the laws of Canonsland, you have violated—"

"Why did they not attack?!" Nesta cries.

Wyndham stares up at the dragon ghosts, holds the rope out, and watches them fly overhead, and says, "What made you believe they may be turned?"

"They were dead!" she says. "And I resurrected them! They owed me their allegiance!" she barks. "If they were my servants, I could use their power . . ."

Wyndham drops his head, shaking it. "In death, good things cannot be turned. They are as they were while they lived," Wyndham says. "And they did not ask to be raised again." Glancing up, he adds, "As well, the dragons will never be our servants," his blue eyes shining, he watches them. "We are theirs," he adds. He takes another step forward, "Now," he says, closing the gap between him and Nesta, "give me your wrists so that I can—"

Nesta takes another step down the stairs, "Don't do it," I say.

Raising her chin, Nesta flashes her eyes at me and says, "Go ahead!" as she sticks her neck against the point of my sword.

As soon as she moves forward, her skin turns white, speckles of frost and ice form in her hair, and her eyes turn dark. When I look up, I see Enisseny is there, and the ghost dragons fade until they're gone.

With Nesta no longer a threat, I lower my sword.

TWENTY-TWO

"How is yu'r train'n?" Gamel says, turning toward me, our horses keeping pace side by side. "With Kemena?"

Groaning, I stare down at the dirt road we're on. Gamel laugh-grumbles as if he's smoked hundreds of cigarettes. "That good?"

My cheeks warm. I know I shouldn't complain about my trainer. It's not the way of a knight. I know I'm lucky to have the opportunity to become one.

"No, it's going good," I say. I don't need to dump everything on Gamel. "Kemena says I move too slowly," I notice that I'm once again not taking responsibility for my failures, "Hopefully, with more practice, I can get better."

Gamel stares forward. His eyes flick in my direction. Tilting his head, he keeps an eye on the dirt path and the eight-foot (I would guess) green shrubs we're passing through on both sides of us. Wyndham, Eustace, and Laurence have returned with Nesta to the King's Acres on Enisseny. They plan to interrogate her there to get to the bottom of the attacks on Rumbling Town and why she lured Wyndham and Enisseny to Winter Dragon's Lake. Sure, we know what the Xyidaks have said, but Wyndham wants to hear Nesta's story.

"You h've made an impression on He'ra," he says, arching an eyebrow, his lips lifting into one of his Gamel smiles. Adjusting my coat, I shift in my saddle and look up to the trees above us, checking to ensure we're not walking into any traps. Unfortunately, thieves and murderers are still on the road. I doubt capturing Nesta would put an end to that.

Gamel asked if I could ride with him and the other Ikansterup soldiers as he lost some of his troops in the battle with the Xyidaks. Thanks to Enisseny, it was fewer soldiers than would have died under normal circumstances. I've always liked Gamel, so I didn't mind. I shift in my saddle, my conversation with Hera coming back to me from the stables. Now I wonder, did Gamel ask me to come along with them for another reason?

"He'ra thinks you are strung and hus offer'd to hel'p you train." I nod. Because honestly, what else can I say? If I argue, I'll sound ungrateful. Also, I can't speak because there's a lump in my throat. I wonder if this is a way for me to become an Ikansterup soldier versus a knight? I bite my lower lip. "You should nut fail because yur teach'r cannut teach!" Gamel's voice booms.

Shaking my head, I smile. "Kemena's not a bad teacher . . ."

Gamel lifts his hand. "I have seen her instruct others. She is short-tempered and has no use for those who are nut abuve her, she in un'ble to change her methuds, and believ's she is *always* right!" Gamel's eyes bulge on the word *always* as he faces me. I can't help myself and turn away to hide my smile.

"I thought it was just me. I thought it was my fault," I say, staring at the road.

"Some of it," he says.

I nod. My mouth opens, and then closes. Staring forward, I remember the time I screamed at Kemena and told her my lunge would have killed her, she disagreed, and because I'd stopped fighting with our stick swords, she finished me off. Sighing, I also recall how I took a beating later in hand-to-hand combat with her because I barely tried. I say, "You're right. I don't know what it is about Kemena—she makes me mad, and then I don't hear anything she says. I don't know why I'm like that. I want to be a knight . . ."

"So, He'ra will teach you wh't she knows ov'r perh'ps a munth or two? After you wul need to learn the rest frum Kemena."

"How am I going to leave in the middle of my training?"

"Well," Gamel says, placing his hand on his thigh and holding the reins with one hand. Our horse's tails swish from behind us as they try to shoo away the flies. "I need to send sum of me men back to Rumbl'n Town to hulp to rebuild. I can send He'ra there for a month, and you go back too. That way, she can train ya in the morn'n and even'n." Gamel bends his head, giving me a sideways look, and says, "I can only have He'ra gun for a short time. So, learn whatev'r you can frum her. Then, when you return to the King's Acres and Kemena begins again with yur train'n, use sum of whut He'ra taught you, and take what ya will from Kemena."

I nod. Gamel's only seen me train with Kemena a handful of times, and he's noticed how Kemena is with me? I let out a long sigh. For the first time, I think I might have a chance of becoming a knight.

"That sounds good," I say. "There's only one problem—"

"Mmm?" Gamel says.

"What do we tell Wyndham? I don't think he'll appreciate me leaving in the middle of my training, even if it's to help with the rebuild of Rumbling Town."

"We will tell him that. That you are going to hulp with the rebuild'n," Gamel says, with a nod.

"No, I don't think Wyndham will like it," I say. I wonder if Gamel's losing his hearing.

Gamel shakes his head. His bushy eyebrows scrunch together, "No, I do nut thenk it wul be a prublm," he says.

I open my mouth to say more, but I decide against it. My jaw tightens. *Ah, right.* Shifting in my saddle, I look over at Gamel and peer out at tall shrubs with orange flowers on them. "If you say so," I say.

Have Wyndham and Gamel already talked about this?

"Good, good," he says, pulling the reins back. "I think we'll stup here for the even'n," he says. He steers his horse off the path and through long grass. We stop our horses when we're under a cluster of yellow-leafed trees and a river. Spinning around in my saddle, I make sure the other Ikansterup soldiers are following us. Behind them are the Xyidak prisoners.

***

I'm one of several Ikansterup soldiers who place food in front of the prisoners. Their helmets are off their heads now, and I see their hair is clementine-orange, and their eyes are black. The odd Xyidak has blue or brown eyes, but they're the exception.

"You feed us?" one of the thinner Xyidak soldiers says.

"Yes," a tall Ikansterup soldier says, with his hands behind his back. He frowns and glances at me. "'Tis part of the Canonsland laws, that a prisoner must be provided with the necessities of life."

A woman huffs, her lips curling, "Are you not the Hunters?" she says. "A people without a home?" she snarls. Even from her seated position, she's looking down at him. I stare at the tall soldier with the dark hair, his tanned skin, the flicker in his eyes, and I see his cheeks flush pink. And I recognize him. It's Elliam . . . Hera named him as her replacement in the tunnels after we had left to travel to Rumbling Town.

"They have a home," I say, "and it's beautiful." Elliam stands there, his hands crossed behind his back. "Enjoy your dinner," I say, turning away from her.

"'Tis beans!"

"Yup. I hope you like beans," I say, walking away.

"You revel in this?" she asks.

"Revel in what? Watching people die?" She looks down at her sloppy brown and black beans, her hair falling onto her plate. "Of course not," I say.

"Nesta said it was necessary," a male voice says nearby.

Looking around, I try to figure out who said it.

"Quiet!" the heavy-set woman, unimpressed with her meal, barks. "You will answer to Xyidak laws if you commit treason!"

"I do not need to return to the Xyidak borders," a young man says, "Do I?"

"No, of course not," Elliam says.

"Xyidak laws will hold your family responsible for any act of treason you commit!" She says, clutching her plate while watching him.

"I have no family," he croaks.

"That is 'nuff!" Gamel's voice booms from behind us. He strides toward the man, "Get to yu'r feet and pick up yu'r plate," he says. The man places his plate on the ground, Elliam helps him stand up with his hands tied, and the young, thin man stares at Gamel.

A *ringing* sound comes from the other side of the young, lanky soldier. I have a second when I see an obese man who's sweating kick the young soldier's plate, sending beans flying into Gamel, Elliam, the only standing Xyidak prisoner, and me. I run my hand across my cheek, wiping beans and sauce from my face.

I suck in the air as the Xyidak soldiers erupt in laughter. Gamel's face changes to the same color as the Red Ocean where he lives. His fists are balled at his sides. He leaps at the robust man, snapping his plate from his hands.

"You must feed me!" the man says.

"We did," Gamel says, "you threw it to the grund!"

"I did not—"

Gamel takes a step forward. The rotund man's mouth snaps closed, but he smiles with Gamel staring down at him. I hang my hands over my belt and shift. Gamel's eyes bulge, and his ears turn red like fire before it gets so hot it changes to orange. All the other Xyidak soldiers sit there in silence. Even the smile from the woman's face has been swept away.

Still, the bean-throwing man keeps on smiling.

"Cum with me," Gamel says, turning to the young man

while he holds the plate with beans in them. The skinny young Xyidak soldier follows behind Gamel.

I'm with Elliam and eight others on the first night shift to watch the prisoners. Standing, I lift my plate to my mouth while keeping an eye on the Xyidak soldiers. Most of them are worn and tired, so they shouldn't be a problem. Still, it's important not to assume anything and stay sharp just in case.

The white glow of stars reminds me of home. Shoveling the beans into my mouth, I hope Mom and Dad are okay and that I haven't been missed yet. Mom would have some explaining to do.

TWENTY-THREE

"Jayden," Petronilla's voice comes from across the courtyard. I search the doorways, look behind trees, tilt, and turn my head on the other side of shrubs and up and down the steps. Oh, and there she stands, holding the sides of her royal blue dress up. Petronilla grins and runs down the steps toward me. In Lydon's Café, under the tree, I stand up to greet her, looking down and wiping crumbs from my shirt. I place my hand on my belt and make sure my white linen shirt is tucked in all around.

Arriving now, Petra wraps me in a hug, and I lean my head against her shoulder.

Taking a step back, she slides a chair out across from me. A waiter hustles over, and Ella waves a hand, saying, "Thank you, kind Sir. I have already had breakfast." We watch as a waiter disappears through the wooden door. Ella says, "Eustace said that you will return to Rumbling Town to help with the rebuild." She swipes a piece of toast from my plate. I hand her my knife, and she spreads yellowberry jam across the toast, biting into it.

Smiling at me, it's one of Petronilla's interesting quirks. She's always stolen food off my plate, ever since we were kids. She never said, *Haha! You don't belong here, so I'm taking this!* It's always been the opposite, with Constance giving me half of Ella's clothes, adjusting them to fit me. Ella never complained. Instead, she would suggest her most billowing dresses with lace and puffy arms, and I'd always shake my head, no. I preferred her pants and plain shirts. Petronilla, stealing my toast, it's more like we're sharing as if we're sisters. "Yes," I answer with a sigh.

"You are not happy about it?" she says, frowning.

"No, it's good," I say. I stare down at my half-eaten omelet and potatoes. I don't want to tell Ella about the conversation I had with Gamel. Ella's good at keeping secrets. But I don't want her to be forced to hide stuff either. "I want to help," I say. "I love Rumbling Town." That's a lot of random announcements without me giving her an explanation. Petra's mouth is closed, mid-chew. She watches me. "Sorry," I say. Placing my elbows on the table and my hand against my cheek, I brace my head against it. "I'm not making any sense. I'm just tired," I say. "We got in late yesterday afternoon." I rub my eyes with my fingers sweeping away sleep guck from the corners. "I just woke up from an eighteen-hour nap."

Petra's lips widen into a grin. She shoves the last piece of toast into her mouth and dusts crumbs off her hands, scattering them across the table. A leaf from the tree falls to the ground, and Ella watches it. "I do not know how you do it," she says. "You have traveled so far with Wyndham and Laurence, fought in a battle, helped Gamel return with the Xyidak soldiers who have surrendered (Xyidak soldiers who have surrendered? I notice Petronilla's choice of words: Gamel, the Ikansterup soldiers, and even I, referred to them as prisoners.), you train as a knight, and I know you have chores you tend to at home, go to school there, and have friends in your other world. How do you manage it all?" she says, her elbows resting on the table.

There's a lump in my throat. I drop my hand and let my head roll to the side before I straighten it and say, "It's not a big deal."

"You are tired," she says.

"Yeah." There's some sense that I'm here at this table, sitting across from Ella and also, not really. My mouth is moving, words are being said, there's a floral scent in the air, birds are singing, and there are mumbles of conversations close by. But everything is whispered.

"You must rest more," Ella says, touching my hand as her dark curly hair falls on the table when she leans forward. "There will be a party in honor of Wyndham," she whispers, her eyebrows lifting. "Today, 'tis grandfather's birthday."

"Really?" I ask.

"Yes!" she says, glancing at the nearby empty tables. Leaning forward, Petronilla says, "Eustace was going through some records and stumbled upon a note with Wyndham's date of birth—'tis planned for this evening. All the people in the King's Court are invited, and it must be done today. Wyndham will return to Rumbling Town tomorrow as well."

"Wait, what? Wyndham's going too?"

"Yes. Wyndham wishes to help with the rebuild. Nesta is caught, and Edric's been found." Tapping her fingers on the table, "The Xyidak and Trygolish issue is, well, still, unresolved. But there is nothing to be done there, for now." Biting her lower lip, she says, "Eustace, some of the other diplomats, and I (as part of my training) will go to the border with Gamel and his men to return the Xyidaks to their home. We will see if we can arrange some peace between the Trygolish and Xyidaks. Eustace, however, is doubtful on whether it will be successful or not. We still must try." She taps her fingers on the table and gazes at nothing. And then, just like that, her eyes sparkle when she looks up at me, and a smile is there again. She says, "I am boring you with politics."

"No, not at all," I say. "You enjoy it, don't you?" I say.

"Enjoy?" she asks.

"Diplomacy."

"Yes," she says, smiling. "I am new to it. But yes, so far, I do. Why do you ask?"

Sticking a finger in front of my eye, I say, "There's a

sparkle there," leaning back in my chair, I add, "even when things aren't easy, you still love it."

"Are you having doubts about becoming a knight?" she says.

"No, it's just—" shaking my head, "—don't worry about it. I was going to say it's not going well. But I just need to work harder." I nod my head, convincing myself.

"You will be successful. I know it. Although, I am not a seer . . . ," Ella says, twisting her lips to the side.

"A seer?" I say, confused. I've heard that word before.

"Yes, someone who can see things that will happen in the future."

"Ah . . . we call seers, fortune-tellers. They charge money to tell a person their future." And now I remember where I've heard the word before . . . Wyndham mentioned that the Xyidaks referred to Nesta as a seer before we'd gone to Winter Dragon's Lake.

"Well," she says, as the waiter returns to take away the last of my dishes. "There are a few who claim to be seers here, but not all truly are." Ella's eyebrows arch, and she shakes her head. "You should get some more rest," she says, squeezing my hand. Nodding, I stare at the top of the table, running a finger across my lips. I'm a zombie from one of those horror movies that I sometimes try to watch with Dad. "Oh. I nearly forgot. Has Wyndham found you?"

"No. Why?"

"He wishes to speak with you. Laurence and Wyndham were together in Wyndham's office the last time I saw them."

"Alright," I say, wobbling to a stand. It's too fast, though, and I nearly fall over sideways. Petronilla grabs me by my arm and laughs. I smile because that's all I can muster right now. Ella lets go, and I steady myself. "Thank you," I say to the waiter who's appeared. He nods and walks away with my empty water goblet.

"I can walk with you part of the way to Wyndham's office," Petronilla says, taking my hand. I place my hand in hers, and we climb the stairs crossing through the main entrance of Stock Castle.

***

There's a man with his hands holding his head, sitting in a chair at the end of the hallway outside Wyndham's office. Even from his seated position and with his body recoiled, I can tell he's a tall man. Worse yet, his clothing identifies him as a senior member of the Royal Family. I still don't know all of them.

Maybe I can dodge him?

"Jayden," the man says, raising his head. "Is that you?" he asks, squinting.

Mander's bite. What do I do? Curtsy? Bow?

"Jayden?" the man says.

Fine, I'm bowing. "My Lord," I say. "Forgive me—"

"'Tis Olin," his voice creaks like a door that hasn't been oiled. I straighten myself up. Oh, oh, what have I missed? "Did you know?" he asks as I try to relax my hands at my sides and inch closer to him.

What do I say? How much should I tell him? Nothing? Something?

"Jayden?" I stare up at the oil paintings that line the hallway. Some of them I recognize: Winter Dragon's Lake, St. Agatha's Mountain, the twelve peaks at Vlerno; others are Castles I've never seen before with soaring animals now extinct, people in fields harvesting their crops, mountains I've never heard of, and I read one description that says, "Children Play Switch Lock" that shows boys and girls skipping through a labyrinth peeking around corners while other children hide behind doors. "You knew?" Olin asks.

My stomach sinks. "I'm sorry," I say, taking another step toward Olin. "My Lord—"

"No, don't!" he says, throwing his hands up. "There will be no, 'My Lord!' no, 'Heir to the Throne!' It's Olin and Jayden. Now sit!" he barks.

I plop my butt in the chair next to him. "I want to point out that by telling me to sit down, you've already taken the role of heir to the throne, and I have no choice but to obey," I say, blinking quickly and giving him a wide toothy grin.

Olin snaps his head from me to the hallway before us and then turns to me again. I keep on smiling.

Dimples form in his cheeks. And then the one comes out in his chin. He huffs. Slowly, a smile gathers in the corners of his lips.

"I'm sorry," I say, staring down the hallway. "All joking aside, I really am. But what could I have said: *King Nicholas believes you might be his son?* We didn't know for sure." I stare at his shifting eyes, his long jawline, and hair that was wispy but now has been trimmed evenly.

Olin's head's bent. "Nesta said I was," his smile disappears. "She cannot be trusted, though. So, Dr. Eastwood ran a test. And he confirmed it. What do I do, Jayden? The King wishes for me to take a role in Canonsland. But he has a daughter. Can she not handle it? I prefer my position at Trepid Divide." He stares down at me, waiting for an answer.

"Maybe you can do both?" I say, shrugging.

"I cannot allow people to escape capture by the King's Knights by way of Trepid Divide and then ask them to share the one thing that they fear the most as the King's son."

I run a hand over my forehead—this is all too complicated. I can't offer Olin any suggestions right now. I scrunch my face, nod, and say, "You're right. You can't."

"I do not even think I can go back—even now. My position," leaning forward, Olin uses both his hands to rub his forehead and says, "has been compromised."

Slouching, I slide back in my chair. But, of course, I didn't think about that, and I can't help but wonder if anyone else did—the King, Wyndham, Laurence—no one even asked Olin what he wanted. Staring at Olin, I whisper, "Sorry . . ."

Olin nods and slouches, and covers his eyes with his hands. Then, looking up again, Olin intertwines his fingers together and rests his chin on his clasped fingers. Glancing over at me, he says, "I suspected something . . . when you said the King wished to see me and then he insisted I have lunch with him here . . . ," Olin's eyes sparkle with moisture.

"I thought perhaps he knew who my father was. Not that he *was* my father."

"Jayden?" King Nicholas says from behind us.

Leaping to my feet, I stammer, "My Lord," shaking my head, "King!" and then bow. *Mander's bite!* I'm to curtsy. *Curtsy!* Stepping back, I lean and cross my ankles. But after that moment, I'm not sure what happens because I stumble, try to catch myself, and grab the chair all simultaneously. I trip over something, falling sideways, and I crash to the ground gripping the chair that's leaning on its side. Somehow, my hands are in front of me, and they've stopped me from landing face-first at the King's feet. Although, I still have a great view of his shiny shoes.

"Jayden! Jayden!" The King and Olin say, together. I'm sprawled out on the ground in a tangled mess.

"Are you alright?" Wyndham says with arms folded across his chest as he leans against his office door.

Peering up at him, I say, "Yup." My cheeks flush hot. *Oh well, another day in the life of Jayden.* Wyndham walks to me, holds out his hand. I grab it, and he pulls me up. Both the King and Olin have a hand on each side of my elbows. "Are you alright?" Olin asks.

"Oh yeah," I say with a wave.

Be cool, Jayden, be cool. And smile! As soon as I smile, I laugh.

Because sure, this is mortifying . . . Still, hey, it's me.

"Thank you," I say to the King and Olin. They smile, nod, and walk down the hallway together. I notice Wyndham didn't bow to them before they left. They probably felt sorry for me and didn't want me to fall over again, so we're off the hook for royal protocol by the King and his son leaving first.

Wyndham and I walk to the door to his office, and before we go inside, he says, "When you are in trousers, you do not need to curtsy," he says, winking at me.

Gaping at him, I roll my eyes. "Are you kidding me?" I say.

"I am not," Wyndham says, opening the door. Laurence is there, with his arms folded, and leans against a wall. He takes a seat in one of two chairs across from Wyndham's desk when he sees me.

***

"I have brought you here," Wyndham says, standing behind a big red oak desk with his palms resting on the top of it as he leans forward. "To share with you the information we gathered from Nesta's interrogation as she was responsible for injuring your mother." Wyndham doesn't live at Stock Castle, but given his long service, the King has always allowed him to keep the room we're in for meetings, and it's where he's kept some of his personal belongings. Or that's what Laurence told me on one of our rides.

I shift in my seat as Wyndham sits down. "Nesta claims she is a seer and said she has had visions of Canonsland burning when our people fight amongst each other for a rare stone that will be found between the Xyidak and Trygolish borders—a stone that will power our world as we have never known. She said that should peace come to the Xyidak-Trygolish boundaries, the stone will be found. But, if the skirmishes and battles continue, it will not." Sighing, Wyndham says, "She ordered Rumbling Town attacked and convinced them to do it by way of her abilities as a seer by first predicting minor events among the Xyidaks. She then used their trust in her to tell the Xyidaks they would be victorious in their land dispute with the Trygolish if they attacked Rumbling Town. Of course, there was no truth to the last part. But it helped her in her plan because another vision she saw warned that Enisseny and I might play some role to bring a peace treaty between the two sides that would then lead to finding the stone."

"Does anyone believe her? That she's a seer?" I say. I can't keep the disgust from my voice. I search in Wyndham and Laurence's faces to see if they believe her.

Wyndham interlaces his fingers together and gazes out a small window. Standing up again, he says, "You know I have never been one to believe in mystical things, even though I am bound to Enisseny." Wyndham glances over at us and tilts his head. Placing a hand against the wall, he leans forward and says, "So, we asked Nesta to prove it." Laurence flicks the buckle on his boot with his finger and stares down at the carpet. I twist myself around in the chair, so I can watch both of them. "And she did. She proved it by telling us the names of each person on the King's Acres who would die over five hours, and she went one step further by telling us how each person would pass."

"Okay, so she knew all that, but she didn't know the spirit dragons would refuse to do her bidding? Or that she would lose the battles at Rumbling Town and Winter Dragon's Lake?"

"We asked those questions. Nesta said she could only see things close to coming to pass. And she thinks Enisseny interferes in her sight and she said the dragon muddies the vision but does not block it altogether. Reluctantly, she admitted the dragon is capable of changing an outcome that was to come to pass. Another thing she told us: She said she cannot see your future or any role you play. She suspects her sight is limited to those who were born in Canonsland."

"How accurate was she in predicting the deaths?"

"She got all of them. Most were elderly, near the end already. One of them was a young man who would have a stroke. I sent Dr. Wretchell to stay with the man and gave her the details of what Nesta said would happen. But, unfortunately, even though Dr. Wretchell was with him, she still could not save him."

"So, now what, we don't even try to reach a peace deal between the Trygolish and Xyidaks? Nesta might still be wrong," I say.

Wyndham stares out the window, smiling, and leans against the stone wall. Then, turning around, Wyndham says, "My thoughts exactly," as he sits back down behind the desk.

"Good," I say, "I just spoke to Petronilla, and she's going with Eustace and the other diplomats to see if they can work something out." I frown and run my hand along the wood of the armrest.

"What?" Wyndham says.

"Does Nesta know where this stone is?"

"She does not."

"Great, so, she knows when and how people will die and knows there will be a stone found that will cause a full-blown war, but she doesn't know where this stone is?"

Wyndham laughs. "It may perhaps be further in the future than she can see for now. And I suspect not all visions are revealed to her at once."

"Maybe she's the one who makes it happen? Maybe it's because of her and her meddling that if there is a war, it's her fault?"

"King Nicholas said the same," Laurence says, nodding.

"He did," Wyndham says.

"And you said that Nesta said Enisseny interferes in her sight, but she knew that you and Enisseny might be able to bring peace to the Xyidaks and Trygolish?" Shaking my head, I don't let Wyndham answer as I add, "That doesn't make any sense."

"I am willing to concede that Nesta is a seer," Wyndham says, letting out a long sigh. "But she sought guidance at the tomb of St. Eithne to see what might be done to stop the world war in Canonsland from coming. There, she said she had a vision of how to proceed, and it was suggested that Enisseny's ancestors be raised." Shaking his head, Wyndham says, "So, there has been meddling from unknown forces— and she may not have the ability to become a sorcerer. Nonetheless, Nesta is in prison now. We will keep in mind what she has said. But we will also work to bring, or preserve, peace on all our borders."

"I thought the tale of St. Agatha and St. Eithne was folklore?"

"Sometimes folklore is based on things that have happened, and while descriptions and such may have been romanticized, much like your world's tale of King Arthur, there may have been some truth to it."

Great, that's what I wanted to hear. *St. Eithne was real?*

"Now, I have shared this with you, Jayden, as I wished for you to have some understanding of the reasons given that your mother was injured because of Nesta—" Wyndham pauses and says, "—and Enisseny. The King wishes to know if you wish to lay any charges against Nesta?"

"Is she going to face a trial for what she did to Rumbling Town?"

"Yes. We have a Xyidak soldier willing to provide testimony against her."

I suspect it's the younger soldier that Gamel removed from the other prisoners. But it's also none of my business, so I don't ask.

"And Edric has been relieved of his position," Wyndham picks up a pen and places it back down on the desk. "He is asking for charges to be laid against her for attempted murder. He is embarrassed to include kidnapping."

"Mom's okay," I say. "I don't need to include charges on her behalf. I suspect I'd have to bring her here and explain it all to my dad. As far as I know . . . ," I scratch the side of my cheek, ". . . he doesn't know—yet."

"And on that note," Wyndham says, "We will return to Rumbling Town tomorrow morning. Enisseny has hinted to me by—whatever you wish to call it—that we must return you home soon."

"Laurence, did I miss anything?"

"No," he says.

"Alright," I say, "if it's okay," I rub my eye, "after my curtsy-fail if you don't need me for anything . . ."

Wyndham laughs, his eyes shining. I shake my head and cover my face with my hands.

Peeking between my fingers, I say, "Can I go?" to Wyndham. He waves a hand at me, smiling. "Thanks," I say, getting to my feet. "Just give me a second to get out the door before you tell Laurence what I did," I say. Standing up, I slam my leg against the corner of the desk in my hustle to leave.

I'm on the other side of the door now, and there are

whispered voices, and there's the roar of Wyndham and Laurence laughing together. I stand there and groan. Then, shaking my head, I shrug to no one.

I pick up my pace and pass paintings with scenes of places and times that were, cities that exist now, and return to my room in the Knight's Wing of Stock Castle.

TWENTY-FOUR

There's *knocking* at my door. "Jayden," Ella's voice comes from the other side. I hop on one foot while trying to step into my heels. My extra two-hour nap seems to have helped, and I do it without falling on my face. Lifting the silk purple dress by the sides, I race across the floor and yank the door open.

Hand on her hip, Petronilla smiles and leans on the door frame. "I heard what you did," she says.

"What, I did?" I say, dropping the sides of my dress.

"How you tried to curtsy and fell into the chair," she says, giggling.

"That's it. I'm not going!" I say with a scowl. My heart thumps, and I say, "Who told you?"

"Laurence," she says. "No one else knows, I think," Ella says, shaking her head, touching my arm. "Well, besides those who were there when it happened—Wyndham, the King, and Olin." Sighing, Ella says, "Laurence only told me because he knew you would be embarrassed and wanted me to be prepared should you resist attending Wyndham's party. Now, let us go," she says, tugging at my wings for sleeves and grabbing the door from my hand. "Do you have your key?"

"Ugh," I say, shoving the door open. I snap my clutch

handbag from the dresser, taking a peek inside to ensure the key is there. How embarrassing would it be if I forgot my key again and had to shimmy up the side of the castle in my ball gown?

Petronilla grabs me by the hand. "What am I doing? I don't belong at parties like this."

"What? At a celebration for Wyndham?" she asks, frowning. I touch the small plum diamonds she loaned me and stare up at the pictures in the hallway. Closing the door to my room, she says, "That is something my grandfather would say."

We walk down the hallway, and Petronilla nods, waves, and has brief conversations with those we pass on our way to the Two White Moons Ball Room.

When it's just the two of us again, I say, "I heard Wyndham found out."

Her nose crinkles, and she smiles. "He did. I do not know how King Nicholas believed he might arrange such a large event without him knowing. But what gave it away was when Constance, Osgoode, Emma, and Hugo arrived, and Wyndham stumbled on them. Of course, it did not help that Hugo wished him many happy returns for his birthday."

Osgoode's already better? How much time has passed? Shaking my head, I say, "I thought the twins went to Ikansterup?"

Petronilla nods and says, "Ah, yes. They did, however, they gave my mother such a terrible time there that they came back." Ella's chin dips, and she says, "But I am doubtful Emma and Hugo did not need to do much. My mother was most likely looking for a reason to return to my father."

I smile. Yeah, that sounds like Idonea. "Did your parents come?"

"No," Ella says, sighing. "My father felt he could not leave too even though some of King Nicholas' soldiers are already there. Constance said my father did pass on his warmest wishes for the happiest of birthdays to Wyndham and to tell him he was sorry he could not attend."

"I'm not surprised." The thought of Rumbling Town on fire, the losses there, I gulp the tears back, "It would have been hard for him to come given . . . ," I search for the right word, placing my hand to my forehead.

"Jayden, do not fret," Ella says, touching my elbow. I just stand there, unable to speak. "Constance said it was difficult to leave. There is so much to do, but my father packed their bags and sent them on their way as he thought it would be good for Constance and Osgoode to come here, if not just for one night. There they are!" Petra cries as she glides through the crowd with her white gown shifting from right to left as she greets Constance and Osgoode. Constance smiles, her hair is done up in an up-do, and her blue dress sways while Osgoode beams with Constance on his arm, and they both hold the hands of one of their two children. "You look lovely, Aunt Constance!" Petronilla says, planting a kiss on both her cheeks. "And you look very handsome, Uncle Osgoode," she says, embracing him. Kneeling down, she wraps her arms around the twins, hugging them at the same time.

"You did not do your hair," Laurence whispers. His breath is warm in my ear. When I turn around, he's grinning.

I eye him over. He's decked out in his knight regalia for official celebrations but not for ceremonies. His medals are pinned to his lapels, a black jacket with the crest that identifies him as King Nicholas' Knight on the right arm of the coat, black trousers, a white vest underneath the coat, a white shirt, and a red tie. Laurence sticks a finger under his collar pulling the fabric from his neck. "No," I say, narrowing my eyes. "I didn't have time. I was busy napping."

"Good evening, Sir Laurence," a tall, slender woman says. Her blonde hair glistens like sunflowers in the sunshine. I run a hand across my dress. "Everyone said this is long overdue," her voice is small, and she smiles at me, but her eyes are fixed on Laurence. Laurence compliments the Cinderella charming beauty on her dress, her hair, and I use the moment to slip away.

"This is . . . ," I hear Laurence say.

I quicken my pace. "Jayden," a hoarse voice says from behind me.

"Osgoode," I say, turning around. "How are you?" I ask, holding my purse in one hand.

"I am well," he says. "I never had a chance to thank you for all that you did."

"Sorry, what did I do?" I ask, shaking my head and shifting in my dress. I want to claw at my chest right now where the embroidery is. Next time, I'm going to tell Ella to get me a dress with no wings! And no embroidery!

"You helped the Ikansterup soldiers find the tunnel to where Alwyn, Idonea, and my childr—" Osgoode stops mid-word to cough into his hand.

"It was nothing," I say, flapping my hand with the purse in it at him.

Mander's bite. Please don't cry. I'm barely keeping it together myself here. A passing waiter offers us a glass of wine, and I opt for some fizzy water instead. In Alberta, I'm not legal drinking age yet, although in Canonsland, once you're sixteen, you can have a glass of wine. But I don't want to give Mom a reason to ban me from visiting.

"No, it mattered," Osgoode says. "Emma and Hugo told me themselves they were happy when you arrived." A pink outline forms around the rims of Osgoode's eyes. "You led the Ikansterup soldiers to where they could find our people." Osgoode runs a finger along the edge of his glass and stares at me. "I have never understood why you risk so much for Canonsland. You have been like that since we first met all those years ago."

I stare at the chandelier and the five-foot candles in the room with the band playing in the corner. In the hall, there are round tables with rainbow-colored floral arrangements at the center, fine china, and polished cutlery in front of each chair. When there's nothing left to look at, I say, "Wyndham's always been good to me." Swaying my head from side to side, I add, "And he's denied it, but I'm sure Wyndham helped my family when I was younger. I'm just paying it forward."

Is that it?

No, there's more.

"As well," tucking my purse under my arm, I hold my glass with both hands. I place a finger on the side, tapping it, and add, "Wyndham's always felt like a second father to me. And Constance, Eustace, Alwyn, Petronilla, and you—all of you, feel like the brothers and sisters I never had." Shifting, I add, "And I do get the chance to become a knight," shrugging my shoulders, I say, "assuming I don't flop out of training."

"You are already a knight," Osgoode says. "If no one else sees that they are fools."

"Well said, Osgoode," Wyndham's voice comes from behind me. I purse my lips as my face heats up, and I'm relieved Constance and Petronilla appear when they do because I honestly don't know how to respond to what Osgoode and Wyndham said. Everyone around wishes Wyndham a happy birthday, and I add my wishes too, and then Eustace arrives, and now most of the Isons-Lydric family have reunited.

Well, except for Laurence, who's still standing on the other side of the room with the blonde beauty with the delicate, refined mannerisms like Constance. Both women are the type who will float into a room with such warmth that others will flock to them, kind of like Albertans in January who escape to Florida.

Right now, I'm really missing my trousers. And my sword.

"I heard you will be returning to Rumbling Town," Constance says. The interruption snaps me back to where I am.

"Yes," I say.

"Good," Constance says. "It would be good to spend some time with you again," she adds while squeezing my arm. I nod, taking another sip of my drink.

I listen to the conversation for a little bit, but I need some time to myself. Too many people, too much expectation, and oh, how I'm suffocating in this dress! "I'm going to get another drink," I say, leaning into Eustace. He nods. I make my departure as Laurence and the woman head toward his family.

Moving through the crowd, I take in large gulps of air and trade my empty glass of water for a refill. Scanning the people, I carry my drink with me as I approach a man standing in the corner who's tugging at his sleeves. I watch as he folds his arms in front of him, leaning against a wall.

I sneak up to him from the side, clutching my purse with one hand and my drink in the other, and say, "Hey," lifting my head.

Grinning, his blue eyes brighten, and he nods and says, "Hey!"

I scan the Ball Room of the nearby people and those that are now sitting in chairs. "Is your . . . ," my eyes flick around the room at my near flub. "Is the King around?" I say.

"No," Olin says. He watches everyone as he says, "I believe King Nicholas, his wife, and daughter plan to come in soon, but they have not arrived yet."

"Ah," I say, as I notice he's omitted himself from the list of Royals. I guess there has been no formal announcement yet. "Well, I just wanted to say hello. But I'm going to find a seat before they get here. I wouldn't want to have another curtsy mishap."

Olin smiles, and I turn to leave. "Jayden?" he says. "I do not know anyone here. May I sit with you?"

"Of course," I say, nodding.

"Jayden," Wyndham's voice comes from behind me again. I roll my eyes. How does he keep sneaking up on me like that? Laurence and Wyndham have the same stealth movements of a cat hunting a mouse! "We are missing you and Olin at our table," he says. "Dinner, I am sure, will commence soon."

I hadn't noticed that most people are already in their seats, so we hurry to join Osgoode, Constance, their twins, Hugo decked out in a mini suit, and Emma with a red bow in her hair that matches her red dress. Eustace, Laurence, and Laurence's date are also there.

"We have taken two tables, and I wish for them to be beside one another," Wyndham says. "Jayden, help me with this table?" he says, snapping his fingers. I throw my purse at Olin, stand, and place my hands on one end of the table. Across from me is Wyndham, who does the same.

"Wait! Wait!" Constance says, throwing Emma at Osgoode, who punches him in the face. Everyone laughs. Osgoode groans. Constance runs a hand over Osgoode's hair, covers her mouth, her eyes wide, and she leans her head against his head and says, "Oh my dear, I am sorry."

Smiling, Osgoode whispers, "I will live."

"Petronilla, grab the centerpiece should it fall," Constance says. Her hand runs across Osgoode's head, Ella stands and grabs the centerpiece, and Constance marches to the same side of the table I'm standing at. Her long hair falls around her arms. *She must have pulled it out.* My lower lip wobbles. On one side is Constance and me, the other is Wyndham. "Gently," Constance says to Wyndham.

"Why is Wyndham moving his side by himself?" Laurence says, throwing his napkin down on his plate, getting up from his chair, and coming over to Wyndham's side.

"I am not so feeble, my son," Wyndham says. "Still, I thank you," he says with a nod. "There was a good chance the King's silverware and china would not make it intact." We place the tables together, and everyone is seated when the band starts to play again after a short intermission. King Nicholas, Queen Mitra, and their daughter, Sahar, enter the room. I look over at Olin, wishing I could think of something to say to him.

Does he feel left out? Alone?

He catches my eye, I smile, and he smiles back. If he's annoyed or feels excluded at not being included as part of King Nicholas' family, he hides it well. "What is on the menu?" he asks me.

"I don't know," I say. "All I really want is chocolate

cake."

"Yes. Let us hope there will be some," Olin says as the band plays.

***

"Would you like a glass?" one of the female waiters asks.

"No, thank you," I say, running a hand over my stomach. "I've had way too much food and too much fizzy water."

Petronilla and Olin are dancing. So are Constance and Osgoode and Laurence and his friend. As for Wyndham, well, he hasn't stopped dancing all night. Emma and Hugo have gone off to bed, and a friend of Eustace's has arrived at our table, and they're now discussing various political problems. I listen and nod, pretending to be interested. But I need to escape. So, I say goodnight and joke that I need more sleep.

I pass through corridors with my head raised, nodding, and smiling to Dame Kemena and Sir Abelard when I see them. Some guards stand at attention nearby because someone still has to work this evening. Others are no longer in uniform. Some I remember their names and speak briefly to them. Other people I can't recall their names, so I simply smile, keep my questions to, "The dinner was spectacular, don't you think?" or "Did you like the band?" as I make my way to the door.

As soon as I'm outside and far enough away from Stock Castle, I take my shoes off. The pavement is cool against my bare feet but not cold as it's a warm night. I tilt my head back, enjoying the breeze and grateful to escape the stagnant air in the Ball Room.

The stars shine bright, and the moon's glow illuminates the marble monument of Wyndham and Enisseny in the center of the square. Tilting my head, I say, "That seems like a good place," and I walk a short distance, and sit on the edge of the monument, and look up to the carved features of Enisseny and Wyndham.

There's the flutter of breeze and flapping wings from behind me. I smile. Then I look up, and I see Enisseny, who now sits in the middle of the square not far from me, and there's the distant sound of the music from the Two White Moons Ballroom.

"This is a better setting than the one in the Ball Room."

Crinkling my nose, I turn around, and there Laurence stands, holding two glasses and a champagne bottle. "Sorry," I say, "I can move on." I pick up my shoes that I'd placed on the ground and stand up.

"Where are you going?" Laurence asks. "I have two glasses and some bubbly, as you have called it," he says.

"Oh," I say, sitting back at the base of the steps of the marble statue. "Where's your date?"

"Who?" Laurence says, handing me a glass and opening the bottle. I take it because I don't know what else to do. "Rosa?" he asks, frowning.

"Yeah—sorry, yes," I say. I'm wearing a formal gown, it's a formal evening, so I should use proper words.

"I introduced her to Yaromil," he says. "I believe she is searching for a husband," he says, one eyebrow arching. He places the bottle on the ground and, as he bends forward, looks up at me.

I pull my hair to the side, laughing. "I can't drink this," I say. "I'm not old enough where I come from. I don't want to give my mother a reason to ban me from visiting."

"'Tis water," Laurence says, with a hiccupping laugh. "I had to bring something. But I knew you did not drink."

"Oh," I purse my lips, frowning. "Is there something we need to talk about?" I ask.

"Yes," he says. "But more of a question, I suppose." He takes a sip of water. "Will you dance with me?" he asks, placing his glass down, standing up, and extending his hand to me.

"I don't know how to . . ."

"I will show you," Laurence says. I look around the courtyard, into shops, up in windows, some with lights on, some without. "There is no one here but us," Laurence says, leaning forward. Enisseny lets out a snort, and I laugh. "See, even Enisseny believes you should dance with me."

"Fine," I say, as my face flushes. My heart thumps when Laurence and I entwine our fingers together. I stare up at him as I try to move with him, then we both look down at our feet as we take one step forward, side to side, back and forth . . .

I step on his toes. He bites his lower lip. I mumble, "Sorry." He sways me back and forth, and when I nearly topple over, I laugh again.

"You are hopeless," he says, grinning. I laugh and look up at him. "So, you will be going to Rumbling Town for a few months?" he says. His hands are around my waist, and my hands are on his shoulders. We move slowly together, not really dancing as they do here. It's more like the type of dancing I've done at school dances. Well, the odd time I've gone to one . . .

"Uh, yeah," I say. "I'm going to help with the rebuild."

"And Hera will help you train," Laurence says, looking at me. "Wyndham mentioned it."

I stare up at Laurence and smile. I'm pretty confident now Wyndham and Gamel orchestrated the training with Hera. But I don't say that to Laurence.

"So, we will not see each other for a few months," Laurence says. Confused, I stare up at him. I don't know why he'd notice my absence. "I am going to the Xyidak-Trygolish border. But I wanted to tell you," Laurence says, "that you are one of my favorite people."

"Thanks." I'm not really sure what he means by that. I stare at his chest. I'm short, awkward, and I don't really belong anywhere. Laurence belongs and is needed everywhere. I must be misreading him. I'm going to need to brush up on my non-verbal communication skills with Eustace. Enisseny flaps his wings, and we both stare at him. "You're one of mine, too," the words catch in my throat.

Staring over at Enisseny, "I enjoy your company much more than Rosa's," Laurence says, turning to me.

My breathing quickens, and we've stopped moving. We stand there, staring at each other. Laurence's lips are a line. *Is this a joke?* It can't be. "I wish to kiss you," he says, running a hand along the side of my cheek. I stand there, speechless. "I would settle, though, for only a heartbeat when my lips might touch your forehead."

"Wait, what?" I say, frowning and taking several steps away from him. I glance around. *Does he have a bet with some of the other knights?*

"I am sorry," Laurence says, backing away. "'Tis Olin, you prefer," Laurence says, nodding. "I had hoped I was not too late and that you might consider me—sorry," he says, running his fingers across the corners of his lips and taking several steps backward.

"No, wait," I say, throwing my hands up. "I like Olin . . . as a friend."

"Is there a chance, or a possibility, you may consider—" Laurence's words are strangled as he takes a few steps toward me.

Laughing, I say, "Wow, you're terrible at this." Laurence's face is unreadable. Crossing my arms, I add, "But the heartbeat thing was sweet." I stare at Laurence. He shrugs and smiles. "Is this how you are with all your dates?"

Enisseny lets out another long sigh. Laurence looks over at the Winter Dragon. "You are not allowed to judge me," he says, laughing. Enisseny snorts again. "As for your question," he raises one eyebrow and adds, "I am normally charming with the ladies. Did you not see me with Rosa?"

"Yes," I answer, "you were very sure of yourself," I say, nodding and looking up at the stars as the leaves on the trees rustle.

"'Tis more difficult . . . with you," Laurence says, his smile fading. The lines of his face are smooth and unreadable as if time has been suspended. And there we stand, staring at each other, waiting . . .

"Yes."

Laurence frowns, his eyes blink, and then his mouth opens. He whispers, "Yes?"

"Yes," I say, nodding.

Laurence rushes over to me and runs a hand across my cheek and chin. We stare at each other like that, and I don't know what to do next. Laurence nods and moves in closer. His warm breath against my forehead, he leans down, placing his hands on my cheeks, and then his soft lips are against my skin, and he leaves them there before he wraps his arms around me and squeezes me close to his chest.

"I do not wish to distract you," Laurence says, pulling away. He takes my hand, and we sit back down beside the steps of the monument. Now though, he sits closer to me with one arm around my waist. "Becoming a knight requires all that you have. But, as well, I have not forgotten," taking a sip of water from his glass, he extends his pinky, pointing at me, and says, "that you wish to train as a fighter pilot in your world too."

"When you are ready, though, I wanted you to know that I would like a chance to spend some time with you, to see if—" he clears his throat, "if we could be more than friends . . . And I would be willing to wait," he says.

"Okay," I say, lifting my glass and sipping my fizzy water.

Tears gather in my eyes. And then, I smile.

TWENTY-FIVE

It's dark. My traveling sack is slung across my shoulder, and I'm standing beside Enisseny. A messenger had delivered a message from Wyndham: *We leave at dawn to return to Rumbling Town as your father is bound to notice your absence. We are short on time . . . 'tis the dragon's fault.*

"Please take care of yourself," Laurence says, touching Enisseny on the head.

"I always do," I say, pulling my coat tighter. "And you too," I say.

"You are here?" Wyndham says, rubbing his eyes. "I do believe I may have had a bit too much wine and other spirits last night. Laurence," he says, his upper lip lifting, "you have come to see us off?" he asks.

"Yes," Laurence says, walking over to Wyndham. My face warms. Sure, we said that we'd wait before we start to officially "court". But at this point, we also don't want anyone else to find out that we have feelings for each other. So we'll tell them after I'm past my studies and there's something to tell.

There's a good eight feet between us, and I keep my eyes on Wyndham. If I look at Laurence at all, I'm sure I'll give myself away. "I met Jayden in the hallway last night," he says, stumbling over his words (okay, that's kind of true except we were with each other already), "and I remembered you were leaving with her, and she mentioned the hour you were to leave this morning, and I came to see you off."

Wyndham raises an eyebrow and gives a crooked smile. "That is very good of you," Wyndham says, climbing up on Enisseny with his bag across his shoulder. "So, I will see you in a few months," he says once he's seated.

"Yes, Father," Laurence says, looking up at him.

"Most likely at the Xyidak-Trygolish border," Wyndham says with a nod. "Jayden," he says.

"Yup," I say, climbing up on Enisseny.

Behind Wyndham, I hold onto his waist. Laurence backs up. Enisseny takes several steps forward, careful not to run into anything, and his wings slowly begin to move back and forth. Laurence watches us as we lift off and sail up to the clouds.

"'Tis good of my son to come and see me off," Wyndham says.

"Yes," I reply. *What else can I say?* I told Laurence he shouldn't stay and that Wyndham would be suspicious. But did he listen to me? *Nope.*

Enisseny glides through the air and then rises higher and higher, and once we're high enough, he picks up speed, and we soar through the clouds.

***

My phone vibrates on the dresser. I flip it over and read the text from Mom: *Jayden, you need to get downstairs! Your father's about to call the police!!!*

"Jayden," Wyndham says, "you have no time to change!" he bellows. "You must go now!" The mirror snaps closed, and they disappear.

"Dad!" I yell from my room. "What's going on?" I say, throwing my jacket off while kicking my boots off at the same time.

"Jayden?" Dad says. I hear his feet running up the steps as he calls me. "Jayden? Are you there?" he asks again.

232

"Yeah," I say. Scrambling, I run to the door and push the button for the lock. *Oh no, I forgot to lock it.* Dad must have checked on me and found my bed empty.

"Open this door!" Dad shouts.

"Just give me a minute to get changed!" My hands stop moving. My boots are off, my jacket is off, but I'm still in my trousers and tunic. My belt with my sword is still in its place too. Back at my dresser, I tap my fingers along the old wood. Then I peel the belt off and slide the weapon under my bed.

Staring at myself in the mirror, my hair is windswept, and my cheeks are red from windburn. Wyndham and Enisseny reappear in the mirror. Nodding at them, I place my hand on the doorknob and throw it open to Dad.

"Where were you?" Dad says. His eyebrows surge together when he sees my clothes. "What in God's sake are you wearing?" he says.

Bob bounces into the room, his tongue hanging out, and he barks into the mirror when he sees Wyndham and Enisseny.

"Robert," Wyndham's voice echoes from the mirror.

"Holy shit!" Dad says, backing up and crashing against the wall.

"There is no swearing, Sir," Wyndham says. His arms are crossed in front of his chest. "Otherwise, Robert, I am delighted to meet you finally," Wyndham says, waving at him through the mirror and with a worn look on his face.

Dad just stares at Wyndham. Then he rubs his fingers to his eyelids, blinks again, rubs his eyelids—

Dad's phone pings, like old people's phone's ping. He looks down at it while he pulls me close to him and reads the message. Leaning in, I read the text too. It's mom. She texted: *Robert, I need to tell you some things about Jayden.*

Dad keeps one hand on me as my stomach grumbles. He hits Mom's cell phone number. "What do you want to tell me about Jayden?" Dad says, keeping one eye on Wyndham and Enisseny.

"Can you put her on for a minute?"

"No," Dad says, looking over at me. "What do you want to tell me about my daughter?

"Have you met her friends?" Mom says. "They're old friends. Friends she's known since she was seven." There must be someone in Mom's room because she's being really cryptic.

"They weren't real," Dad says, loosening his grip on my arm.

"No, they were. And they are . . ."

"You knew this whole time!" he says.

"No, I found out when she was eleven. She never visited them before that," Mom says. "Or, at least that's what I was told." Dad has the volume on the phone up because he's lost some hearing in one of his ears. But it also means I can hear both sides of the conversation over the cell phone.

"On the life of my King," Wyndham says. He stands in the mirror with one hand raised and his head held high.

"Queen," Dad says, annoyed, glancing at Wyndham.

"King Nicholas," Wyndham says.

Dad stares at him through the mirror, his head tilted, his mouth open. Dad's face is pale, and he lets go of my arm.

"I will give you some time to speak with your wife and Jayden," Wyndham says. "If there are any questions, you may call me through the mirror. I will answer any inquiries you might have," Wyndham adds.

And in a flash, they're gone. Now, it's only the reflection of Dad with his phone to his ear, me, and Bob the Dog in the mirror.

"So," Mom says. "I'm getting out of the hospital at three today. Come and get me, and we can talk about it then. Hand the phone to Jayden, Robert."

"Your mother wants to talk to you," Dad mumbles.

"Hello," I say, holding the phone to my ear. Mom lets out a long sigh from the other end. There's a pause, so I say, "I'll tell him," I say, nodding.

"Sorry," Mom says. "I should have told him before. It's not fair you're stuck with this."

"It's okay, Mom. I'll explain everything," I say, staring at Dad. My stomach rumbles again, and I laugh. "Mom, I'm going to let you go. I need to get something to eat."

"Okay," Mom says. "Oh, Jayden?"

"Yeah,"

"If your dad's really angry with me and won't come and get me, can you make sure someone else does?"

"Don't worry, Mom. We'll be there to pick you up at three." Dad frowns and slouches. I flap a hand at him to make him stop.

"Thanks, Jayden," Mom says.

"Bye, Mom," I say, clicking the *End* button.

"Okay, Dad," I say, sighing and handing him back his phone. "I'll make breakfast, and you can ask me anything you want to." Dad stares at me, turns to face the mirror, looks around my room, and scans my clothes from top to bottom. His mouth gaping, he's still clutching the phone in one hand. I grab Dad's free hand, and pull him towards the stairs and say, "Come on, Bob." My ten-year-old pup bounces along, his mouth widening into one of his smiles.

Dad, on the other hand, is not smiling.

And I know it's going to be a long morning . . .

ACKNOWLEDGMENTS

Thank you to my readers, editors, and cover designer. Without my readers, I would be nothing but a rambling person with many, many imaginary friends. I'm grateful to my editors for your sharp eyes for grammatical mistakes and your broader insights into how I could improve the overall story. Many thanks to my cover designer, who again created a beautiful cover based on a few vague ideas that I offered as direction. Sorry. I'll try to do better next time.

Special thanks to all my regular supporters: friends, colleagues, neighbors, and my family. Some of you have seen me at my worst when I've been stumped, discouraged, or struggled to write. On those bad days, I can't begin to tell you how much it meant to me when I received encouragement through emails, messages, or face-to-face conversations.

Finally, I want to thank my husband for his ongoing support. Without him, I wouldn't have had the courage to even start this journey. And to my other favorite boy, who was never second, Hershey—because without him and our trip to the pet store on a spring day in 2016, I may never have written the original short story.

ABOUT THE AUTHOR

Penelope Hawtrey is the author of the Dragon in the Mirror series. Her first full-length novel, *Dragon in the Mirror: Into Canonsland*, was released in 2019. *The Bridge of Olin* is the second book in the series.

To find out more, visit:
http://penelopeshawtrey.com
https://www.goodreads.com/penelopeshawtrey
https://www.instagram.com/pshawtrey

9 781777 247560